In memory of Auntie Eileen, much missed,
who always said I would become a writer.

And for Gethyn – I love you millions.

Prologue

Sally

As soon as we got him home, it started; I obsessed about him dying.

I had been all bravado in the hospital, smug with my dark-eyed little bundle, and dosed up on painkillers. Holding him felt like the beginning of everything. I kept whispering his name – 'Oliver, Oliver' – relishing the taste of it on my lips. I breathed his new-born scent, stroked his tiny fingers one by one.

We hadn't known we were having a boy. When we brought him home, via an alarming car journey (had other drivers always been so careless?), I showed Oliver his bedroom. Everything seemed too neutral now, too mild, too magnolia, to contain this spirited, coal-eyed boy. *I'll repaint it*, I promised him silently, *I'll buy a blue rug, and big animal stickers for the walls, and a height chart so we can watch you grow*.

Richard believed in putting babies in their own room from the start, so I dragged a single mattress down from the loft and lay curled on it that first night, my arm outstretched at an awkward angle so that I could reach his basket, touch his hand, feel his chest rise and fall.

I started to see danger everywhere. Stairs were terrifying. Ours, in our Victorian house, were steep. I would stand at the top with my little boy tight in my arms, frozen for minutes on end. I counted each tentative step, wondering if it was better to hold him in both arms (but what if I fell?), or hold the bannister with one hand (but what if I dropped him?) Which outcome would cause him the least injury?

One of Richard's friends made a throwaway comment during his not-altogether-welcome visit on day three. There was a lot of manly backslapping and clinking of beer bottles going on.

'Now, all you've got to do is keep him alive,' he said with a booming laugh. 'How hard can that be?'

Sick fear instantly pooled in my stomach. Suddenly the idea that Oliver might be taken from me morphed into a possibility, a probability, a near certainty.

Richard took him away from me on the fifth day.

'I'm taking him out. You need a break,' he said. I didn't think I did. I wrapped my baby up, layer after layer.

'He'll overheat,' he said, but I insisted on the hat, the extra blanket. I watched through the curtains as my husband walked down the path, swinging the car seat.

I counted the minutes while they were gone. Thirty-seven, thirty-eight …

'Have a bath,' Richard had said. 'Read a magazine. Rest.'

I didn't rest; I paced. I gnawed at my nails. I saw car crashes, abductions, fires. When they returned I felt as though the missing piece of me was back and I could finally exhale.

Over the coming weeks and months, the fog lifted and the fear abated slowly. I felt myself again, albeit a changed version of myself. Life took on a slower pace than it had had before. I saw the world in a different way. I watched with a new parent's tireless fascination as Oliver learned to smile, roll over, grip his toys. I clapped and cheered every minute achievement and instead of seeing him as a breakable doll, I've now come to think of him as a clever, strong, bold boy who can and will conquer everything in his path. I suppose what I'm saying is, I've relaxed into motherhood.

More fool me.

Chapter One

Sally

I'm out. That's all that is running through my mind. I'm out I'm out I'm out.

It's exhilarating to be walking to the train station, unsteady in ridiculous heels. My arms are almost weightless without a pushchair to lean on, a child to carry, bottles, plates, baby wipes and nappies to balance. I swing my newly light limbs as I walk.

I am waiting on the platform and the phone rings.

The cry in the background is high-pitched, different. Richard's voice is irritable and terse as without preamble he fires questions at me:

'What time was he fed?'

'Did he eat it all?'

'Have you given him any Calpol or anything?'

'Has he slept today?'

The undercurrent of it all: *this is your fault*.

'You're his dad.' I try to keep my voice even. 'I'm sure you can manage without me for a couple of hours.'

A better wife, a more patient person, might lay on the reassurance at this point – add something like, '… and you're a great dad' – and I try for this, honestly, I reach for it. When it doesn't come I hang up instead because what I really want to say is: *You're the experienced one, after all. You're the brilliant parent. Can't you work it out?*

I flick the phone onto silent, slip it into my bag and step onto the train. I put away the guilt, the fear, but most of all, the fury, as though into a drawer. But the conversation, and worse, Oliver's cry, haunts me.

Parenting is still all new to me, but not to Richard. He already has a fifteen-year-old daughter, Martha, from his first marriage. The whole time I was pregnant I had felt the ghost of his ex-wife over my shoulder. My attempts to engage him in the pregnancy were futile. I would read to him from magazines: 'this week your baby is the size of a pomegranate', and so on – they always seemed to compare the foetus to food, for some reason – increasingly exotic food, too. Still, at least it gave me ideas of things to try to eat that might not make me hurl.

Richard just appeared bored and, worse, provided what seemed to be daily commentary:

'When Zoe was sick, she ate ginger nuts.'

'Oh, Zoe wasn't sick past thirteen weeks.'

'Zoe's ankles never swelled.'

'Zoe never had heartburn.'

'When Zoe was pregnant …'

'When Zoe …'

Et cetera. Et bloody cetera. Bloody Zoe.

Zoe is an artist. And an alcoholic. That's why Martha lives with us. She was with her mother for a while but Zoe needed 'space' for her art, she said. She couldn't focus with a teenager around.

'She needs space for her vodka bottles,' I'd muttered at the time, to no one in particular, and I'd agreed to the new arrangements, of course.

It's only the third time I've been out alone, I mean without Richard, since Oliver was born ten months ago. On the other two occasions I've had drinks with my antenatal-group friends, or as Richard calls them, the MMG (Mad Mothers' Group). The first time, we managed a full ninety minutes before we ran out of baby updates and Melinda started checking her watch and yawning. The second time, Esme announced she would be leaving early because she had to get back for the 'dream feed', also known as the desperate 11pm stuffing of the baby with milk in the hope they would sleep until morning. Julia scoffed and sank her fourth gin, declaring that she had expressed that night and the baby could have a bottle and like it. The two of them stared at each other in a kind of breastfeeding face-off, and Melinda and I shuffled awkwardly into our coats.

But tonight I'm meeting people from work, for a chance to be the old me, to reconnect with my old life before my maternity leave ends and I go back in a couple of months. It's a chance to feel like more than a mother, to feel like a person again. If I can only remember who that person is. A bubble of anxiety rises in my throat, and the closer the train gets to the station, the closer it comes to choking me. I do my best to swallow it back down.

We're meeting in a pub on the river. It's warm and there's a festive air, loud voices everywhere suffused with that almost-weekend, almost-summer joviality. People are flowing between the bar and the outside terrace, shouting to each other across their clinking Mojitos and capturing toothy grins and headlock-hugs on their phones.

I see my old team almost immediately; Jamie catches my eye and waves. Within seconds the four of them are crowding me, chattering and slinging their arms around my shoulders. Jamie kisses my cheek. It all feels a bit odd, like I'm not really supposed to be here. Like I need permission to let go and enjoy myself. I remind myself: *I'm out*. It's supposed to be fun.

'How's it feel to have a night of freedom?' Helen, the youngest of the team, grins, giving me a nudge with her pointy elbow.

'I'm on maternity leave; I'm not in prison,' I say, and it's meant to be a joke, but it comes out all wrong, a bit too sharp. I try to smile an apology and add, 'It's really nice to see you all.'

The railing overlooking the river is strung with fairy lights. I lean against it and watch the water rushing by. It's not quite drinking-outside weather, not really, but here we are, like animals just out of hibernation; the evening is mild, and dry, and after a horribly wet winter it seems right to venture, blinking, into the light. I draw my cardigan closer around me and at last allow myself a smile, breathe in this new-found liberty.

'You've got your figure back, I see,' says Charles, a smooth hand on my back as he passes me a drink. I shrug and look back at the river. Charles can be kind of creepy and usually best ignored, but even though it's supposed to be a compliment, I can't ignore it and it stings. He couldn't know, of course, just what a sensitive subject 'my figure' is, or the way a certain voice in my head wakes up and throws out its prickly commentary as soon as anyone mentions it.

'Some people are just lucky like that,' muses Shirley. 'Of course, I've had three. You'll discover it's a lot harder to get it off after the second and third.'

I smile. 'Oh, I don't know that I'll have any more.'

'Oh, you will, you will.' She shovels peanuts from a little glass bowl into her mouth with claw-like hands. 'You just can't help it. Some things are bigger than –' she looks me up and down '– vanity.'

I swallow, hard.

Being pregnant was terrifying at first – I had no control over my body, I felt like I was being invaded – but in time it became liberating. My competitive side had a new focus: I had to beat Zoe – or to match her, at least – and that meant delivering the healthy baby Richard wanted. So I ate and took care of myself, for the baby. I ate probably better than ever in my life. It was acceptable to have curves. It was actively encouraged. For the first time ever, I was praised for growing. Even my mother looked at me with something like approval.

I thought that once the baby was born, I would get my control back. Little did I know I'd feel less in control than ever in my life.

It starts to feel a bit like I don't know these people. I certainly don't have much to say, so instead I drink. They talk about work; of course they do, because that's their common thread. But it's not a thread I can get hold of any more.

The wine starts to taste unpleasant. It's a bit too warm, a bit too acidic, and it's leaving a coating on the roof of my mouth, but I go back to the bar again and again, hoping the next glass will be as refreshing as the first one. Out on the terrace, someone – Jamie – offers me a cigarette. I haven't smoked in years but I take it, flicking the ash into the river and squinting in an effort to watch it float off downstream. I lean over the railing and Jamie takes my arm, saying something like 'Woah there' and pulling me back. I stagger to a table and place my palms on it, trying to get centred, but everything around me is unsteady. The cigarette has made me feel sick.

'You look a bit queasy,' Jamie says, and he gestures to the others. Charles offers to walk me to the train station and I smile and nod, and say I'll just go to the bathroom and meet them out front in five minutes, but instead I nudge my way through the crowd, back into the bar, straight out of the door and onto the street. I unsteadily make my way to the station.

When I get there, I look at the screen and see that my train is due to depart in two minutes. I do the calculations and I know that even if I move fast I won't make it. I know this, but I barge through the barriers and break into a stumbling run anyway.

As I cross the bridge I hear the train doors shutting, the screech as it pulls away hurting my ears. I sit on the platform feeling as though the world is swaying around me, and want to sob. Eventually I stagger out of the station and into a taxi. As we round the corner into our road, twenty minutes later, I pull out thirty quid from my purse and think, *Richard is going to bollock me for this.* He hates wasting money. *Was it worth it?* He'll ask, *For that one extra drink? Really? That last wine has cost you thirty quid!*

I close the front door behind me and perform the elaborate tiptoe dance of the drunk. My handbag, as I drop it to the floor, makes a ghastly clatter and I hold my breath waiting for a shout, a cry, but nothing comes. I sink to the floor with it and close my eyes, wishing for a glass of water to materialise next to my hand.

What should happen next is that I go upstairs, and on my way to our room look in on Martha as I always do, glance at her sleeping face lit by the fairy lights that hang over her bed, maybe cover her spread-eagled limbs with her duvet. When I look at her sleeping I could almost love her. Next I should walk into Oliver's room, lean over the cot, kiss him and whisper 'goodnight'. Maybe I watch him for a while, stroke his face. I see all these things playing out, but I can't be sure if they are real or part of a dream.

Richard is shaking me awake. Somehow I've made it to bed, still wearing last night's top, my knickers, and nothing else.

'Sally,' he urges in a hoarse whisper, and above it, I hear Oliver's wail, right in my ear. 'SALLY. Come ON.'

I fumble my way out of my fog, aware of a bright light at the edge of my eye. The lamp is on, and below it, the clock reads 4.20am.

'No …' I moan, bringing my arm up to my face in protest. My tongue searches my mouth in vain for moisture. The front of my head throbs and thuds.

'SALLY!'

My eyes spring back open and I suddenly see, in the haze of lamplight, my husband, his hand gripping the top of my arm, and on his face, something I've never seen there before: fear.

Cradled in his other arm is a whimpering baby. Our baby. My boy. Oliver.

I sit upright, the movement seeming to cause my brain to rattle inside my head.

Oliver is flushed, his face tear-streaked. His hair clings in wet strands to his forehead.

'What is it? What's the matter with him?' I reach out my arms but Richard yanks him away from me.

'You stink of alcohol,' he mutters. 'Put come clothes on.' At this, I realise that he is already dressed. 'I think something's really wrong. Come on. You can sober up on the way to the hospital.'

'Hospital?'

I fumble into my jeans and, still fastening them, follow Richard onto the landing to see Martha standing there, blinking, her dressing gown pulled tightly around her.

'Shall I come?' she asks.

'Don't be silly,' Richard snaps. 'There's nothing you can do.'

'But—' She's staring at Oliver with a haunted look.

'You've got school in the morning. Back to bed.'

Richard has left Oliver in his Babygro and wrapped a thick cardigan around him. He peers out from under its woolly hood, whimpering. I sit in the back seat to be next to him, the motion of the car bringing warm bile up into my mouth.

'It's his arm,' Richard is saying, 'the left one. He's … done something to it, I think. It's … I don't know, it's bigger than the other one.'

'You mean it's swollen?' I lean over and try to look under Oliver's layers, but the car seat makes it awkward and even touching his left wrist causes him to let out a shriek. Fat tears spring from his eyes and I draw back, chanting, 'Ssh, it's OK, sorry, sweetheart, it's OK, it's OK.'

Arriving at the hospital under a pale-grey, pre-dawn sky makes me think of the last time we were here, ten months ago. Richard drove with a similar urgency that morning, swearing under his breath as he struggled to get a ticket from the machine at the car-park barrier, swooping the car into the nearest space with a loud screech. Then he jumped out and ran around the bonnet while I watched through the windscreen, half-sitting, half-lying on the reclined passenger seat, listening to the long breath I was blowing out through pursed, drying lips.

They say you forget the pain, but I haven't. It was a fire, a tidal wave, a steamroller through my insides. It made me want to sink, lie on the floor, crawl under the earth. I felt like an animal. Nothing existed but this pain. There in the car, in that instant, I would have done anything to make it stop.

Then Richard took a moment; it was only a split second, but he took his own deep breath and then opened the car door and everything was suddenly slower. Calm. He took my hand and helped me up, then held my elbow all the way to the hospital doors. We had to stop halfway while another contraction washed over me. My knees nearly gave way but his arm was there, and his voice, murmuring words I couldn't make out, but the tone was reassuring.

Today is different. Today we are both entirely focused on Oliver, even jostling each other to be the one to carry him.

'I want to hold him,' I say.

'Leave him in the car seat,' Richard says.

'But I want to pick him up, I want to carry him.' Oliver is wailing, now.

'It will be easier, and quicker, to take him in the seat. You can hold him when we get inside.' I have a wild notion that

Richard is trying to keep me away from him for as long as possible, and we form an awkward trio as we shamble into hospital, my husband carrying the car seat and I stumbling next to them, trying to keep my hand on Oliver's head, the slightest of contact, the wool of his hood, the warmth of his skull a comfort.

We are ushered from the main casualty desk into children's A&E. It's quiet, none of the usual injuries at this time of the morning, I suppose. No adolescent rugby tackles gone wrong, no toddlers with marbles up their noses. Most kids, right now, are safe in their beds.

Although there's hardly anyone there, we find ourselves speaking in low voices to the tired-looking receptionist who logs our details.

'This is Oliver Townsend. He's ten months old—' I start to say.

'It's his arm—' Richard interjects.

'He's very distressed.'

'OK, OK.' She holds up a palm. 'One at a time, please. What happened to Oliver?'

'We're not exactly sure,' Richard says, 'but his arm looks swollen and he's crying a lot more than usual.'

'I see. And when did this start?'

'A couple of hours ago,' I murmur, at the same moment Richard says, 'Yesterday evening.' He frowns at me.

'It started before you went out,' he says. We're now addressing each other, while the receptionist waits with her head tilted.

'If he was that bad earlier I wouldn't have *gone* out,' I hiss.

'And what time did you get back?' the woman asks me. I'm sure she looks me up and down, and I regret not brushing my hair before we left. I wonder if I look like an ordinary anxious, frazzled mother ... or a drunk. I remember Richard saying *you stink of alcohol*, and I put my hand over my mouth.

'I'm not sure,' I whisper. 'About one in the morning? He was quiet then.'

She glances down at Ollie in his car seat, shifting and moaning although no longer screaming. 'He doesn't look too happy now, poor poppet,' she says, 'I expect you'll need to see the doctor, but a triage nurse will assess Oliver first.'

'It's probably nothing,' I try to smile. Richard flashes me another annoyed look.

'It's *urgent*,' he tells her, 'please let them know.'

'Take a seat, please,' she says, nodding towards the plastic chairs. 'It shouldn't be a long wait.'

There is one other couple with a baby, a little girl younger than Oliver, huddled in the corner. The baby is pale, whimpering. The mother looks as though she hasn't slept in days. We all smile at each other in a sad, awkward way.

Grinning safari animals populate the walls. Brightly painted lions, zebras and giraffes all co-habit happily in long, lurid green grass, under a huge sun. No hunting or eating. No vultures overhead awaiting a carcass.

'Oliver Townsend?' A nurse's voice breaks the silence and we all look up. 'This way, please.' As we follow her I'm aware that I do still smell of alcohol and slip a mint into my mouth, although I know it's futile. The smell is in my skin, and cigarette smoke lingers in my hair.

We go through the same, somewhat hazy story, with the triage nurse and then again with the doctor who comes in to look more closely at Ollie's arm. He doesn't say much, but takes the nurse out of the room for a few moments and speaks quietly to her before slipping away down the corridor when she comes back into the room.

'We'll give him a nice strong painkiller,' she says with a smile, taking out a syringe. 'It might help him rest a bit while you wait for the radiographer. He looks shattered, bless him.' She eases the syringe into Oliver's mouth and he scowls at the taste of the medicine, and some of it dribbles down his chin, but he hasn't the strength to push the woman's hand away. I stroke his face.

'Radiographer?' asks Richard.

'Oh, it's just to rule out a fracture,' says the nurse. 'It's very unlikely he's broken it, though. Babies' bones are usually far too pliable.'

Richard and I look at each other but say nothing.

Those first weeks, after he was born. What do I remember?

I remember walking up and down our hall, rocking him, saying 'Why does he hate me?' Richard laughing at this but then taking him from me, at which point Oliver promptly fell into casual silence on his shoulder.

Part of the reason I was so elated in the hospital, holding Ollie when he was a few hours old (apart from the oxytocin, obviously) was that here, at last, was a person who was mine. Because even then, it was apparent that Richard wasn't – well, of course he wasn't; he had a history (with Zoe) and he had to be shared (with Martha). Here was a person who would be my friend, always.

So when it started to seem that Ollie didn't *like* me very much, it was crushing.

People tried to reassure me that he was unsettled with me because he could 'smell the milk', but this was a joke, surely. My milk came reluctantly, shards of pain yielding nothing but dribbles except in the night when I would wake in useless puddles, the smell of it high in my nostrils. When bout after bout of mastitis, my breasts red hot and rock hard, made it too difficult to feed him myself, I remember spending almost an hour expressing a few pathetic millilitres into a bottle, to have them guzzled by Oliver in seconds.

I felt the oppression of being expected to be happy. My own mother, when I stood weeping in the kitchen, said in her old, exasperated way, 'How can you be sad? You have a beautiful, healthy baby.'

I remember feeling that everyone else knew what to do – with their babies, and with mine. These new 'friends' who were not friends, not really. We didn't actually know anything about each other, had been thrown together by an accident of timing, of biology.

It was a weird intimacy – we shared birth stories, in all their bloody, wrenching glory, but we each didn't know what the others had done for a living, or how they met their husbands, and so on. We only found this stuff out months later when, as though stumbling out of a war zone, we remembered we'd had lives before and it occurred to us to ask questions that weren't related to nappies or feeding or sleep.

There were weekly meet-ups with these 'friends' and when it came around to my turn to host, I spent the morning whirling around the house (wipe, hoover, mop, spray air-freshener). I was conscious that on her turn, Julia had baked cakes. I reviewed the contents of the fridge, smelled the milk, noted I had only four teabags left in the cupboard. I couldn't imagine how I could get Oliver to Waitrose and back in time and finish cleaning the house. Maybe if I stuffed them in a teapot and let it brew for ages, it would be OK. I put a few Penguin biscuits onto a side plate.

One of the girls, Esme, was a real earth mother, and really was a girl, it seemed to me, although she was all of twenty-nine so actually a little older than me. She was barefoot most of the time, her baby peacefully and angelically nestled in her sling.

My baby had a misshapen head and bruised face. He looked like he'd been in a fight. I felt as though I'd been hit by a truck.

I looked enviously at the others who seemed capable of applying mascara, lipstick even. Stared at them, fascinated. I was barely able to brush my own hair. In fact I remember, one day, making the conscious decision to brush my teeth rather than my hair, because that seemed the more important of the two and I felt I only had the time, not to mention the energy, for one of these tasks. Mascara? How?

I remember the tears. Tears that came every day and became normal.

Everything falling out of me. Blood, ridiculous amounts of blood. Pieces of clotted blood that I kept on mattress-like pads to show to the health visitor. One was almost the size of a chicken breast. She inspected it but didn't appear concerned. I felt wrecked.

Then, in time, handfuls of hair. *I'm losing myself*, I thought, *soon there will be nothing of me left*. This was actually a soothing prospect.

Only eating what I could hold in one hand, and not really tasting it. Sugary biscuits melting on my tongue and bringing brief bursts of energy, followed by guilt. The return of the old, ugly voices: 'you're fat, you're disgusting, you're useless'.

My new shape, in the bath. My body sack-like.

Everything hurting. Breaking.

'I'm afraid Oliver has sustained what we call a torus fracture. It means the bone is twisted. Do either of you have any idea how it might have happened?'

We look at each other. We're in a doctor's room, a behind-the-scenes kind of place, which is not used to seeing members of the public. It has taken some minutes to get chairs organised and to make space for us.

'No,' Richard says; the doctor glances at me and I shake my head. He sighs, as though this was the response he expected but he'd hoped for something else. His next words sound a bit like lines from a script.

'We're going to put Oliver's arm in a cast and make him as comfortable as possible. We need to run a few more tests so we'd ask that you stay until the morning.'

I look at the clock. There are no windows in the room but I know that outside it must be light. We should be at home, getting up, getting ready, making breakfast. It's already morning.

'What kind of tests?' Richard is asking.

'We'll be looking for … any other injuries,' the doctor says. 'In these types of cases, because fractures in young children are so … unusual, I'm afraid we have to treat the injury as suspicious.'

'What does that mean?' Richard's voice has the slow, stone-like quality I've heard many times. *Don't get angry*, I will him silently, *please*. His knees bounce up and down beneath the table, causing his heels to hit the floor with a rhythmic clack, and I resist the temptation to put my hand out to steady him.

'There will be a social worker along to talk to you in a few hours. And the police.' At this I feel Richard start to rise from his chair, from the corner of my eye see his mouth open and then close again. The doctor turns to me and says, 'It's routine. Please understand. Your son's safety is of the greatest concern to us right now.' He starts to get up from his desk, raising a hand to indicate the door, then almost as an afterthought he adds, 'We'll let you see Oliver just as soon as he's settled.'

Let *us see him? He's my baby*, I think. *The world is upside down, this is all wrong.*

I can feel the rage coming off Richard in waves. He's biting his lip and a strange sound, between a cough and a growl, is forming in his throat, but he says nothing.

'Thank you, Doctor,' I mumble, and we are led back to the waiting room.

Chapter Two

Richard

There are some rooms in a hospital you hope never to go into. Like the windowless, airless room they take you to when they think you've hurt your own child.

What with her job, Sally should be more at ease in medical places than I am, so it's annoying me how much she is deferring to the doctors. I'm sure she wouldn't always have done that. Something about her has changed, I think since she had Ol. She's not the same girl I married.

We're taken to separate rooms, once the police and social workers arrive. It reminds me of when we gave our notice of marriage. Then we sat in rooms not unlike these ones, clean and sterile and featureless, together and later apart. I remember I had felt Sally flinch when the registrar referred to me having been married before. *Still?* I'd thought. *Still pissed off that there was someone before you. Really?* I'd produced my divorce documents. Grounds: adultery with an unnamed woman. I never have been able to work out whether Sally was relieved or annoyed not to be named.

When the time came for us to be interviewed separately, I couldn't remember Sally's date of birth. It had taken me ages. Eventually I did, of course, and the registrar kind of laughed with me, and as we left the room I had whispered to her, 'Don't tell her I forgot, or there'll *be* no wedding!'

This time there is no laughing and joking. There is a policeman, grey hair and a low voice, business-like and reserved. He doesn't say anything or take notes and I'm a bit unsure why he is here. I keep looking at him expectantly, but he's impossible to read. He sits a little way back from the desk, just watching. I try to keep my expression neutral, not remotely aggressive, but people are always telling me my emotions show all over my face, and right now my blood is boiling. His silence is making it worse.

The social worker is all friendly at first, urging me to relax, making sure I have water, oh, and am I comfortable? Is there anything else I need? I resist the temptation to reply that, yes, there is actually: I need to get the fuck out of this room and get home. She is probably in her forties but looks older; her hair is a mess and her blouse strains open at the middle buttons. I can see the pale skin of her stomach. She has a wide smile but a big crease between her eyebrows. There is a folder on the desk and she holds a notebook and pen, but she doesn't write anything down.

I've very nearly calmed down when she asks, 'Have you ever hit your children, Richard?'

There is the briefest of pauses, and then I look her in the eye. 'No.'

There is silence from the other side of the table. I know why they're doing it, to try to get me to speak, and I want to resist but I can't help filling the space.

'Of course not. Oliver's ten months old, for God's sake.'

'What about your daughter?'

'I was counting her as one of my children, funnily enough.'

I met Sally when she was really young. I was in between two businesses, snowed under, and I took her on to do a bit of clerical work; she needed the cash while she was in the final year of her pharmacy degree. No, I didn't bang the secretary – I'm not *that* much of a cliché. Besides, Zoe and I were pretty happy at that time. But Sally and I got on well, and after she graduated we met up for a drink, and … you know how it goes.

She was fun, then. She's ten years younger than me and her life had a simplicity to it that was attractive. When I first went to her flat I couldn't stop grinning at how clean and ordered everything was. I know it sounds crazy, but after years of living with Zoe, and all her mess and clutter and madness, not to mention the chaos of a young child, Sally and her first apartment – small and simple but full of barely used things and alive with promise – were pretty appealing.

It was about the sex, really (for me anyway, at first), but Sally was funny, sort of old-fashioned: she wanted us to date. I would remind her that I was married (as though being married meant I definitely couldn't go on dates – illicit sex was OK, but not dating, no way – I know, mad logic) and that I wasn't about to leave Zoe, not while Martha was still so young. She was ten at the time.

Sally said she understood this but still insisted, and so I found myself taking her out, to country pubs, to the cinema, the theatre, nice restaurants. It was hard – I had to choose places we were unlikely to bump into friends of Zoe's – but Sally knew what she was doing. She was making me court her; it made me feel young again, and it made me fall in love with her.

And once you fall in love, you *have* to leave your wife.

And then, in time, Ol came along. Sally struggled, for a while. Motherhood didn't really fit her as maybe she'd hoped it would. She'd worked with children for years by this time so I guess she assumed it would all come naturally to her, but it didn't. She was tired, and tearful, and always grateful when I got home at the end of the day. I liked it, when she needed me. I liked it when I was useful.

And then all of a sudden it was like they became a unit: a self-sufficient world on their own. Bonded, to the exclusion of all else. Hermetically sealed.

Sometimes it seemed like they were laughing at me, plotting against me, even, so tight was their togetherness. I know this sounds ridiculous. I know this, now.

They get us together to break the news that they aren't going to let us take Ol home. They say we aren't to be with him 'unsupervised', not until they complete their investigations. No one can tell us how long that will take.

'What does supervision mean, exactly?' I ask.

'But … where will he go?' Sally whispers. The social worker's eyes flicker from her face to mine, then back again.

'Well, we have foster families, of course. But if there were a family member he could live with in the short term – a grandparent, maybe?'

'My mother,' I murmur, feeling Sally stiffen at my side. The social worker seems to brighten.

'That might work. Do they live nearby – your parents?'

'Yes, yes, they do. A mile or so.'

'OK, then. We'll let you make the call. There'll be paperwork to complete, but … it should be straightforward.'

'How long?' I ask, not for the first time. 'It will only be days, right?' I feel Sally's hand on my elbow, as though trying to steer me away, and I shrug it off, irritated. The social worker's and doctor's faces are impassive.

'It makes no sense,' I tell Sally, as though they aren't in the room. It feels as though there's something I'm getting that no one else can see. 'They can't just take him. They can't keep him.'

Sally looks at the doctor and says, in her most professional voice, 'Could you give us a few moments, please?' He glances at the social worker, then nods.

'They've got the X-ray,' Sally says quietly, once they've left the room. 'That's all they need.'

'So based on one X-ray – one flimsy bit of paper – they can take our son away?'

She looks at me and frowns. 'It isn't just a piece of paper though, is it? It's Ollie.'

She's right; he's his own piece of evidence, with his little arm now in a cast, the plaster white as snow but far from innocent. Somehow I'd forgotten to see him, or not let myself see him, as a whole, but instead like the X-ray itself, as a disembodied arm, unnatural in black and white, the twisting crack hardly visible.

'The doctors saw the break; the social workers see the child,' Sally says, hanging her head.

It's a measure of how much Sally wants to keep Ol from going into care that she's willing to consider him living with my mother. Let's just say they aren't each other's biggest fan. But her own mother, the only possible alternative, is too far away, in every sense of the phrase. And at least this way, I reason, Ol will be close to us, and he'll still be with family rather than strangers. I have to take a few deep breaths before I make the call, though, and can hardly let myself hear my mother's responses, which are initially startled but quickly controlled and composed. That's her style.

'Mum. It's me. Yes, I know it's early, I'm sorry. You're up, though, right? OK. Well, I need to ask a favour. That is, we do. It's Oliver. No, no, he's fine … Well, actually he's not, not really … That's the thing. He's had an accident. He broke his arm. We don't know how it happened and … No, I know … Look, social services are looking into it and while they do, we can't take him home.' I move the phone away from my ear while she has a momentary rant. But if there's one thing my mother finds irresistible, it's being useful. When she realises what I'm asking, the enormity

Joanna Barnard

of the favour, of the responsibility, she reverts to type and comes over all efficient. She sounds pleased, even. 'Thanks, Mum,' I say, feeling the need to swallow but finding my mouth too dry. 'I'll talk to you again a bit later.'

Walking out to the car, we compare our separate 'interviews' (I can't think of a better word; that was what they felt like) in self-conscious whispers.

'Did they ask you where you were?' I say.

'Of course.'

'You told them you went out?'

She looks at me strangely. 'Yes, I said I was out all evening.'

It was one of the first things they asked me, of course, and it should have been a warm-up question, with a simple yes or no answer, but it keeps resurfacing in my mind as we drive back to the home that will feel a little less like home, without Ol in it.

'So you were in the house, with your son, all night?'

'And my daughter.'

'And your daughter, yes. But you were there all night?'

'Yes,' I'd lied.

~ 29 ~

Chapter Three

Martha

I come home from school, drop my bag in the hall as usual and call out, 'Hello?'

There are murmurs coming from the kitchen. I stand in the doorway, watching Dad and Sally. He's standing up, his shoulders hunched and tense; she's sitting at the breakfast bar, her head in her hands, her hair all mussed up.

'Don't say hello then,' I mutter, walking to the fridge, but halfway there I stop and look at them again, then up at the ceiling, as though I can see through it up into Ol's room. I notice how quiet everything is. He can't be here.

'Where's Ol?' I ask. Sally lays her head on the marble without a word, and for a moment I think the worst. Nausea swells in me.

'He's not coming home,' Dad says; Sally, lifting her head, shoots him a look through her hair. 'Not yet,' he adds. 'He's staying with Granny and Grandad for a while.'

'But why? Is he OK?'

'He's got a broken arm, it seems,' says Dad as though he doesn't quite believe it, that it's just a rumour he's heard. But they don't make mistakes about this kind of thing, do they?

'Look, Martha,' he continues, 'could you just go to your room for a bit? I'll be up shortly and we can have a chat.' Something about the emphasis on the word 'chat' and the unblinking look he gives me tells me that what he means is: *don't say anything, just leave the room and stay out of the way until I tell you otherwise.* So that's what I do.

Sally is closer in age to me than to my mother. This must really piss Zoe off. Yes, I call her by her first name, at her insistence – she's *that* kind of mother.

At first I thought me and Sally might be friends; it seemed cool that Dad had a new girlfriend, I thought it might even be fun.

When he wasn't looking, I used to read the texts and emails she sent him. She seemed nice. It didn't occur to me, back then, that she'd been on the scene much longer, that she was the reason Dad had left.

But then I met her and she wasn't cool at all, or even that nice. I was a bit gutted, to be honest.

She tried *really* hard to be matey with me. We met for the first time in an arty little café in town that Dad knew I liked, and I knew he hated. It's the kind of place that has no menu, just scribbled 'specials' on a blackboard and whatever drinks they happen to have in the fridge that day. There are mismatched chairs, stained tables, benches with cushions on them, and flyers everywhere for local bands, poetry slams, jewellery and craft sales.

Dad looked totally awkward hunched over his lemonade. Sally had a green tea. After some general chat Dad announced, 'Well, I'll leave you girls to it,' and with a sickly grin, got up to leave; I scowled at him.

Almost as soon as the bell had tinkled to signify his exit, Sally got all serious, and gave me the whole 'I know no one can replace your mother' speech. I said nothing.

To tell the truth, I'd hoped she could. I'd hoped she would be the one I could do all the clichéd things with: go shopping, gossip about boys. But she wasn't. Maybe it wasn't her fault; maybe no one was. But I didn't like the skirt she was wearing, and I didn't like the way she went to pat my hand at one point, then changed her mind. She had chipped nail polish, too.

Then along came Ol. Or, first, the threat of him. I knew she was pregnant way before they told me. They must have thought I was stupid. I'd already moved in with them by then and I used to lie in bed listening to her chucking her guts up in the bathroom, which is right next to my room. She made this hideous hawking sound and then a spitting that seemed to go on for ages. It made me want to throw up myself. She'd come out, all pale and sweaty, smile at me as though nothing was going on.

I was kind of sick (ha!), by now, of being bullshitted by adults.

The baby was, like Sally, a bit of a disappointment. He cried all the time. Oh, I know, that's what babies do, but I'm talking *all the time*. He would frown at me. 'Look, he's smiling,' Dad would say, and I looked, I really did, but he just seemed bloody grumpy to me. His little face was permanently scrunched up in fury.

He stank of shit, too. No one else seemed to mind this; in fact they were obsessed with talking about his shit. They had this plastic nappy bin thing that was supposed to be hygienic but it didn't stop the house from reeking, it just added a layer of synthetic baby powder smell on top of the shit. I walked around with my breath held half the time. And every other day they'd empty the plastic bin and I'd trip over a bag on the landing filled with squashed up nappies, streaked with shades of mustard and brown, and if I could stand it I'd pick it up between two fingers and run, arm outstretched with the bloody thing trailing behind me – the 'shit snake', I called it – out to the wheelie bin to get rid of it.

Sally would be pathetically grateful – 'oh, thanks for doing that, Mar', with a big wet smile – and I'd shrug and get out of the house as quickly as I could.

I hate it when she calls me Mar.

Dad has been and now it's Sally's turn to come and question me. She knocks softly on my bedroom door.

I do love my bedroom at Dad's. It's a bit girlie and kind of childish, I suppose, what with the fairy lights and all, and it's smaller than the one I had – still have I guess, in London – but it's my space. I love the sash window that looks over the garden; the fireplace that isn't a working fire, not any more, I suppose it was once but now it's crammed with candles; the rug I bought myself from a craft fair in town; the sink in the corner with its corny gold-plated taps and a little mirror above.

Sally comes in and sits on my bed and I shift as the weight of her (not that there's much of it, she's gotten pretty skinny since the baby) tips the mattress slightly. I take off my headphones and bring a pillow round to my chest, to hug.

She looks really tired. I guess she's still a little hungover, and I do feel sorry for her, for that.

'So, Martha, I just need to ask you a couple of questions about last night.'

'OK.'

'What was Oliver like, after I left?'

I shrug. 'Whingey. Crying, like, a lot.'

'More than usual? Different crying?'

'I guess. I dunno. He went to bed all right, though.'

'Hmm. That's what your dad said, too. And after that? Did you hear anything odd? Notice anything?'

'I was in my room.'

'Of course.' She sighs and looks around as though the answers are on the wall, or out the window.

'You know, this could be pretty serious,' she murmurs, but it's as though she's talking to herself, so I don't bother answering.

We both sit there for a while and I start to fidget with my headphones. Suddenly she looks up.

'You know,' she says again, 'I had two missed calls on my phone last night. Pretty late on. While I was out. From the house phone.'

My breath catches in my chest. I don't say anything.

'I just thought it was odd. Your dad usually rings me from his mobile.'

I shrug.

'There's *nothing* else you can think of.' She pauses. 'Nothing you aren't telling me?'

'Nope.' A decisive shake of the head.

'You won't get into trouble,' she says, the way you would to a little kid standing next to a broken vase.

'There's nothing,' I say. 'Sorry.'

Then she takes me in an awkward hug and leaves the room.

Turns out I'm a good liar. It must run in the family.

There's this guy. Isn't there always?

Brendan Lowe. Should've been Brendan High, that's what his mates say.

He's a dealer, small-time stuff really, but he's pretty popular, put it that way. He's a sixth former, well-built, gorgeous. Everyone knows him. We girls call him 'him with the eyes'.

So last night, Brendan Lowe texted and asked to come over. Brendan Lowe wanted to come to my house. This didn't happen. And I was alone; well, apart from the baby. As soon as I'd sent the message back, as casually as I could, saying, 'yeah, come over whenever' (I re-drafted at least eight times and *that* was the best I came up with), I crept up the stairs and into Ol's room.

He was asleep but his breath was all raggedy. I looked closely at him; his eyelids were fluttering, his face all red. I wondered if he had a temperature. Aside from his shit, his temperature seemed to be Sally's main obsession.

Sally is one of those irritating people who suffers through a headache (and whines to everyone else about it) rather than just taking a pill. So when people say to her, 'Oh, dose him up with Calpol', in response to every bout of sniffles or sleepless night, she frowns at them. I half-expect her to say she plans to try milk thistle or camomile or something; for a pharmacist she's kind of snooty and suspicious about drugs.

Luckily Dad has no such issues and at the side of the cot, on the changing table, was a half-empty bottle of the magic pink stuff. And a syringe, or a dropper-type-thing. Anyway I didn't know how big a dose a full one of those was but it couldn't have been much; it was tiny. And baby medicine couldn't actually be harmful, could it? Probably just keep him asleep. Hopefully. I told myself all this and only had a short moment of doubt, leaning over the cot with the dropper in my hand, but then he stirred, opened his mouth in a kind of sigh, and I took my moment and pressed the plunger and shot the gooey liquid right into the back of his mouth.

* * *

'Wanna try some of this? New shit,' he said. 'I could use a second opinion.' Brendan Lowe was in my house and we were sitting opposite each other, cross-legged, in front of the fire in the den. It wasn't a cold night but I'd lit the fire thinking it would be atmospheric, or something. It did look nice although it smelled kind of dusty and weird.

Brendan was looking at me through narrowed (but still gorgeous) eyes and I wondered if he knew, knew I was a fraud, that I was not the person to test his gear on, that I wouldn't know if it was good or not, because I had nothing to compare it with. But I wanted to be that person, so I said, 'Yeah, all right,' with a bored sigh, like I was doing him a huge favour, 'but you can roll it.' Ha! As if I knew how. He grinned, pulled a plastic bag out of his jacket pocket and set to work.

I watched his fingers fill the joint, watched his tongue snake along the paper, and then with a flick of his wrist he snapped open his lighter. It was one of those old-fashioned, fat, flat, ones; it looked like it should belong to a much older man, somehow. And it let out a huge flame. I was afraid it would singe those beautiful eyelashes right off. He took a drag, exhaled and passed me the joint, which I took between my finger and thumb, trying to hold it just the way he had.

As usual, I knew all the right things to say but I didn't have the moves. I felt slightly behind. I'd always felt like this, maybe it's because I was an August baby and so I was young in my class, or maybe it was because I missed out on a few years of primary school during The Home Schooling Experiment That Is No Longer Spoken Of.

With the first drag, I coughed, and he laughed. I remembered someone telling me about pot etiquette, that you were supposed to pass it around after one drag, so I tried to hand it back, but he gave a little wave, and said 'S'OK, you carry on.' He leaned back on the floor, his hands behind his head.

When the joint was half-smoked I lay on the sofa and it was wild because I realised all in a rush that although I could speak, could hear and understand, and although my thoughts seemed to be working normally, I really wasn't able to move. I had the sense of being glued to the sofa. I said this to Brendan; he didn't seem concerned.

I thought about what my friends would say if they knew Brendan Lowe was here, in my house. Sitting on the rug with no shirt on. I wondered when he took his shirt off. I realised it was very hot in the den, with the fire and everything. I laughed and the sound that came out seemed to me to be like a bubble that was rising, rising to the ceiling, and this made me laugh even more.

Some time passed. It might have been minutes, or hours. It was probably just minutes. It would be later that I'd remember the click, and the flash, and the sense that my head was being pulled, gently, into an unnatural position. So gently, though. And then he was gone.

I crawled to bed and was aware of noises that seemed to be in the distance. I dreamed monsters were climbing the walls outside, reaching for my window with tentacle-like fingers. I heard the front door open and close twice, presumably once Dad, once Sally.

When I woke up in the early hours and they said they were taking Ol to hospital I remembered the Calpol and panicked, so I was kind of relieved when they said it was his arm, because that couldn't have been my fault.

There's another knock on the door. I groan and consider pretending to be asleep. Then I hear Dad's voice: 'Martha, you awake? It's just a quick one.' Is he going to ask me what I said to Sally? She clearly wanted to know what I said to him. I wish they'd just talk to each other and save all this cross-examination.

'Come in.' I sigh.

'Hey, squirt,' he says, which is something he hasn't called me in, like, eight years. I give him my best 'get to the point' look. He takes a breath and says, 'Listen, we just had a call. The social services people need to talk to you. I said they could come tomorrow.'

'What? What will they ask me? What will I have to say?'

'You'll do fine. Just like we talked about before. But listen, you need an adult present, for your protection, and it can't be me or Sally.'

'Grandma?' I ask, with what I'm not sure is hopefulness.

'No, Grandma's . . . ah . . . well, she's already very involved.'

It suddenly occurs to me how much Sally will be *hating* this fact, and I almost snigger. Almost, because next Dad says, 'So your mum is coming. She'll be your, ah, your appropriate adult. I think that's what they call it.'

My stomach drops. So Zoe is coming. Here, to the house. Great.

Chapter Four

Sally

At the hospital, I'd got the young, pretty social worker and Richard had the more matronly one, and even with everything that was happening it occurred to me to be grateful for that, at least.

She'd asked me how I felt about my son. It seemed an odd question and it took me a while to answer it. She held me with her glittery green eyes while I scrabbled for the right words.

It was protectiveness, first. Pure, animal protectiveness. An urge, with no idea how I would fulfil it.

Then, for a while, confusion. Bleakness. Fear and an awareness of my own inadequacy.

Then came the love, finally. Love that hurts. Love that fills your heart right up to exploding point.

'Love,' I told her, 'I love him. Obviously.'

Love, as it turned out, that left no space for anything, or anyone, else.

'What's that?' I asked, pointing at a blue folder.

'They're the notes from your health visitor.'

I'd almost forgotten the stream of people who came to the house in the days and weeks after Ollie was born. Sometimes unannounced, or had they told me they were coming and I'd forgotten? I would whisk around the kitchen, hiding boxes of formula as I made tea, because I was 'supposed' to be breastfeeding.

One of the health visitors had asked me a series of questions and filled in a sheet with ticks and crosses. I'd studiously lied to most of them. Richard didn't like this succession of visitors and wanted to put paid to them as quickly as possible. But then she'd asked me about crying.

'How often do you cry, or feel like crying, would you say?'

I looked at her.

'Every day,' I whispered. *Several times a day*.

'Baby blues,' she nodded and patted me on the arm but she wrote something in the folder and before she left she handed me a leaflet. I can't remember the details now but it had a woman's silhouette on the front, oddly menacing, and a quick glance at the contents revealed it may as well have been called 'Don't Shake Your Baby'.

I put it in the bin.

It turned out a few of us in the MMG had been given these leaflets, and we all laughed about it, over cups of tea.

I didn't know then that almost a year later, that folder would come back from the past to berate me.

All those tears, reported by me in innocence, now contained in a folder that might be used to prove that, at best, I couldn't cope, and, at worst, I'd hurt my son. Tears on tears, wrapped in paper, which would surely become damp and weaken and burst open.

So now I find myself at home with, it seems, nothing to do, so I decide to go to bed early. Although Ollie is ten months old, I'm still in the habit of sterilising his bottles and taking one upstairs with me, along with a carton of ready-mixed formula, just in case he wakes in the night and needs a drink to settle him. I have to stop myself in the kitchen; I find myself standing in front of an open cupboard, just staring.

The kitchen is the only room in the house I allowed Richard to make modern, and he's gone to the extreme: all stainless steel, glass and cold edges. Elsewhere, I was fanatical about keeping the original features: the floorboards, fireplaces, ceiling roses and picture rails. I love the sense of history in the house, the feeling for previous inhabitants and just the aesthetics of sash windows and high ceilings. It was, still is, my dream home and I've poured my heart and soul into it. It's my castle, my cave, my escape.

My mother, when she first visited, had walked around wearing a bemused expression. 'I don't hold with this so-called "shabby chic" craze; it just looks tatty,' she'd said. In her home, cushions have to match curtains, rugs have to suit wallpaper, and so on. Everything is co-ordinated and each room has a very definite colour scheme. You feel uncomfortable in the determinedly green-and-gold sitting room if you're wearing a colour that clashes.

Our house is more muted. Nothing matches, but I like that, and nothing jars either: pale-grey walls, tones of mauve, mocha, occasional splashes of blue. Antique furniture in natural materials, all wood and slate, some chipped, some scratched, all loved. Grudgingly my mother said it was 'tastefully done, though', as she ghosted from room to room, bewildered as to how this had been achieved, or that her daughter was capable of putting together a home at all.

As I move through the house from the kitchen up to the bedroom, I become aware of a whispering lack of something, as though the soul of the place I so care about is leaking, very slowly, away. I climb the stairs with empty hands, thinking, as I've been thinking every minute, all day, *Where is he now? What is he doing? How is he feeling?* And the question I can't bear and keep pushing down, down: *Is he missing me? Does he, in his tiny heart, also feel this lack, this loss?*

I am so surprised to see Richard already in bed that I actually stumble a little as I move into the room. He usually comes up at least two hours later than I do.

'Oh,' is all I can muster, as I start to peel off my clothes. He is sitting up, pillows propped behind him, his reading glasses on, looking at something on his phone.

'It says here babies don't break bones,' he says. 'They just don't. Not normally. There has to be real force applied. They don't break a bone just lying in their cot.'

'I know that, Richard.' I resist the temptation to snap at him. I'm the healthcare professional, after all; does he think I'm stupid? What's more, I'm the one who did the baby and toddler First Aid course – not him. He was too busy to concern himself with how to dislodge a grape from Ollie's throat or treat a burn or a bee sting. I want to shout but instead I say again, calmly, 'I do know.'

He puts down his phone and looks at me. 'You haven't asked me,' he says. 'You haven't asked me if I hurt him. You haven't accused me.' I stare at him, incredulous.

'Of *course* I haven't.' I start to move towards him, to comfort him and tell him *I know you couldn't, you wouldn't,* but then it occurs to me it could be an accusation in itself and I stop. What if what he's really saying is: 'You haven't asked me if I did it because you know I didn't, because *you* did'? And is he thinking the same about Martha right now? I just stand there, mouth opening and closing, because I haven't formulated any words.

'I think that's extraordinary,' he says. 'Thank you.' I nod and sit down on the bed with my back to him, pull off my socks.

'Big day tomorrow,' he murmurs. As though I have a job interview or something. In a way I suppose I have. Tomorrow I'll be auditioning for the role of mother.

'Yes, we get to visit our own son.' I sigh.

'Not just that,' he says, 'I mean, that, yes, but something else. Afterwards. They're coming here. Social services. They have to talk to Martha.'

'Well, OK.' I frown, feeling exhausted at the prospect of more questions, even if it won't be me answering them. 'Will that be OK? I mean, for Martha – will one of us be able to stay with her?'

He shakes his head. 'It can't be us. And I didn't think you'd want Mum.' He looks at me pointedly.

All I can do is shrug; I'm not sure what's coming next.

'Zoe is coming over. She'll be Martha's appropriate adult.'

Of course.

I haven't seen Zoe, since. I don't relish the thought of having her here and I itch to ask: Really? Does it have to be her? Does it have to be *here*? But I don't bother.

I pull on my pyjamas, avoiding my reflection in the full-length mirror in the corner of the room, the glass that seems to see everything. I am aware I am doing everything more slowly, more carefully, than normal, as though afraid of breaking something myself. I brush my teeth in the en-suite, briefly glancing at my face, certain I can see new lines there. By the time I creep into bed the light is off, Richard's phone and glasses are on the bedside table, and I assume he is asleep until his arm snakes across my stomach.

I wriggle but he holds me fast, and moves closer, whispering, 'Let's have sex.'

'What?' His hand is creeping along my pyjama top, undoing the buttons I've only just fastened, and his breath is on my neck.

'Come on,' he says. 'Let's have sex, you know, like we used to. In the beginning.'

'What, you mean missionary, with kissing?' This is only half a joke.

Richard is unlike any other lover I've had, not that there have been many. He's astonishingly selfish in bed. I think he hid this selfishness at the start, or it wasn't there at all until I released it; I'm not sure. To be fair to him, I cast myself in a role where I was all about pleasing him – nothing else mattered. I don't know why I did this, but it became a habit I couldn't break. I suppose I wanted to impress him, and I wanted him to need me.

But before our sex life evolved (or degenerated) in this way, he used to be tender and attentive. He is touching me in that old way now, and in spite of a head full of the pain and questions of the day, my body starts to relent. I'm torn up with guilt at the idea of doing anything for pleasure, am not even sure I can feel pleasure, not today, but some dark part of me knows that these moments of being held, possessed, covered, will distract me.

'Yes,' I whisper, and that word is all he needs to peel off my pyjamas, to be on top of me, inside me, moving, grunting softly, his face turned away.

In a way, I was waiting to meet Richard, or someone like him. I'd had a few boyfriends: the ultra-runner with his 'plant-based diet'; the Iranian dentist with his fabulous cooking and total absence of any sense of humour; the lovely, kind, generous, unambitious IT programmer who was so desperate to marry and have babies I found myself running from him in something like terror. I liked them all, in a vague sort of way; but I didn't love them.

Richard was older than all of them; maybe that was part of the appeal. Ten years older than me, which, when you're in your early twenties, seems like quite a gap. And he was unavailable, or so I thought.

I met him and his wife on the same day, and as soon as I saw him I thought *oh, shit*.

When you become someone's second wife it seems the accepted thing to hate the ex, but I didn't always hate Zoe. In fact, when I first met her I really liked her, which made it very inconvenient that I fell in love with her husband almost instantly.

It was Zoe who answered the door when I turned up for the interview. They lived in a narrow, mint green-painted townhouse in Notting Hill. I got off the tube at Ladbroke Grove and shuffled through the market crowds, eyes desperately seeking street signs, no idea whether or not I was headed in the right direction. Whichever way I looked, the multitude of stalls and the throngs of people, traders shouting in singsong voices, punters chattering and haggling, seemed to fill every possible space, giving the effect of being in the midst of a living, humming mass that looked the same whichever way you turned.

A couple of dreadlocked guys on steel drums gave Portobello Road a tropical feel that belied the grey skies and drizzle. I resisted the temptation to duck into the pub on the corner and while away the afternoon soaking up the west London atmosphere. I needed a job – I was in the fourth year of my studies and was finally, truly, skint. A friend said her uncle's friend's golf partner (or something) was looking for someone to do admin. I held my jacket over my head in a vain attempt to stop my hair from frizzing. I didn't own a suit but had figured that jeans and a smart jacket would be OK.

The only other interview I'd ever had, apart from academic ones, had been for a job in the bus station café back in my hometown, so I wasn't really sure what the protocol was and my stomach was fizzing with nerves. It seemed a bit weird to be interviewed in someone's house but the guy had sounded so nice on the phone that I went for it. Plus the money was good – a lot better than I could make in the union bar – and better hours too.

She was beautiful, although her skin, clearly weathered by too much sun, made her look older than she was. She was wearing a long, purple tunic over skin-tight flowered leggings, her feet were bare and her toenails painted fluorescent orange. I remember thinking two things: it's a bit early to be drinking (she was holding a glass of white wine and it was only just before 2pm), and, I'd love to be like her when I'm grown up, even though I was already twenty-two and knew I would never, ever look so bohemian or so effortless.

She welcomed me warmly, told me Richard was 'on a call' and wouldn't be long, and led me by the arm into their bright sitting room full of unhung paintings and huge plants.

I've often thought since that if she'd known what was coming, she'd have slammed the door in my face. If I'd known what was coming, perhaps I might not even have knocked.

It was the thing people called 'banter', I supposed, the easy interaction between Richard and me, bouncing back and forth of chat, of ideas, conversation that flitted easily from politics to art to science to travel. Conversation that flowed so naturally, so quickly that had there been other people in the room it would have excluded them almost immediately, and suddenly I became self-conscious, remembered why I was there and with a hesitant cough, brought him back to it with some mumbled sentence that included the word 'job'. He sighed as though he didn't really want to bother with all that.

'You're clearly a bright girl; you can handle a bit of filing. I'm interested in what you are passionate about.'

'Well, I like my work. My studies, I mean.'

'Oh, yes – pharmacy. What made you choose that career?'

I fixed myself back into interview mode and had to hold myself back from telling him all the real reasons, all the madness of wanting to please my dad, all science's obsessive learning and listing and numbering and labelling that made me feel safe in a world that was not safe.

'I liked biology, and I was good at it, and I wanted to help people.'

'So why not a doctor?'

'I wanted to help people but I didn't want to clean up their shit.' It just came out; thankfully he laughed.

'It's probably nurses that do that.'

'I didn't want to hold their hands either. I'm probably not a very ... touchy-feely person.'

He raised an eyebrow.

'And you were too clever to be a nurse, I guess.'

I frowned. 'There's nothing wrong with being a nurse.'

'Of course not.'

'I've met plenty of clever nurses.'

'I'm sure.' He looked amused.

'I'm saying they have skills I don't have.'

'Well, you're skilled enough for this job. Do you want it?'

I realise I'm making him sound a bit unattractive, now. It's only now I see his comments as a bit sexist, a bit patronising. I suppose through the glass of years together, he looks different. But at the time here was a man, not a boy, not an awkward student, an actual attractive, successful man paying me attention.

On the tube ride home, a one-page employment contract rolled up in my bag and my immediate money worries receding, I allowed my thoughts to turn to Richard and felt my heart hit the floor.

I tried to rationalise it. Maybe I was just a bit lonely and was latching onto him.

But this was just an excuse. The truth was, my head was pounding with something like shock. The exhilaration of seeing exactly what you want; the sorrow of knowing there is no way you can pursue it. He belonged to someone else, someone I'd liked even though we'd only met briefly, and was more than a little intimidated by.

And here we are now. We lie side by side, breathless, not touching.

I decide to say something, a whispered admission, but the kind of thing you should be able to say to the person you're meant to be closest to in the world.

'I feel like a terrible person,' I say, 'because up until now, I would have loved for someone to take Ollie away for a night.'

'You never said,' he says, twisting round in bed to look at me.

I shrug.

He frowns. 'How can you say that?'

'Quite easily, Richard. It's all right for you – you're not the one who's been here with him, day in day out. It's hard work. It's boring. It's ...' And I look up to the ceiling to stop myself from crying. 'I needed a break, that's all.'

I thought I was opening up, trying to bridge the space between us, but he's looking at me and something is passing across his face, like it's occurring to him for the first time that I could have hurt Ollie. 'I didn't do it,' I whisper eventually, but he's already asleep, or not listening.

I wake up feeling as though I've only just fallen asleep. Light streams through the bedroom windows, illuminating their dust and streaks. By the time Richard stirs I have a bucket of hot water and am cleaning them. I use the chamois leather to polish them to a shine until my arms ache.

'Don't forget we have to be at Mum's in an hour,' he mutters; I scowl at him. As if I could forget our first 'visit' to our own son. As if I am not feeling the great yawning absence of him with every second.

I too always think of it and refer to it as Richard's mum's house, not his parents', because his mum is such a force and his dad so ... well, inconsequential, in comparison.

Cynthia wears her hair in an ash-blonde bob that skims her chin, the fringe sitting neatly on her perfectly sculpted eyebrows. She likes to control everything, as far as I can make out: the house, the garden, the finances. Her only son.

Since retiring she's amassed a formidable array of hobbies including Pilates, flower arranging, jewellery making, not to mention a book club, walking club and all her work with the church. She can't abide idleness.

'Busyness is next to godliness,' I've heard her say on more than one occasion. Not long after I had Oliver, I overheard her say to Richard that he should watch out because I could get fat 'just laying around the house all day'. I heard the echo of her crisp tones later that night when Richard said to me, in an irritated way, 'I just don't know what you *do* all day.'

Ah, yes – the great divisive line, the barbed cliché that so many husbands trot out after the birth of a new child, as I soon learned. At first I thought it was just my husband, and it was just me; I took my daily exhaustion as proof that there was something fundamentally incompetent, maybe lazy, about me.

While Cynthia is loud and opinionated, David, Richard's dad, is low-voiced and gentle. I suppose he has to be. He dresses smartly, shirt collars and jumpers, and moves carefully, as though in anticipation of reprimand. He's always been kind to me, and I'm fond of him, but on our visits there his son barely acknowledges him, Richard's energy and attention so thoroughly absorbed by his mother whenever she is in a room that there are no fragments left to go anywhere else.

Whenever Richard rows with his mother (or, to a lesser extent, with The Ex), these are the best times. He seems to need me, then.

I've learned quickly, though, to be diplomatic. You can't say 'Yeah, she's a bitch', because it's OK for *him* to say that, but no one else; you just nod, and soothe, and listen.

When they are getting on, though, I find myself edged to the fringes of the picture. The strength his mother's approval gives him is visible, it's physical: he walks a little taller after a compliment from her, a shared joke, praise, a confidence.

I get dressed slowly, mindful of the scrutiny that will come from Cynthia as much as, if not more than, from the social worker who will also be present. I am standing staring at myself in the mirror when Richard comes in.

'What are you doing?'

'I'm wondering if I look like the kind of woman who would hurt her baby.'

'I don't know, what do those women look like?' His voice is sharp, the brief intimacy we shared last night now wholly evaporated. I feel disgusted that we rolled under these sheets, momentarily carefree, so I lean over and smooth out the creases. But each smoothing motion seems only to create another crease, another crumple, somewhere else on the sheet, and I feel tears rising in my throat. Richard is just staring at me.

'For fuck's sake, Sally,' he mutters. 'What's the matter with you? First the windows, now the bed … just leave it. Leave it. It's time to go.'

* * *

The social worker, the older one, is already there when we get to the house. She is in the conservatory with Cynthia, drinking tea. Her hair looks unwashed and she has bags under her eyes. Her blouse, presumably once white, is grey and ill-fitting. She stands up and with an uncertain smile shakes our hands.

'I'm Mary,' she says.

'I remember you,' says Richard stiffly. 'We met at the hospital. Yesterday.' Was it really only yesterday? I look around.

'Where is Oliver?' I ask, my voice sounding far away. Cynthia pats my hand with her papery fingers.

'He's in the other room. David is with him.' Then she turns to Mary and says to her, 'One of us is always with him.'

The 'other room', the front room, is rarely used except for very special guests. Cynthia keeps plastic covers on the arms of the sofa. The mantelpiece is home to an army of figurines, meticulously dusted, who seem to follow you with their tiny painted eyes, and a bowl of artificial pink peonies in the window clashes with the flowers on the curtains, the flowers on the carpet. The room makes my head ache.

We troop in to find David perched on the end of an armchair, teacup on his knee, and in the centre of the room, a playpen filled with brightly coloured plastic balls. It looks brand new. They must have been out this morning to get it; they've not wasted any time. They hadn't much baby stuff in their house before, only a few toys. In the corner of the pen, his healthy arm raising a red ball to his mouth, sits Oliver. My Ollie.

I look at him, at his little face in the second before he notices me, worlds of thought behind those dark eyes, and I know in a rush how *passionately* I love him. The longing, the deep need to breathe him in, to place my lips on his skin.

'Mmma!' his triumphant cry, the closest he has come as yet to 'mummy', a cross between an appreciative sound made while eating something good and the noise some people make when air-kissing. Then that smile: two bottom teeth, little perfect white squares; dimpled cheeks. His hair is freshly washed and combed, but not, of course, by me.

I rush over and he drops the ball and holds both arms up to me. The plaster cast looks awkward on him, too big, wrong.

'He's getting used to it,' Cynthia murmurs, as though reading my mind, but I can't believe it.

'Hello, baby,' I cry and as I lift him, careful not to touch the cast, I glance at Mary, silently asking her permission, I suppose, with a sick feeling in my stomach at the possibility she might tell me to put him down. Instead she gives a brisk nod. But she's watching me.

I inhale his powdery, milky smell. He clings to me like a baby monkey, his good arm and his feet little magnets on my body. I try to keep my voice light as I coo and chatter to him, but it comes out a bit high-pitched. I wish everyone else would leave the room so I could have him to myself.

There is no chance of that. Mary is talking, her head bobbing as she glances alternately at me, Richard, Cynthia, David.

'I thought I'd explain what's going to happen next,' she says. 'We'll be arranging a child-protection conference as soon as possible.'

'And what's that, Mary?' Cynthia asks. I fling her a resentful look. All pally with this woman, topping up her tea.

'Well, the purpose of the child protection conference is purely to make a decision as to whether Oliver is at risk.'

'It seems like that decision's already been made,' says Richard, leaning over to stroke Oliver's head. 'Otherwise he would be at home with us.'

Mary takes a deep breath.

'Well, given that Oliver sustained a serious, unexplained injury, I'm sure you can appreciate that our primary concern is for his safety. I know how difficult this must be for you all.' *Do* you? I think. *Do you know?* 'You'll receive a report in the next week or two which will form the basis for the conference. You'll have the opportunity to talk it through with me.'

'And what happens on the day itself?' Richard again.

'Various professionals will be there to give their view as to the degree of danger Oliver is in.'

'He's not in any danger,' I mumble, but as I do, I squeeze Ollie a little too tightly and he lets out a squeal. Richard puts out his hands and I reluctantly hand him over.

'You'll get the chance to speak at the conference too,' Mary says. I feel the emptiness in my arms and all I can think is soon, soon, they're going to take him from me again. She is already glancing at the carriage clock on the mantelpiece.

Oh yes, don't think I haven't seen you, Mary, clock-watching.
Her words are starting to become a blur.

'And these professionals –' Richard is looking at me
although he is addressing Mary '– presumably we can get our
own experts involved? A second opinion, I mean, something
like that.'

'Well, of course. You're also entitled to have a supporter
present.' At this, Cynthia opens her mouth as though to
speak, is actually raising her hand, but slams her lips shut
when she catches the look I give her. 'Or an advocate. There
are agencies you can use for that.'

'I'm not sure that will be necessary,' I say.

'Well, we'll discuss it . . .' says Richard, frowning.

'Could I please just have some time to play with my
son?' I look at Mary, and at all of them.

'Of course,' she replies. 'If you've any other questions,
just ask.'

I have no questions; I just want to be near Ollie, to
pretend for a few minutes that things are normal, to look at
his smile and see nothing else in the room. Richard places
him carefully on the floor and I sink off the sofa and down
onto the rug to his level.

He only just started to crawl a few weeks ago. At first
he'd moved backwards, which had caused him to cry in
frustration as the toy he was trying to reach got further
and further away despite the frantic scrambling of his little
limbs. Richard had videoed him, then played it in reverse
and laughed as the film showed him going the 'right' way.

But within a day or two he'd mastered it, more or less, one leg dragging slightly with the effect that he would move in circles, but the delight on his face was infectious.

Now, with the cast, it is tricky for him. After a few thwarted attempts, and heart-tugging squeals when the broken arm touches the ground, Ollie just sits, his big eyes staring, blinking.

'Nee-naw,' he says, pointing. 'Nee-naw.'

I lean across the floor and bring him his 'emergency vehicles garage', from which, if you press the right buttons, little police cars, fire engines and ambulances will come out whizzing and wailing their sirens. I flinch when he picks up the ambulance, but I keep the smile on my face.

Mary looks for what seems like the fiftieth time at the clock and then at her watch, as though for confirmation. She starts to smooth down her skirt, pointlessly it seems to me, as it's full of stubborn creases. My insides drop.

'I think that's all for today,' she says. 'I'm happy for Oliver to continue to stay here as long as it's OK with you.' She glances at Cynthia and David, who nod. 'But I think it's time for Mum and Dad to leave now. You'll get another supervised hour tomorrow.'

'Swimming,' I say suddenly. Everyone looks at me. 'He usually goes swimming on a Sunday. I usually take him. That's tomorrow.'

'He can't go swimming, sweetheart,' says Richard. 'He's got a cast on.'

'Of course,' I mumble. 'Stupid of me.' At that, everyone gets up and heads for the door. It's all happening quickly, too quickly. I scoop Ollie up into my arms and carry him, nuzzling his neck, his ears, until our odd little procession gets to the hall and Mary opens the front door.

'Bye bye, sweetheart,' I whisper, 'Mummy will be back tomorrow.' Ollie's good hand grips my collar and his face starts to crumple and redden. *Oh no, he's going to cry, and I just will not be able to leave him.*

'Don't drag it out,' says Cynthia. 'You're upsetting him.' She peels him from my arms and Richard has to steer me out of the door and onto the path, both hands on my shoulders, and I crane my neck all the way to the car, watching my son get smaller and smaller.

Richard waits until we're in the car to tell me he's going to work.

'What?' I spin my neck towards him so quickly it gives a twinge.

'I have to,' he says, tapping the wheel as we meet traffic. 'I've already had too much time off. Don't forget, if I don't work, we don't earn.'

'But it's Saturday.'

He looks at me. 'It's hardly the first time I've worked on a Saturday.'

'But what about Zoe coming? Martha, and social services? You're going to just leave me to it?'

'You're a grown-up.' He gives a chilly little laugh. 'I'm sure you can manage.'

I've never seen Zoe since our first and only meeting, in Notting Hill. It's weird because she has been such a huge presence in our lives, especially over the period of the divorce, and yet, for me anyway, she was like a ghost, never physically there. And in my mind, she's fixed as a kaftan-wearing, floaty artist waving a glass of wine around, so it's odd to find her sitting in my kitchen wearing jeans and Converse boots, a mug of tea in her hand.

She's cool with me, and I'm almost relieved when Mary arrives and ushers them both into the living room and closes the door. After about half an hour, the three of them troop out again. Mary says something quietly to Martha and hands her a business card, with a pointed look at me, then leaves. I look at my feet.

'Martha, hon,' says Zoe, her voice every bit as confident as if she were the woman of the house, not me. 'Can you leave us for a minute?'

Martha nods and I find myself alone with my husband's ex-wife. We're standing in the hall, surrounded by framed photographs of me and Richard, Richard and Martha, and the three of us. I try not to look at them, in the hope that she won't either.

'Probably time we cleared the air, isn't it?' she says.

I look at her; at her shiny hair, her barely made-up face. I have no idea what to say so I point back at the living room door and mumble, 'Do you want to go in there and sit down?'

'No, this won't take long,' and then she starts looking around, and I wish I could tear all these photographs off the walls; I'm like an impostor in someone else's life and I'm surrounded by evidence of my guilt. I steal a glance at my watch;

Richard won't be back for about an hour. I feel her studying my face. 'I suppose he told you this was different, special, he'd never cheat otherwise.' She pauses but I don't say anything. Am I supposed to? 'Don't you think he said that to me too?'

'But . . . he wasn't married before you.'

'No, but he did have a girlfriend.' This is news to me, but I try to keep my face neutral. She plucks her jacket from the coat stand. 'He said it to me, he said it to you, he'll say it to the next one.' She shrugs. 'I think he believes it, too. Anyway, if you're OK with that, then good luck to you.'

'Martha,' I call, or try to call, but my voice is too quiet to be heard upstairs, so I try again. 'Martha! Your mum's leaving now.' I turn to Zoe and say in as business-like a tone as I can muster, 'Thanks for coming.'

Martha hovers at the top of the stairs but doesn't bother coming down them. 'See you,' she calls down, with a half-hearted wave.

'Bye, sweetheart, and remember you can call me any time,' Zoe shouts back, but her daughter has already turned on her heel, back towards her room. I open the front door and just as she's about to step out, Zoe turns around and says to me, 'One more thing. Sorry about the baby. I hope you get it sorted.' She pauses. 'Richard's a bastard but he wouldn't hurt a baby.'

The visit this morning must have invigorated Richard. When he eventually gets home from work he practically races to his laptop, props it on the kitchen worktop and stands over it, as though even sitting on a stool might slow him down or represent an unacceptable level of relaxation. *My husband, the doer*, I think, moving around the kitchen as though through deep mud, picking things up, putting them down. I run the tap until the water is very cold and fill a glass. I stare out of the window. Everything, everything, feels very far away.

Richard's voice.

'You know what that retinal exam was about, don't you?' he demands, index finger jabbing at the screen. I look up. 'They were trying to see if we shook him. That's one way you can tell if a baby has been shaken.' He starts to pace and mutter to himself, curses pouring out one after another, 'For fuck's sake', 'Jesus Christ', 'Fucking hell' ... a mantra of profanity.

Then he gathers himself and goes upstairs to talk to Martha, leaving me alone with my babbling brain.

It doesn't even stop when I sleep. In my nightmares, there are endless different settings and scenarios but what they all have in common is that one minute I am holding Oliver and the next he escapes me, slippery as an eel through my hands, and falls. Falls inexorably onto cold flagstones, his head splitting like a watermelon, or down sharp-edged wooden stairs at the bottom of which he lands, twisted and in pieces, or once, memorably, over the side of a huge boat into a frothy grey ocean that swallows him up.

And in the morning I get up and make breakfast and drink coffee and attempt to function as a normal human being.

Chapter Five

Richard

Zoe had left by the time I got home, but of course I'd spoken to her briefly on the phone. She said Martha did great. And of course I didn't mention this conversation to Sally.

It suits Sally to think I hate Zoe, but I don't. Obviously we're in touch because of Martha, but as a rule I like to keep in touch with exes. Why wouldn't you, when you've shared so much together? Sally doesn't get this.

At first Zoe said I was selfish for wanting to be friends. She said I was using her to assuage my own conscience, or something. I didn't really understand what she meant. But anyway, we get on all right, now.

I give Martha's door a little tap. She mumbles something that sounds like 'Min', which I presume to be an abbreviation of 'Come in', so I do, settling myself on the edge of the bed.

'Your mum said you did really well today. Proud of you, squirt.' I move as though to ruffle her hair, like I used to when she was little, but think better of it.

'I said everything I was supposed to say.' She's sitting in a huddle, knees pulled up to her chest, and she looks fearful, and very young.

'It's over now, hush. I know it must have been really hard.'

'Dad? Whoever ... did this. To Ol. Whoever gets the blame. Will they go to prison?'

'Oh sweetheart. No one's going anywhere. You don't have to worry about that.'

'But I do. Don't you see?'

'Well, I mean, I know you're worried. Of course you are, he's your brother, but Sally and me, we're doing everything we can, and—'

'It's not that.'

'Then what? I don't get it.'

'I don't know!' she cries. 'They asked me outright, after I answered all the questions about you, they said Martha, did you hurt your little brother, just like that, all serious, and I said I didn't but the truth is I don't *know*!' She bursts into tears.

'Martha,' I say, slowly and as gently as I can, 'how could you not know? What do you mean? You would know—'

'I was—' Suddenly she stops herself.

'Martha, anything you tell me, I'll trust you. And you can trust me. You know that, right?'

'Right.' But she doesn't look certain. I just look at my hands and wait.

'I was ...' she begins again, shaking her head miserably. 'He ... I was ... well, I was drunk.'

'You were looking after your brother and you were drinking?'

'Sort of.'

'How could you be *sort of* drunk? Or was it something else?' I look at her closely, remembering her spaced out expression that morning on the landing. 'Drunk, Martha? Or stoned?'

She looks up, wide-eyed. 'Just drunk.'

'Jesus,' I mutter. 'Am I the only one around here who was sober?' And for a second the little girl my daughter was and has always been, to me at least, disappears and a cloud passes over her face.

'But you weren't "around here", were you? You weren't here.'

'Hang on a minute, lady. This is *not* about me now. You're telling me you were off your face on whatever,' I give her a pointed look, 'and you "don't know" if you hurt your brother or not?'

'Half-brother,' she mutters, and I lose it.

I grab her wrist and pull, just hard enough that she has to spin around, turn to look at me. She snatches her arm from my grip as though she's been stung, and sits rubbing it, tugging the sleeves down over her hands, and glaring at me.

'I don't want to hear you say that again,' I say. 'Got it?' She says nothing but rolls her eyes in the teenage way that can be universally translated as 'whatever'. I'm about to get up, get out of the room, the house, clear my head and work all this out, when something like a delayed echo comes back to me. 'Hang on a minute.' She looks up. 'Martha, earlier you said "he", then you stopped yourself.' She stares, unblinking. 'Was someone else here that night?'

'What? No!' Too quickly.

'Martha.' She flinches at the sternness of my voice. I try again, more gently. 'Come on. It's me. If there's something you need to tell me ...' But she's just staring into space, as though she's not hearing me. 'Who's "he"? Martha!' That was too sharp. Damn it.

'I meant ... Oliver. When I said "he". I was about to say something about Oliver. He was crying, then he was fine ... then I don't remember.'

I study her face, trying to work out whether she's telling the truth. It's difficult; her fringe is hanging into her eyes, her eyes looking anywhere but at me.

All the thoughts I've had about Martha growing up, the fears I've tried to ignore, are surfacing. Boys. She doesn't talk about them, but of course there are boys. But is it really possible she smuggled one of them into the house that night? Called someone to come round the minute I was gone? It seems pretty unlikely. I know they say the apple doesn't fall far from the tree but I really shouldn't tar her with my own brush. Not my little girl. Should I?

'I'm sorry,' I say. 'I'm tired.' And my mind is racing; I'm also thinking, if there *was* someone else here, where does that leave us?

'So am I. I don't know what I'm saying, Dad. I don't know anything.'

'Look, it's a really tough time. For all of us.' And as I say 'us', a picture of our little quartet swims before my eyes, fissures and all. We're still a family. But I don't know who to protect. We're programmed to protect our kids, look after the gene pool, but what if you have two and their needs don't match? What if you think one could have hurt the other? Do you just turn your back on them? Or do you protect them, even if that might mean incriminating your wife, or yourself? If Martha really is capable of harming a baby, then she's obviously damaged, and whose fault is that?

She's staring out of the window; she looks wretched. I look at her skinny arms, recall the feel of her tiny wrist in my hand.

'I'm sorry I was a bit rough,' I mutter; she nods. 'I don't think you would have hurt Ol, sweetheart. I don't believe you *could*.'

'Thanks,' she whispers, and lies down, drawing a pillow to her and curling her legs up, looking as though she's just going to go to sleep here, in her clothes. I guess this is my cue to leave.

I've made mistakes in my life, sure, but doesn't everyone? It just seems ridiculously unfair that this is happening to me. I'm basically a good guy. All I ever tried to do was get by in life, and I've done all right too, with not that much help.

I ran the tuck shop at sixth form college and realised I liked the feel of money. I learned about margins, profit on return, cash rate of sale, stock turn. Suddenly there was a world that made sense to me in a way that school never had. The only trouble was, it wasn't me making the money. Every week I handed over the profits (which more than doubled over the year I was in charge) to the student council. Don't get me wrong, they spent it on worthy causes and all that, but I felt resentful that my hard work didn't bring me any personal reward.

It was then, aged seventeen, that I knew I wanted to work for myself. The fact I'd announced this at home made things a little easier when I didn't get near the grades I needed to go to university. That had been my mother's dream anyway, not mine, and in time she came to understand that. Well, when I started making money, and handing over large chunks of it as rent, she came to understand it.

When I set up a cleaning business, I thought she might turn her nose up, but instead she said. 'You know, people will always want to live in clean houses. I think it's quite brilliant, darling.' And she promptly lent me the deposit I needed for my own premises, and that was my start. And then the new millennium came and with it, I don't know, a new optimism, or boldness or something, and all around me I kept seeing that people were making big money out of property. More specifically, I saw that people with less intelligence than me and few discernible skills were making really, really big money from buying houses, holding onto them for a bit, maybe decorating along the way, then selling them on. The cleverer ones were renovating, knocking down walls, adding extensions. Adding value.

I spent a few hundred quid on a plastering course. Best return on investment ever. Later, I learned about electrics, and even trained as a surveyor.

Houses became like a drug: I kept looking for something bigger, more of a challenge, more of a wreck. A bigger and better profit opportunity each time. In some cases I got emotionally attached, of course. But not often. When I bought the Notting Hill house, I remember really feeling like I'd made it. But even that soon felt too small, too ordinary.

I became a success because I'm a grafter. I'm a fixer, always have been; and I'll fix things again.

Here it comes. The fight that's been brewing since the hospital. Three days have passed, each of us engaged in our separate distraction tactics: I've been mainly on the laptop, making furious Google searches, desperate for information. Because what do we do, in times of uncertainty, but turn to the Internet? It's always on. It will give you answers, unblinking, any time, day or night. Of course it will also lead you down holes into vast warrens of misinformation, but sometimes, that's all there is and when you're desperate it's better than nothing. Sally, meanwhile, has been engaged in a frenetic, sleepless round of cleaning, tidying, ordering. She shadows me, picking up every crumb, every stray hair I dare to moult. My coffee mug barely hits the counter and it's spirited away and into the dishwasher. We've danced around each other for three days and nights, hardly talking, although we have had sex, once, which made a change. But now Sally has something to say. My head is buried in some notes I've printed from the website of a charity that helps parents wrongly accused of abuse. She is standing at the sink and she suddenly throws down the dishcloth she's been holding and narrows her eyes at me.

'Anything you want to tell me, Richard?'

'No,' I say while the voice in my head notes: *Lots of things I don't want to tell you.*

'Sure about that, are you?'

'What is this? Are you accusing me of something?'

'All I know is, Oliver's hurt and it happened on your watch.' Wow. I was wondering when this would start. We've spent months having a go at each other for every tiny misstep. Now we've got something really serious to argue about. I take the bait.

'Yeah, after he'd been screaming like a lunatic for hours on end. Seems to me there's a good chance he was already hurt when you left him. So, anything *you* might have missed?'

'No way. If something had happened I'd have known.'

'Oh, really? With him every second of the day, were you? Or were you drinking tea and gossiping with your little mummy friends while he crawled around getting up to Christ knows what?'

'I didn't even see anyone else that day, it was just us.'

'Well, why don't you just talk me through *that day. Were* you with him all the time?' She shrugs and I seize my chance. 'You left him alone? Why? How long for?'

Joanna Barnard

'Yes, Richard, I left him alone on a few occasions.' She is speaking very slowly, as if to someone new to the English language. 'To answer the door to the postman, or to take a fucking piss. What do you want me to do, wear a fucking papoose?'

'Yes!' I slam my fist onto the worktop. The laptop rattles against the marble. 'Yes. If it means my son won't end up in hospital and in plaster, yes, wear a fucking papoose. For fuck's sake, Sally.' I barge out of the room and I'm halfway down the hall when I hear her start to cry. I realise it's the first time in the three days, that I know of, that she's shed any tears. I don't turn around but walk straight out of the front door.

I go for a drive. Driving is my thing, it's how I clear my head. For Sally it's running – or it used to be, anyway – not so much since we had Ol. I pull away from the kerb and I don't know where I'm going but I know I need to get out, get away, so I head out of town. I've got a sensible car these days, Jaguar estate. What's worse, it's an automatic, so I can't rally the shit out of it like I would have done when I was younger in a faster, crappier car. But I can still get up to a good speed, still feel that weightlessness, like flying. I can focus on this for a bit and it's the only way I have of blocking everything else out.

It's dark and I find myself squinting at the road, the blackness stretching and winding ahead of me, an uncomfortable contrast to the bright white screen I've been glued to for the last couple of hours. There are cases on the websites I've found that make my head ache. They are so complicated I can barely keep up with them, even though they're told in such a way you can tell the parents are trying to put them into simple terms. So far we've only met a couple of social workers, and one policeman, and they seem unthreatening enough, but the more I read the more I get the sense that we are only at the edge of what will turn out to be a horrible labyrinth with no foreseeable exit.

I miss Ol, of course, but from tomorrow I can escape to my office and pretend things are normal. I'm so grateful I don't work at home any more.

It's harder for Sally, I get that. Her days will suddenly be empty and quiet. We'd agreed she would take the full year off from work with Ol – this had worried me, money-wise, but I never would have let Sally see it. It strikes me now, having seen case after case of parents whose separation from their child ran into weeks and even months, that Sally is in the last two months of her maternity leave and will never get this time back.

The divorce from Zoe battered me, financially. I suppose I should say it battered us, but as I say, I never really let on to Sally just how bad things were. Thank God she had a decent job and by then I had a couple of properties I could sell. I'd bought them at the right time and made just enough to pacify Zoe, who was also desperate to stay in the Notting Hill house, so I used this for quite a lot of leverage.

In an attempt to save money, which I sold to Sally as 'finding a quieter lifestyle in which to bring up our baby', we moved out of London and into leafy Surrey, into a Victorian house in the so-called 'favoured south side' of Farnham. 'Favoured' is right; houses were bloody expensive considering the town is an hour away from Waterloo. Probably getting me away from Zoe was part of the reason Sally agreed to the move to Farnham. Her enthusiasm surprised me at the time, especially as it meant being close to my family. Then again, she's more of a small-town/suburb kind of person, really. Me, I'm all city. I miss London like a lost friend.

Sally got a job at the Royal Surrey Hospital and fretted about me finding work, but there are always houses to be bought, and in this part of the country, always money to be made out of people too lazy to do it themselves. It's easy; it's a cliché now but you just buy the worst house in the best street. That's what I did with our house, the Farnham Victorian semi that was half the size of the Notting Hill place but that, thankfully, Sally fell in love with, even in its wrecked state. I did the same with a couple of others, got a decent rental income coming in, and felt I could breathe again.

I'll go back, of course. In one of the cases I've read about, the wife says she felt like the social workers were trying to pit her against her partner. They kept interviewing them separately and saying to her things like 'Does he have a temper?', 'Has he ever hit you?', 'You don't have to protect him', and the insidious 'Is there anything you want to tell us?', over and over again.

I do have a temper, I'll admit that, and I've been trying really hard not to let it show, ever since the hospital. I know if I lose my rag they'll put two and two together and get to five. I also know how ... *compliant* Sally can be, and I'm terrified that if they ask her just the right question (or the wrong question, as I see it), she could get me into a whole lot of shit. I know that if we are going to get through this, get Ol back home, we have to present a united front.

I've seen Sally do the mirror thing, the thing she was doing the day we went to see Ol, once before. I only snapped at her the other morning because it gave me shivers to see what she is now and compare it to what she'd been. Back then she'd stood in front of a mirror in a hotel I'd taken her to in the middle of the day, and cried, 'Look at me. Do I look like the kind of woman who sleeps with other people's husbands?'

I'd coaxed her into bed eventually, said something like 'you're not any "kind" of woman. You're not "like" anyone else. You're you, and you're wonderful, and this situation is not your fault.' (I worked out early on with Sally that this was something she needed to hear a lot: 'It's not your fault'.)

That's what we called it, you see, the 'situation', as though my marriage to Zoe was an external event over which neither of us had any control. The situation was a tsunami rolling in, about to break.

There are basically two types of women. There are women who take their make-up off before bed, and women who don't. I have done a lot of research. I'm not saying this as a boast, it's not as though I'm especially proud of it, it's just a fact. There it is.

You marry the women who take their make-up off. You have affairs with the ones who leave mascara streaks on the pillows.

The exception was Sally. She was the affair who became a wife. But she was always a wife, really; I knew this because of the making-me-date-her thing, and I knew the first time she brought her clean face to bed.

Look, all men do it, or think about doing it. Or would do it, if they could be sure they wouldn't get caught.

There was this TV programme; they had hidden cameras in a hotel bar and this woman went up to twenty different men, told them she was a bit pissed and a bit horny, and asked did they want to come outside with her for a blow job.

Nineteen out of the twenty said yes (I can only assume the remaining guy was gay). Seventeen out of the nineteen were married. You see? Everyone does it.

The difference is, every time I do it, I genuinely think it will be the last time. Because I may be a faithless bastard but I do fall in love, you see. And I'm many things, but when it comes to love, I'm not a cynic.

I pull onto our drive and sit in the car for a moment, ignition off, listening to the engine hum and settle, before stepping out onto the gravel and pressing the key. The car locks with a reassuring click. I come through the front door quietly and walk into the lounge.

She's on the sofa. No TV on, no radio. Everything still. She seems kind of distant. Her face is dry but still has the signs of tears, white streaks through her make-up, as though once she started crying she really let it go. When she speaks all she keeps saying is, 'He's my baby, Richard,' so much so that it actually starts to piss me off. Eventually I point out, as gently as I can, even though I'm gritting my teeth, 'Well, he's my baby too,' but she looks at me strangely, doesn't seem to want to hear this. 'United front,' I tell her, quietly, and carry my laptop into the kitchen, listening to the sounds of her taking herself off to bed.

My baby. Not *our* baby, *my* baby. And both of us saying it. What was that about? It was like we were competing for him. It wouldn't be the first time.

From the moment a woman gets pregnant, it's all about her. Well, her and the baby. After the scans, the midwife appointments and so on, everyone asked Sally about it but not me. Then they would ask *me* about *her*, as though she wasn't there, as though she was some kind of mute invalid, or just a baby carrier, which I knew she hated as much as I did.

It's even worse after the birth. No one cares about the dad. No one asks how he's doing. 'Grow up,' Sally said to me when I tried to talk to her about it. 'You're not the one who needs looking after just now. You're an adult.' I didn't mention it again.

Then we'd got into the usual pissing contests. I remembered them well from when Martha came along, but I couldn't seem to stop them from happening. You know, 'I'm more tired than you,' all of that. 'I've been working all day' versus 'Oh, so you don't think looking after a baby is work?' And on, and on. It was so clichéd it was almost embarrassing. It was like we each had a script we were compelled to follow.

And now the stakes have been hiked up and the competition has got an even darker side: suspicion is growing between us, like a weed.

Chapter Six

Martha

I love baths. The so-called grown-ups never seem to have time for baths, well apart from Sally when she was whale-like towards the end of her interminable gestation (and presumably couldn't hold herself up for long in the shower on her fat ankles).

I can spend hours in the tub, topping up the hot water to near-scalding, making my skin flush bacon-pink. Watching my fingers wrinkle, the tips soft, white, numb, like I could peel the top layer of flesh off them and not even feel anything.

I started hiding out in the bathroom not long after Dad left my mother. Zoe and I were not much more than mute housemates then, circling each other in uncertainty. It was a hot summer and I got my first period, but didn't know how to talk to her about it. The balled-up tights I had hidden in the back of my drawer, stained red, then brown, disappeared, presumably disposed of by her, embarrassed or disgusted, for all her so-called liberalism. They were my favourite pair, too. I would go to the bathroom to escape my mother's pained eyes and doleful expressions; I couldn't really stand how pathetic she was and I always felt I was supposed to do something about it but I never knew what.

So I would lock the door and lie in the bath for ages, my wet hair hanging over the back, drip, drip, dripping onto the tiles.

When I moved in with Dad, I adopted the same routine, just in a different bathroom.

I don't really know why I agreed to move in with Dad and Sally, or even whether I was given much of a choice. I do know that Zoe had moved on from silence to rage. She'd taken to playing Alanis Morissette at full volume. There were heated phone conversations between her and Dad. I didn't have to read far between the lines to gather that having me there was a pain in the ass.

Each fresh revelation – they were living together, they were getting married – had seemed to unpeel an extra layer of composure and she got more and more demented. She hid the bottles but I knew. She'd be slurring her words by 11am and I'm not an idiot. God knows what she did when she heard Sally was pregnant. I'd gone by then, Dad insisting I'd be 'better off' with them and that Zoe needed 'space', and I was caught up in my own feelings about it all (disgust, mainly). I suppose her art must have gone off the scale. She always 'produced' more when she was miserable and bitter. She was pretty prolific.

So one time after I'd just moved, I was pulling my bath routine at Dad's and I cut myself shaving, badly, for the first time. At that time I would spend ages shaving my armpits, my legs, once my arms because some of the girls in my class did, although thankfully *that* was a craze that didn't last. When I tried it they looked weird, like scalped animals, pale and bald and out of place, like the creature I'd seen in the pet store that the man there said was called a 'skinny pig', basically a guinea pig with no fur and it was just *gross*, reminded me of one of those sphinx cats, you know.

Bikini line, obviously. The mania, of course, was for 'everything off', but I've never done that. Just, ugh.

Anyway I was shaving my legs this one time, and it was a new razor or something and I nicked myself just above the ankle, right on the bone, where there seemed to be hardly any flesh and the skin was paper-thin but apparently there was a lot of blood underneath because from that tiny slice it billowed out in bright red flowers into and all through the water.

I felt a massive surge of peace watching those scarlet blooms. It made me realise how easy it is to do yourself harm, and how no one might even notice or know.

By the time I got out of the bath, there were no traces.

All through the social services interview – that Mary woman all earnest and probing and Zoe with her hands practically over her mouth to stop herself from butting in – I tried to answer the questions in such a way that I wasn't technically telling a lie. It reminded me of that 'yes/no' game that you play as kids, when you end up giving convoluted answers like 'of course I would like to do that' or 'I don't think that is true'. When they asked if I noticed anything unusual, I said I didn't remember. They didn't seem too fazed by this answer generally, almost as though it's expected of me as a teenager, as though I'm a doddery old woman. When Mary asked a question I couldn't not lie to I looked at them blankly and waited it out until they rephrased it, which they mostly did.

I've no idea where this sudden skewed moral compass came from. Zoe flirted with Catholicism for a bit when I was about eight. It didn't last long and I think she mainly liked the paintings, statues and so on. I don't remember too much about it except that a nervousness around telling lies has lingered around me. I'm always waiting for the lightning bolt to strike me down.

The question I *had* to answer with an out-and-out lie was whether Dad was here all night. Mary said it almost as an afterthought; I'm sure she'd already heard his version. I knew he wouldn't get in trouble for going out as such because I'm fifteen, nearly sixteen, and I guess it would be OK, legally and stuff, to leave me babysitting my little brother. I knew that the lie was not for social services, but for Sally. He didn't tell me that in so many words but I worked it out.

I looked the woman in the eye, nodded and said, 'All night.'

I worry about things a lot. Zoe calls it anxiety.

On good days, all I worry about is how big my thighs are, and whether I'll ever actually get a boyfriend.

The idea of Brendan Lowe as a boyfriend is absolutely terrifying – because he's older and experienced and I always imagined myself hooking up with a cute, shy boy who no one else had really noticed – and at the same time absolutely thrilling, for exactly the same reasons. But it's never going to happen. Never, ever.

On bad days, I worry about everything. If we don't worry about the world – our generation – who will? Our parents don't care, they'll be dead by the time it really kicks off. They've fucked everything up and they're leaving it to us to sort out.

I worry about the planet. About North Korea and nuclear weapons. Islamic fundamentalism. I might be fifteen but I watch the news. Hard to avoid it, with 24-hour streaming on every social media feed. I might be fifteen but I care about more than nail varnish. Some nights I lie in bed and I can't move, can hardly breathe, I'm so terrified.

The world is fucked and even in this country, I keep hearing how prospects are worse for our generation than that of our parents. No jobs, or shit jobs. So you go to uni and saddle yourself with debt. Crazy house prices. Crazy food prices, even. I can't imagine how most people even manage to live. It's depressing.

Dad would tell me not to worry about this stuff, but he thinks I'm just a kid. He doesn't see the reality that in a few years I will be on my own, potentially. It does happen: my friend Pip's mum threw her sister out as soon as she turned eighteen, and plans to do the same with Pip. So she knows she has three years to work out how she'll survive. She's trying to fix herself to a boyfriend with a nice, respectable family who might take her in (I reckon this is pretty pathetic, not to mention unrealistic: Pip is not exactly a nice, respectable girl, and most guys stick with their own kind). Like I said, depressing.

I know my family aren't quite like that, but my mum has made me feel pretty unwelcome and my dad left us, so it doesn't feel so far off.

That's why I've decided to not need anyone, ever.

It was a huge pain in the ass leaving London, but like I say, not sure it was really my decision. I started at the new school and met my friend Del and she was pretty much in the same place, an outsider too. Del sounds like a boy's name but it's short for Delilah, which she hates. I think her parents are Bible freaks or something. They've moved around a lot, something to do with her dad's job, and finally settled in England. Even the things that make me vaguely interesting – I used to live in London! My mum's an artist! – are overshadowed by Del's life.

She was born in the US but has also lived in France, Hong Kong, Sweden. Her dad is a diplomat! None of us really know what that means, but it sounds seriously cool. So Del was the cool girl and I was just the new girl, ripe for mild bullying and whispered comments behind hands.

But me and Del found each other in this Surrey school where it seemed like everyone knew everyone and definitely everyone *wanted* to know everyone's business. Compared to school in London, it seemed to me that there was a lot more gossip and rumour and all that crap;

as though, because their lives were actually so boring, people had to make up twice as much shit about other people just to entertain themselves.

My 'cool levels' have ratcheted up a notch, though, now that Brendan Lowe has started talking to me at school. And not just talking, either. He'll come up to me and hook his arm around my neck; today he even gave me a kiss on the top of my head and then, without saying a word, swaggered off.

'He *likes* you,' our friend Lynsey whispered today, kind of awe-struck.

'Well, I don't even really know him.' I shrugged.

'And he's a *sixth-former*.'

'I mean, he did come over to my house one night last week...'

Even Del looked shocked and impressed.

'You never told me that,' she hissed, nudging me.

I know you have to be careful when talking about boys. Don't get me wrong, I can and usually do say anything to Del. We hang out at one of the pubs in town where we know the older lads from the art college go. We have fake ID, but we're never asked for it. We both look older and besides, it's just that kind of a pub. We flirt with the guys, and sometimes Del will go out back with one of them, although I can never be sure if that's for something sexual or to smoke or just to score some Adderall off them. She definitely has a bit of a reputation, which doesn't seem to bother her, though it would bother me. It's a fine line in the Farnham rumour mill: you're either a slag, or frigid, and neither label wins you any passes. It's best to keep your head down and stay unnoticed.

So I hesitated for a few moments but, looking at Del's and Lynsey's faces, couldn't help filling in a few gaps for them. It felt kind of good being the centre of attention for once.

'Yeah, he came over. We smoked some weed,' I said as casually as I could. Lynsey's eyes widened.

'And then what?' she whispered.

'I don't really remember, I was off my face.' I laughed, but I wasn't really laughing inside, because it was true that I didn't remember, and the nagging feeling in the bottom of my stomach made me feel really, really not cool at all.

Chapter Seven

Sally

He's been gone for six days.

There's a whole obsession with dates that starts as soon as you get pregnant. 'When are you due?' people ask, even strangers.

Then the baby comes and they ask 'How old is he?' as they gaze at his tiny form sleeping in the pram. And you answer, first in days, then weeks, then months. There is a new sense of the timing of everything.

And now there will be a new calendar, won't there? There will be the days and weeks and months before it happened, and the days and the eternity after.

'Don't drag it out,' Cynthia had said as I hugged my son. 'You're upsetting him.' It seems she isn't alone in this opinion, as a report materialises from the social worker, stating how our visits are 'distressing' for Oliver and that she recommends they be reduced to every other day. I tear up the letter and throw the pieces into the recycling.

I would have held him even tighter if I'd known that was coming.

My mother rings.

'Cynthia called me,' she says. *Of course she did.* Shit. How had I not predicted that? 'How could you not have told us?'

Well, 'us' is a bit of a joke for starters, I want to say, considering my father never shows the remotest interest in my life. Instead I murmur, 'Sorry.'

The truth is I'd hoped it would be a storm in a teacup. I'd assumed Oliver would be back with us in a matter of days, because that was the proper way of things, there was a rightness and order to it, our little family unit, a completed jigsaw that couldn't miss a piece for long. Of course jigsaws, even when complete, are full of tiny cracks.

The second truth is that I'd feared exactly what I am getting now: my mother's judgement, disguised as questions and advice.

My mother had three miscarriages, after me. I don't know why she told me this when I was a teenager. My mother was too present, treating me as an adult before I was ready, smothering me with a love that was both sickly-sweet and thick with conditions.

My father was absent, both physically and emotionally. He worked long hours and he didn't 'do' hugs and kisses. He'd wanted a son; my mother made no secret of this either. He didn't deny it but at least he had the decency to appear embarrassed. A Boy. Scientist Footballer Boy.

This was why they'd kept trying, she said, even after the second failed pregnancy when she'd cupped the tiny foetus in her bloody hands, sprawled on the bathroom floor.

This was why I'd cut my hair, got good at maths and biology, worked hard to stave off the curves and bumps of my treacherous female body.

This is how it goes:

First they tell you to eat. It's like telling a depressive to cheer up.

They cajole, bribe, bully.

They don't get it.

They take you to see the fat, sleazy GP with blobs of white stuff at the corners of his mouth. His breath makes you feel sick and he doesn't meet your eyes.

He treats you like a silly girl. He says things like: 'Taken the diet a bit far, have we?'

He keeps saying 'we', even though he's nothing like you. But to escape him all you have to do is smile and promise to try harder, this is easy, you've been doing it all your life, then he sends you away. Be a good girl.

Be a devious girl. Conjure tricks: food up your sleeves, food stuck to the roof of your mouth, buried in the nooks between your gums and your cheek, and spat out at the first chance.

You beg them to leave you alone. And eventually, for a while, in desperation or exasperation, they do. Then you collapse one day trying to walk upstairs, tumble straight back down, hurt yourself, so they have to take you to hospital.

And there you stay, for quite a long time.

I told it to Richard just like this, hardly taking a breath, and he held me, and I felt safe.

'I didn't want to be thin,' I told him. 'That's what nobody understood. I never cared about that, not really.'

'What did you want, then?'

'I think I wanted to make myself as small as possible.'

Richard never did what people usually do, which is treat you as a curiosity. Even those in the medical profession – actually, especially those people; they want data, they want numbers. Just how thin *were* you? What weight did you get down to, exactly? It's like some creepy competition and it takes me right back to where I was, and I hate it. Because the voice in my head says, 'Don't tell them, they'll think you're pathetic. You couldn't even do that right. If you do tell them, knock off a few pounds, exaggerate a bit. That will impress them. Because the truth is you were even a failure at being a freak.'

There was another precursor to my interest in Science, though it sounds silly, now. As a kid, I loved comics – they were one of the things that bound me to my dad. He had kept stacks of them from his own youth and every Saturday he took me into town and bought me a *Beano*, or a *Dandy*, and then we'd sit in a café and read it together, laughing and eating cakes. I especially loved the Numskulls. Reading them was the first time I became aware of myself as a physical being; a machine. I became fascinated with how the body and the brain worked.

There are worlds inside of us.

Who could fail to be interested in that?

So I wanted to study Science – had to, really, to meet Dad's aspirations for me – and I wanted to help people, do something good. I ended up spending a fair bit of my own teenage years in hospitals, in clinics, and for a while wondered if I should go down the psychology or psychotherapy route. I would look at the counsellors, one after another trying to untangle the knots in my head, and I would think *I could do that*.

But in the end the mind was just too nebulous a concept for me. I wanted to work with nuts and bolts, with fixable components like bones and skin. Of course, I would realise these things weren't always fixable, but they did at least tend to behave in predictable ways. The mind was an altogether different beast.

So I stuck with the knowable beauty of the body, the machine.

I qualified as a pharmacist and when I moved in with Richard, took a job at the Royal Surrey Hospital, in Children's Oncology. Oncology sounds so much better than cancer, doesn't it?

But it was cancer that interested me, more than children, that's for sure – at first, anyway. If you're interested in disease, as I was, you want to go for the biggie.

People warned me that my line of work might make me hyper-vigilant when I became a parent. In fact it sort of did the opposite – I felt I *knew* cancer, was ready for it in the unlikely event it came knocking, because I also knew that in childhood it's thankfully rare. That can be hard to remember when you spend your working day surrounded by sick kids, but my logical brain won out and I repeated facts to myself on a regular basis. Statistically Oliver had only a 1-in-1000 chance of developing leukaemia before his nineteenth birthday, for example.

No, my worries were more pedestrian: the pan on the stove, the stairs, the slippery floors, the dog in the park, the choking hazards. The everyday dangers were what troubled me.

I might not have studied psychotherapy in the end but I read a lot. I understand attachment theory – the importance of the primary caregivers in the first months of life. I wonder now what unknown future damage is being done to our son. I've read books, even, that preach how early years childcare is A Bad Thing. Especially for boys, apparently – you can find plenty of books that will tell you a boy should be with his mum for the first three years. I once hurled one such book across the room with so much force it left a mark on the wall. What if the mother *has* to go back to work? I shouted at it. What if she needs to work for the money or, I don't know, for her *sanity*? Who the hell can take *three years* off? Who would want to?

Guilt on anxiety on fear on more guilt. This is the club I've joined. I now wish that the biggest thing I had to worry about was returning to work and putting Ollie in nursery. If only.

'How could this have happened, Sally?' my mother is asking; she's been delivering a monologue, really, up to this point, but she falls silent and I suppose I am meant to answer.

'Well, if we knew that, it would be all right,' I say.

'How the hell can you not know?' She's angry; she hardly ever says 'hell'. It's the nearest my mother ever comes to swearing. 'Where were you?'

I hesitate. 'I was out.' There is a long pause at the other end of the line.

'Out?' Her voice drips with disgust.

'Yes, Mum, out. You know, that place people sometimes go when they have a life. I was out.'

'So Richard did it.' Something triumphant there; she never liked Richard. I roll my eyes and feel myself ready, as ever, to leap to his defence, notwithstanding the fact that over the last few days I've looked at him differently. I've wondered more than once what he's hiding.

'Well if you're going to go down that route,' I say, 'what about Martha?'

Mum tuts loudly. 'Blaming the poor child. How can you?'

'I can't win,' I say. 'What if no one *did* it? What if it was just an accident?'

I hear background muttering from her end, which I suppose is Dad. Mum says 'yes, yes' to him and then comes back to me. 'Your dad says it's common, is it, for a nine-month-old baby to break his arm?'

'You can tell Dad his grandson is *ten* months old. And no, it's not common. Which is why we're in this mess. But what's my alternative? Believe that one of my family hurt Ollie on purpose? Who would do that?'

'If only we were closer,' she murmurs, and I know she means geographically – my parents live in St Albans, just far enough away as far as I'm concerned – but the other meaning of the comment is not lost on me.

'What difference would that make?' I snap, the coldness in my voice surprising me.

'There's no need to take that tone,' she says. 'I just meant, if we lived nearer, we could have shouldered some of the burden for you. You've clearly been under a lot of pressure ...'

There we go, I think. When she says *How could this have happened?*, what she really means is *How could* you *have* let *this happen?*

'Look, Mum, I'm going to have to go,' I say, cutting her off. Not bothering to conceal my sarcasm, I add, 'Thanks for the call.'

People are always surprised – shocked, even – when I describe my mum as critical. She is so publicly effusive with her love they can't believe she can be equally forthcoming with her disapproval. Some people say I'm being over-sensitive. Maybe I am.

I suppose she knows me so well she can pinpoint my faults and go after them with her scalpel words.

I am too slow, too clumsy, too awkward. I can't dance; she always points this out. I was too fat, then I was too thin.

When I was heavy (not fat, I know that now, I was never fat, not really), she would poke my hips and my stomach, make jokes. She stood behind me when I got on the scales. She taped pictures of stick-thin models, cut from magazines, onto the fridge, under the pretence of 'motivation' for herself and whatever madcap diet she was on, but I knew they were for my benefit, really.

The disapproval when I was thin was different, though. Behind it lay a sort of grudging respect for my self-control, a quality she'd always lacked. She was jealous.

Richard saw it straight away, the day we went 'home' for a family lunch and to tell them we were getting married, and I loved him all the more for it. He recognised the hypercritical mum from his own family model, I suppose, though I've never put this to him directly.

While I was ill, under the advice of some counsellor or other, Mum had got into the habit of serving food all in the middle of the table so I could help myself to what I wanted and not feel 'over-faced' by a piled-high plate. Even once I'd got better, mealtimes retained a feeling of awkwardness as Dad basically stared at me and Mum provided a running commentary every time I picked up a serving spoon. On this particular day it went like this:

'Oh, I didn't know you liked broccoli, Sally.'

'There's no point just having one potato, is there? Take a couple.'

'Do you want a chicken leg? Stay there, I'll get a leg.'

'Since when do you like broccoli?'

'Don't have too many of those carrots; there's honey on them.'

'Wow, you must be hungry.'

'You won't be wanting any pudding, then.'

Polite and charming to their faces, as soon as we were in the car Richard said, 'You don't ever have to see them again.'

I cried with relief.

I knew I would never cut them out, of course, but I felt like I'd been given permission to tone them down, like adjusting the brightness of a screen or the volume of a radio. I could tune them in or out, it was up to me.

That's what you have to understand about Richard, and why I love him so much: he's been my protector. And he released me.

I'd been so nervous telling Richard about my illness but I said, 'This is part of me. If you're going to love me –' I swallowed then, avoiding his eyes '– I need you to know this.'

'It's part of you,' he replied, 'but it isn't who you are. And yes, by the way, I am going to love you.'

The only other person who ever made me feel quite as safe as Richard did was Ben.

When I told Richard my best friend was a man, his reaction was: 'He's gay, right?'

He's not gay. He had a girlfriend when we were at uni, and though that didn't survive living apart he's had relationships since, although nothing too serious or long-term. As far as I know, anyway – we haven't spoken for a while.

When I call him and he doesn't answer, my first thought is 'that's unusual' (Ben is the kind of guy who is constantly connected, whose phone is virtually another limb), and my second is 'That's probably a good thing as I actually don't know what I was going to say'. For this reason I almost hang up when his answer phone kicks in, but at the last moment I say, too cheerfully, 'Ben! Hey. It's me. Give me a call. I need you.'

It's only later that I realise how odd 'I need you' might sound.

When you have a baby and you're on maternity leave, a world of social events opens up that you never knew existed. Events that are meant to be for the babies but are actually for the mums because, really, how much does a three-month-old get out of sitting in a circle, propped against his mother's knees while she sings and forces his little hands into uneven clapping? Oliver for one seemed to hate 'Rhythm and Rhyme'. He would scream and shake his head wildly as soon as the music started. At the end the teacher would hand out plastic maracas and drums and tambourines and let the babies shake and bang them while the parents smiled at each other, trying to work out how to strike up friendships as adults. Oliver would shriek above the din.

Then there was 'baby cinema'. Never heard of it? Well, it's just like normal cinema except it's hardly any fun at all. The lights are up higher, the sound is lower and, as the poster cheerfully informed us, it doesn't matter if anyone cries! They meant the babies, I suppose, and not the mothers, but I found myself filling up on a few occasions.

I would go with the MMG to baby cinema most Friday mornings, sitting through not-quite-new releases that we weren't that interested in, stuffing popcorn into our mouths (OK, it was 10am, but we'd been up since four or five, so it seemed acceptable) and stuffing our boobs into little mouths to silence them during the good parts. I watched more movies in the first six months of Ollie's life than I had in the previous ten years.

I know that once word gets out on the snaking New Mum Grapevine, the invites will dry up and I will be marooned. There's not much of a social scene for parents whose baby has to live with someone else. As much as I've resisted the 'forced fun' of all those mother-and-baby activities, now I long for them. Or for any kind of company at all, in fact. Any kind of friendship.

Julia lives in a sprawling bungalow on the north side of town, so close to the park it's practically her back garden. She claims that when she looks out of her kitchen window every morning, she sees deer mooching about in her roses.

We've fallen into a routine of coming here every Thursday. Our days out in the late summer while the babies were still small and sleepy – Buggy Fit! Bootcamp! Fitness for Mummies! – glided into winter afternoons around Julia's cosy fire. We laid the babies a safe distance away, still in our line of sight, although none of them were crawling then so danger was still an externalised worry, not yet something they could inflict on themselves.

As the evenings got lighter again and the weather milder we carried on using Julia's house on Thursdays as our go-to place for the weekly catch up. I missed last week, of course, preoccupied with getting ready for my night out, and I'd promised I would come this week. But I didn't know I'd be baby-less and would need to talk to them about something that a week ago didn't seem possible.

The side gate is open and I can hear voices from the garden, so I slip through, standing out of sight for a moment to listen to the conversation. I hear Melinda say she's dreading going back to work. She is the only one, apart from me, who plans to go back full-time. The other two, who have rich husbands and will stay at home at least until the children start school, make supportive noises.

'I mean,' Melinda is saying, 'it's weird, isn't it? When they're with you, all you can think some days is "Give me a break". You long for time on your own. And then any time they're not there, it's like your bloody arm's been cut off!' Everyone laughs and murmurs agreement. I put my hand against the wall of the house for support, then take a breath and round the corner, forcing myself to move into view.

The scene that greets me is oddly comforting: the trio of women whose faces have become so familiar to me: Julia, Esme and Melinda. A pot of tea and plate of cakes on the garden table.

'Bloody baby-led weaning,' Melinda mutters, as she prises a piece of cake out of her son Joshua's chocolatey hands. I freeze, staring at him, then notice the other two babies, Henry and Freya, on the lawn, each intent in their own game of pulling up grass and digging in the soil.

Snapping me out of my spell, a chorus of voices chimes 'Hi! Hi! Hi!' like an echo, accompanied by little waves although I'm only a few feet away. I try a smile but it feels at best weak, at worst like a grimace. As I step forward, three pairs of eyes skim over me and the inevitable question follows. I think Julia gets there first, but they are all looking at my empty hands.

'Where's Ollie?'

How can I not have thought this through? Not rehearsed my lines? This was a mistake. This isn't one of those days when we sit around moaning about our husbands not helping, our hair falling out, our lack of sleep. For a moment I consider just telling them he's with his grandparents, which technically isn't even lying, but then I realise that if I try to hide or embellish anything at this point, it will end up looking really, really bad.

This isn't gossip. This is real. This is my life.

I do start by saying he's with his grandparents, but quickly (before they can respond with comments about how lucky I am to have a break) follow it with 'I've got something I need to talk to you about'. I try to explain what's happened in a matter-of-fact way. I'm getting better at it. They have questions, I can tell they do, bucket loads of them. But they don't ask. I suppose once I'm gone they'll all say what they really think. Esme picks Freya out of the grass and brushes soil from her hands and lips, pulling her close in her lap and wrapping an arm tightly around her. As though having children taken from you might be contagious. I should have worn a bell, should have called out a warning. Unclean!

It feels a bit like a circus, and I'm the freak. Roll up, roll up, see the woman with the disappearing baby. I always hated being the centre of attention, even when it was for something 'good': passing my exams, marrying Richard. I can't tolerate it for this.

So I get on with the business of why I'm here. I take a deep breath and say: 'Look, social services might contact you, I don't know, but I thought I should make you aware in case they do. I thought you should hear it from me, first.'

They each nod in a solemn way, these people who I don't really know, yet in whose company I've spent more time over the last few months than anyone apart from Richard and the kids. I've seen these women far more regularly than I've seen my parents or any of my so-called 'real' friends. These are the people they will say know me. I look from face to face.

What kind of report will they give me?

Chapter Eight

Richard

My mother must be agitated when she rings, because she opens the conversation without any greeting. It's as though I've accidentally picked up the phone on a stream-of-consciousness ramble.

'It's ridiculous,' she is saying, 'that you can't even pop in for a cup of tea without making an appointment.' This is interesting, since I've always had the impression that an appointment system for visitations is exactly what my mother would prefer. 'I don't enjoy being *dictated to* by these social so-called services people.'

'Hello, Mum,' I say. 'How's Ol?'

'Oh, he's precious, just precious,' she says in a distracted way. I can hear her stifling a yawn. 'She hasn't sleep-trained him very well, has she? He was up three times last night.'

'Well, I expect he's a bit unsettled. Unfamiliar place and all that.'

'Nonsense. He's been here *weeks*. And he loves it. And if the rings around *her* eyes are anything to go by, he doesn't fare any better at home.'

'"She" has a name, Mum.'

'Anyway, he's napping now. Looks positively angelic.'

'Well, that's good. We'll see you all tomorrow – at the *appointment*.'

'How long is this likely to go on, Richard?'

'We don't know, do we?'

'Your father and I are very tired.'

'I understand. We do appreciate it.' I take a deep breath and utter the line she can't help but respond to with a shudder. 'None of us wants to see Ol in a foster home.'

'You'd better speak to a solicitor, you know.'

'I intend to.'

'Without Sally. On your own.'

'Goodbye, Mother.'

My mother sees kindness as weakness. The one time I made the mistake of putting someone else first (not ahead of me, that would have been bad enough, but ahead of her), she was furious.

We were in an antiques shop in Lewes and she was looking at china. A good-looking woman in a long coat suddenly picked up a teapot in the same design as the saucer Mum was turning over in her hands. 'This is it, this is just it,' the woman was murmuring to herself, and her happiness as she held it up to the light was causing little pink dots to appear high up on her cheeks. I couldn't help smiling. It was like she was in her own world.

'You should take the whole set,' I whispered, leaning over to her.

'It's just like one my grandmother used to have,' she replied. What followed was a bit of low-level flirting, then I went off to get a basket and helped the woman load her treasures into it. My mother was still holding the saucer. I'll never forget the look she gave me.

When I told her Zoe was pregnant, she sighed and said, 'You do realise what having a child means, don't you? It means there will be an expectation, for the rest of your life, that someone else is more important than you.'

'I already have that – I have Zoe,' at which she laughed. She knew me well.

And when Sally got pregnant, she said, 'I thought you would know better by now.'

She told me she wished she'd never had a child. She said it just like that, 'a child', as though that child were nothing to do with me. 'It's very difficult for intellectual women to cope,' she's often said, 'when they have a baby.' My mother's evidence for her own superior intellect is the fact that she passed the eleven-plus and went to grammar school. She likes to say that 'opportunities' were not the same for women when she was young, by way of an excuse for not ever having much of a career. Then she had me and I became the excuse.

I think this is why she was disappointed that I chose for both of my wives women she might term 'intellectuals'. She said they wouldn't be natural mothers. God knows, in a way she's been proved right.

When I call my solicitor, he says in a jovial sort of way, 'Not getting divorced again, are you?' I explain the situation and he immediately switches to thoughtful and sympathetic mode. 'Come and see me,' he says, and we fix a time.

Philip Lingwood is a specialist in family law. I know him, outside of him handling my divorce and one or two business issues, in a golf-club, rotary-club sort of way. He is a straight-talking kind of guy and while I know that's what I need just now, I'm not sure Sally would appreciate it. She's never been keen on him, although they've only met once or twice. That's why I go there alone. It's nothing to do with what my mother said. I can always update her later, I tell myself, although guilt nags at me.

'I'm going to be upfront with you,' Philip begins, once we've settled in his office and I've outlined the case again. 'This is not going to be easy. It's the duty of social services to protect the welfare of the child, and I won't lie, they have a hell of a machine in place to help them do that. There've been too many high-profile cock-ups in recent years for them to risk making a mistake; they won't back down easily.' He pours us both some water and sits back, steepling his fingers.

'But they have to prove we did something wrong, surely?'

'Well, no. The burden of proof isn't on them. It's on you to show that you didn't. And in the family courts, that isn't easy.' He pauses. 'What have you said so far?'

'Well, we've both denied hurting him, obviously.'

'I see. You won't like what I'm going to say, Richard,' he says. 'But in cases like this, when there's medical evidence pointing to your guilt, you might come off better if you admit blame.'

'What? Admit to something we didn't do?'

'I said you wouldn't like it. I'm just telling you how the system works. I've only had one other case like this. In that one, social services had a heap of evidence on the guy, and the woman only got the baby back once she left him.'

'I won't have my family broken up when we've done nothing wrong.'

'And you're sure about that, are you? That you've done nothing wrong?'

'What do you mean?'

'Can you speak for Sally? And Martha?'

'I know my wife and daughter.' *Do I?* 'And I'm not going to be making any confessions.'

'You may not have a choice. And, Richard?'

'Yes?'

'You'd better advise Sally to get her own solicitor.'

I drive home with Ol's face swimming in my head. I keep remembering all the overwhelming feelings when the midwife placed him in my arms, saying, 'Meet your son.' Something about the word 'son' had caused a huge lump to form in my throat. At first I'd felt foolish, stripping off my shirt, because since Martha's arrival things had changed and these days it was all about 'skin to skin' contact as soon as possible after birth, not just for the mum, for the dad too. Martha had been delivered to me all cleaned up and wrapped in a pink blanket. She was beautiful, perfect, but she was 'other', somehow. The feeling of Ol against my bare chest, his tiny, warm body seeming to cling to me, his hair still sticky, his face scrunched up, was different. There was an immediate connection.

Is it wrong to prefer one gender of child over the other? My mistake was telling Sally, before the second scan, that I 'hoped' we were having a boy. 'Well, we don't always get what we hope for,' she said, and when the sonographer asked if we wanted to know, she immediately said 'No, thank you'.

You have different expectations, different plans, for a boy as opposed to a girl. Oh, I know, these days no one's supposed to say that, but it's only natural. Sure, I've read all the rubbish about bringing kids up 'gender neutral', but you know, some stuff's in our nature, whichever way you cut it. Girls will choose dolls and dresses – Martha did, although not recently, obviously; she's eschewed all that now and seems to dress in the most androgynous way possible, turning her nose up at anything remotely feminine or frilly – and boys will choose ... well, what will my boy choose?

I suppose there's a chance I might not find out. I got Lingwood to outline all the worst possible scenarios. He said if Ol ended up in long-term foster care there was a chance he would be adopted. 'Adoption in the UK is irreversible,' he said. 'You wouldn't even have the access you have now. That would be it, ties cut.'

So there is a chance I might never get to see, first-hand, whether my boy prefers guns or princesses, football or make-up. I've already applauded everything he's ever done with a ball, even though at ten months old his skills mostly extend to rolling balls, catching them (more by luck than design), and lying in a pool of them at soft play, gurgling madly.

I feel guilty now that I've ever wished for him to be anything. Boy, handsome, sports star, genius. It doesn't matter. It's enough for him to just *be*. And be with us. He has to be. That's just how things should be.

The thing about kids is, they take away all the 'what if's. You're not allowed to wonder 'what if I'd taken that job, moved to that country, met that woman and not this one?' because you'd be wishing your kid away, removing the seemingly random pattern of events that led to one in a gazillion sperm meeting an egg and becoming your brilliant, lovable child.

When I get home I find torn-up pieces of a letter from social services in the recycling bin. I pull them out and tape them back together, and round on Sally when she comes in the kitchen.

'We're supposed to keep everything,' I say. 'What are you playing at?'

'Sorry,' she says in a dull voice that sounds not sorry at all. 'It was a spur of the moment thing.' She studies me. 'Sometimes my *feelings* get the better of me.'

'Oh, here we go.'

'What?'

'The old heart versus head BS. Just because you're emotional and I'm being logical, practical. That doesn't mean anything. It's me being practical that will get us our son back.' I stare at the taped-up letter then, regretting my harsh tone. 'Lingwood says we might even have a case when this is over. We might be able to litigate. Against social services.'

'Lingwood's a snake,' Sally mutters.

I bang my fist on the table. 'A snake who made sure we weren't on the street after I left my family for you,' I snap.

She looks at me as though she's been slapped, blinks slowly, shakes her head and leaves the room.

I offer to take Martha up to London, shopping. She rolls her eyes at me and mutters 'lame'. Our earlier confidences and the closeness of only a day ago are clearly forgotten, but eventually she agrees.

On the train, she reads to me from one of those grotty gossip magazines and I pretend to be interested. She whoops and laughs at ridiculous stories of infidelities, weight loss, weight gain and fashion faux pas. Every now and again she turns the page towards me and shows me some 'papped' picture, exclaiming, '*Look* at that.' I'm cast back, madly, to the days of fairy tales before bed, her freshly bathed and snuggled in the crook of my arm in her soft pyjamas, eyes wide at some fable or other. As the train slows on the approach to Waterloo, she cranes her neck to see the Eye and Big Ben. I see a glimpse of the little girl she used to be. I smile. It will be OK.

I'd forgotten the horrors of Oxford Street on a Saturday. Swarms of people shoulder into each other, faces set into masks of grim determination. In Top Shop I stand outside the changing room, a pile of clothes over my arm, ready to faint from the heat. Semi-dressed girls, groups of friends, buzz from one cubicle to another, squealing at each other over this or that pair of jeans or 'perfect' top. I've asked Martha to come out and 'model' everything she tries on, partly to save me from total boredom, partly to stop me from looking like the most gigantic pervert. She does so in a stomping, resentful way, muttering, 'How would you know what looks good anyway?'

She is right, of course; I tell her everything looks good, and after a while she stops showing me.

We stop for lunch in one of those places that sells burgers but charges twice as much as, you know, a standard burger restaurant, because you get some fancy relish and your tiny portion of chips comes in a little silver bucket. Martha likes it though; that's the main thing. She orders with hilarious exactitude.

'I'll have the black and blue burger, please, but I don't want the bun, just the burger. Yes, I still want the cheese, but can I have the relish on the side? Yeah, in a little dish. And no mayo. And I want the waffle fries, not shoestring. And a side order of coleslaw and a Diet Coke. Thanks.' The waitress turns to me.

'And for you, sir?'

'Err ... burger and chips?' I grin.

'That'll be the standard cheeseburger and shoestring fries?'

'I guess. And a beer ... thanks.'

She nods, takes the menus and turns from us with a disdainful shrug.

'Wow, no one smiles in London,' I say. 'Not even people in the so-called service industry. I'd forgotten.'

Martha is scowling.

'That's probably because you were, like, blatantly flirting with her. Honestly, she can't be much older than me. That's disgusting.'

'Oh, come on, I so wasn't.' I laugh because this is the kind of teasing that used to go on between us, but looking at Martha's face, it seems she is serious. That wasn't a mock-scowl; it was for real. I know flirting, I want to say to her, and trust me, that wasn't it. 'Hey, what have I done?'

'Nothing.' She sighs and looks around the restaurant as though she's never been so bored. I decide to change tack.

'How's school?' There it is again: the eye-roll. 'Hey –' I lean forward but keep my balled-up fists under the table '– what's with the attitude?'

'No attitude, *Dad*.' She says 'Dad' in an exaggerated way, like she means *allegedly* I am her dad. 'School is fine. Actually it's not; it's shit. But y'know, I'll be out of there soon.' God; I haven't really had the time to think about Martha doing exams, and finishing school.

'When's your first exam, again?' I ask as casually as I can, as though I know but it has just slipped my mind.

'Couple of weeks. They're all on the calendar.' She nods at the waitress who has just delivered her Diet Coke and my beer to the table with as little ceremony as possible.

'Well, you'll be fine,' I say. 'You've been busy revising, haven't you? Going to the library and all that?' She stares at me.

'Yes, Dad,' she says. 'Yes, that's what I've been doing. I'll be fine.' She sighs. 'And what about you?'

I look at her, a bit startled.

'Me? Well, I'm OK.' I take a swig of beer. 'I'm sorry, I know I've been preoccupied with all this Ol stuff. You understand, don't you sweetheart?'

'Of course. You've made up for it today, haven't you?' She gestures at the pile of carrier bags on the seat beside her. 'With all this?'

'What do you mean?'

'Well, that's what it's for, isn't it? To buy my silence?' The defiance in her face brings a wave of anger up to my chest.

'Of all the ungrateful—'

'Tell me I'm not right. That that's not what this little outing is about.'

'Of course not.' I soften as my anger is diluted by guilt; I've put a lot onto her. And I've been ignoring her. I just don't have enough time to deal with her, and Ol, and everything else.

'I don't even understand why you don't want Sally to know,' she says, folding her arms, eyes wide with mock-innocence. 'I mean, if she knew you went out, she'd know you didn't hurt Ol. Right? Then she'll stop suspecting you.'

'She doesn't suspect me,' I say quietly.

'Oh, *Dad*. Of course she does.' She looks around, unfurls her arms into an exaggerated stretch. 'Then again, she might turn the blame on me. Hmm. I see your quandary, really I do.'

'Martha. I'm not sure what you're trying to say, but I really think ...'

'I lied for you. Not just to Sally. To the police, to social services. That's serious, isn't it?'

'Martha, you're just a child. I really don't want you to worry about any of this.'

'I'm not a child!' She bangs her fist on the table, making me jump, making the people on the next table jump. I offer them a placatory smile. I suppose we just look like any dad and daughter, having a row.

'Please let's try to be normal,' I say through clenched teeth.

She laughs and she looks a lot older than fifteen; I really, really don't like it.

'Oh, yes,' she says. 'Let's try.'

The train journey home is virtually silent. When we get in the house, Martha stomps to her room and slams the door behind her.

'Wow,' I say to Sally, 'I'm really winning at this parenting game.' But she's not listening.

Chapter Nine

Sally

The empty cot is the worst thing. I feel the lack of him deep in my bones.

We'd built the cot in the nursery; well, Richard built it and I mostly observed and handed him things, as my stomach was beach-ball sized by then. After four hours that consisted mostly of him sweating and swearing, Richard had stood back to look at his handiwork and joked, 'Well, we're never moving house, because we'll never get this damn thing through the door and I'm not taking it apart again.' I'd laughed and thought, it doesn't matter, because it's a cot bed and will last the baby for years, hopefully. Those years stretched out ahead of us, the idea of them bizarre while he was still curled up, high and safe, under my ribs.

And now that solid oak cot, heavy and reassuring, is empty and he's sleeping somewhere else in a hastily bought, flat-pack plywood thing that I can only hope with all my heart is temporary.

The pain of Oliver not being here is physical, brutal. It feels like a lump, and I can tell you exactly where it is: right in my solar plexus. I could swear there is something there, it feels like a growth, a tumour; invasive, unignorable. At times it feels like it is spreading, growing, and it is bound to rise up into my throat, and come out of my eyes in tears that aren't like any other tears: they are hot. They are tears of acid, of poison.

I've been in the habit of checking on Oliver every night before I go to bed, around 11pm (the same time I used to nudge him awake, when he was smaller, for a 'dream feed', in the vain hope of eliminating the 2am and 4am cries). Now that he's gone, I still stand in his room at 11pm. Every night.

I still wake up at 2am and 4am, to silence.

I miss watching him sleep. On his back, his arms flung above his head, or as he has got bigger, on his front, bottom in the air, knees pulled under him.

At first, in the early months, I was too fearful to enjoy those moments, consumed by the idea that my breathing, his sense of me in the room, would wake him and the whole rocking and shushing and soothing drama would start up again. I was dogged by weird contradictory fears that he would wake, and that he would never wake.

But once I relaxed, Richard and I would watch him together. I'd asked him, 'What do you think he's dreaming about?' and he'd frowned.

'I don't think babies dream,' he said.

* * *

My son, by the age of ten months, has already made a hoarder of me. This is a source of stress for someone who, to put it mildly, likes things neat. But throwing away anything he has worn, played with, or made (babies don't actually make things, of course, but they do have their little fingers and feet pressed into paint and clay so we can pretend they do) would feel like throwing away part of him. At the same time, the curating of this fathomless array of items is overwhelming.

The 'Baby Memories Book', presumably meant to be helpful, adds to my stress and lies like a reproach on Oliver's bedroom shelf, its pages a record of my slow decline as a parent. I pick it up, in the middle of another restless night, in the middle of a 2am vigil in his empty room, and turn on the pale-blue, elephant-shaped night light. I sit on the feeding chair I persuaded Richard to spend several hundred pounds on, my head having then been full of visions of peaceful, blissful night feeds, just me in my special nursing pyjamas and my happily suckling child. When I gave up breastfeeding, exhausted, at six weeks, I'd felt a fraud sitting on this chair, as though a bottle-feeding mother didn't deserve the same comfort.

I open the book. The 'pre-birth' section is meticulously populated: scan pictures, twelve weeks and twenty; potential names, neatly transcribed in fountain pen (funny, I don't remember making that list – he is so *Oliver* it seems impossible that we ever considered calling him anything else); a photo of me, hands resting on my enormous bump, grinning. Glowing. A second picture, taken barely a week later, shows me with pale cheeks and terrified eyes, clutching a white blanket-wrapped bundle whose face you can hardly make out. A shaky hand has recorded his time of birth and weight, and a tiny envelope stuck to the page contains his hospital bracelet bearing the same information, but after this point the pages have been only sporadically completed.

I consider for a moment handing the book over to Cynthia, but the thought makes me shudder. Not only because I can see the smug look on her face, and the meticulousness with which she would complete it, shaming my clumsy efforts, but because such an act would be like admitting to myself that she is his guardian now, and that this situation isn't going to change any time soon. I can't accept that. I hold the book a bit tighter.

You are supposed to record all the 'first times': first smile, first tooth, first steps. First steps.

It strikes me for the first time that I might miss his first steps.

Of course, in the alternative universe in which the broken arm had not happened, I would probably have been back at work when the magic moment occurred and missed the steps anyway. I'd been thinking about it before that night, wondering if he might manage a little totter before my twelve months' maternity leave was up, but given he'd not been crawling for long it didn't seem likely.

But missing out because of work and missing out because of *this*: they are entirely different things. I think of everything else I might miss, *am* missing, and they come at me all in a rush, a dam breaking, a flood raging.

We've been advised to get separate solicitors. I don't have a solicitor. I've never bought a house on my own, been divorced, been in trouble with the police, dealt with probate. I suddenly feel very, very young.

Richard isn't keen on the idea. I understand the reason for the advice, of course, although I don't say it aloud. We both know it's because when something like this happens to a couple, more often than not they wind up separating. All that pressure. Guilt, doubt and recrimination.

Not us, though. We won't break.

I can't let Richard go, however tough things get. I fought too hard to get to this point, even bore the recriminations of my own mother (who shook her head and kept repeating the word '*married*' in a disapproving whisper, to which I kept responding '*separated*', to such a degree that it felt as though for a while we had entire conversations consisting of single words being batted back and forth). It had seemed impossible to win him, but I did, and I am going to keep him.

I will appoint the solicitor though, because when your baby's been taken from you and someone offers advice, you take it. And so much feels stacked against us that it seems wise to gather as many allies as possible, even if those allies do charge £250 an hour. I have a feeling we'll need them.

But how do you choose? I look at websites, at faces and credentials. They all look the same to me, and their qualifications are meaningless. In the end I choose a woman, because in some way I think she'll provide balance, a counter to Richard's precious Philip Lingwood and his oily brand of manliness. Her name is Sarah Taylor-Smith, and she looks approachable but tough. Her biography says she has two children. I hope she'll understand.

Julia calls to check how I am.

'That was intense,' she says. 'At my house, the other day. I've been thinking about it and I just wanted to make sure you are coping.' I'm immediately prickly.

'Oh, I'm sorry,' I snap. 'Sorry if it was uncomfortable for everyone.' I knew it: as soon as I left, I bet they all started bitching about me.

'Oh! No, no, that's not what I meant at all. I really just wanted to see how you are, and whether I can help in any way.'

This is possibly the first one-to-one conversation we've had. Up to this point the MMG has always been the foursome: me, Julia, Esme and Melinda. There were five of us in the actual NCT group but the fifth woman didn't stay in touch – we speculated that she'd attended the classes actually to learn about birth and babies rather than to make friends, could this be right? Or maybe she just hadn't liked us very much. The rest of us had a WhatsApp chat group set up so that we could communicate in group texts, often in the middle of the night, feeding and bored, so all contact was visible to everyone.

You shouldn't rank your friends, of course, but Julia is kind of my favourite of the group. She's always quite 'together' and matter-of-fact. She's clearly one of those capable people, a manager, but equally is unselfconscious when things go wrong, like if we go round there and the house is untidy, or like the time her baby was wearing odd socks and Melinda pointed it out, a bit unkindly, I thought. Julia had just shrugged and said, 'He's lucky he's dressed at all.'

'Actually,' I say, thinking about this and softening, 'I would really like it if we could meet. You know, just to talk.'

'Shall we go to that little coffee place just off the High Street?' she asks. 'It's the only place where I don't get the evil eye if I whip my boob out to feed his lordship.' Julia is still breastfeeding, unlike the rest of us, but she complains about it often and her accounts of her attempts to wean little Henry are entertaining despite her exasperation. 'I mean, he's got *teeth*,' she'd say. 'It's ridiculous. As soon as he starts being able to *ask* for it, I'm definitely stopping.'

'Actually, could we go out, *just* me and you?' I ask. 'I mean, no babies. Baby.' *Obviously there will be no Ollie.* There is silence at the other end of the phone so I carry on. 'In the evening if that's easier, when Henry's in bed?'

'Well, I can't really do that, can I? Who's going to look after H?'

'Er, his *dad*?' I really didn't mean my tone to be as acerbic as it sounds, but I have been getting a bit weary of the 'all dads are useless and can't be trusted with the babies' routine that we seem to have subscribed to for the last ten months. Me included, to be fair.

When I first met Richard, he told me he didn't want any more children. Nappies and night feeds were behind him, he said. But then, when I first met Richard, he had a wife. So, you know, things change. He didn't do too many nappies or night feeds when Ollie came along, as it happens, and I suspect he didn't do much with Martha either, though I'd never dream of asking Zoe. That's the thing with Richard. It's hard to know how much of what he says is true and how much is just the most spectacular bullshit. I recall for a minute what Zoe said about his philandering past, and resolve to ask him about it, but not yet.

Anyway, so I'd joined in the husband-bashing as gleefully as the next woman when, a few months into our friendship, it started, but it is wearing a bit thin now and I'm beginning to suspect that some of us, particularly Julia, are actually just control freaks who can't bear the idea that their baby might not combust without their constant attention. I suppose they might get even more protective now they know Ollie was hurt on Richard's watch.

Equally I can't really stand the idea of trying to talk to Julia about everything that's been going on while she bounces Henry on her knee, or he munches on a banana or a rice cake, looking every inch Oliver's twin (they were born two days apart and have uncannily similar thick hair and dark eyes).

'Are you OK, Sally?' she is asking. I've drifted off, as often happens these days, and look down to find I've been drawing ever larger circles on a piece of paper in front of me, the pencil digging deeper and making a darker line with each one.

'Yeah, you know what? Don't worry about it. Another time, maybe.' I hang up before she can say anything else, and realise that maybe these people aren't my real friends, and I should be brave and try Ben again.

'We have the same ruling planet,' Ben once told me. A lifetime ago.

'I'm sorry?'

'Mercury. You're a Virgo.'

'Um. I guess so.'

'Gemini.' We shook hands. 'Mercury, you see.'

I met Ben at university, in Halls. His room was next door to mine. 'Halls of Residence' had sounded grand; I'd imagined oak panelling, maybe even chandeliers. No one told me it would be a 1970s building whose design, it was rumoured, had been based on plans for an open prison. Twelve identical rooms, shoulder to shoulder, and a corridor too narrow for two people to walk down at once.

The others made fun of him, especially The Lads, as they called themselves. They formed a testosterone-fuelled group that excluded Ben. Was it bullying? I don't know. I walked a strange tightrope between the popularity that would guarantee me a drinking partner, late night secrets, maybe kisses, and the doomed world of the outsider. I like to think I protected him, a little bit.

For all his fascination with the heavens, Ben didn't believe in God. When late-night Halls kitchen talk would turn to the Big Questions, usually accompanied by copious slugs of cheap whiskey, he would say things like 'I believe in Zeus' and then argue that this was no more ludicrous than belief in an Abrahamic God and act all affronted, with his best saucer-eyed, sincere look, when everyone mocked and challenged him.

'Is he for real?' they would say, their conspiratorial winks inviting me to fully join their side.

'Oh yes,' I'd say, and always go back to him.

After a while I enjoyed playing the cynical friend, the Scully to his Mulder, the sceptic to his wide-eyed believer.

'Look. Take the moon. It controls the tides, yeah?' I nodded my agreement. 'It controls the tides! You see. The thing is, the moon … pulls and pushes every body of water on this planet, from the Pacific Ocean to the sea at Brighton, all that water rolling in and out like clockwork, perfectly, perfectly controlled … even down to the tiniest, muddiest puddle, the moon has an influence. That's where we come in. What are you made of?'

'What?'

'What are you made of?'

'You're asking a biologist?' I laughed. 'A pharmacist? Skin, bones, blood—'

'Water. Two-thirds water. You see.' He pushed on, talking about lunar cycles, onto menstrual cycles, and I blushed a bit, then he was onto linguistics, talking about the word lunacy, joking about his girlfriend's PMT, and hysteria, coming from the Greek word *hustera* for the womb. The wandering womb.

He was full of excitement for the enormous choreographed dance of the universe. He told me I was an earth sign and he was air. We liked swapping facts.

'Mercury,' he said. 'Allied with the Greek messenger of the Gods, Hermes. Master of words, language and travel.'

'Smallest planet,' I said. 'Closest to the sun. Diameter three thousand miles. Daytime temperatures up to four hundred degrees.'

'Bloody scientists.' He laughed.

We fell out fairly spectacularly on the day I married Richard. My usually easy-going friend got hideously drunk and dragged me out onto the terrace to slur at me.

The *Telegraph* would later run a piece reviewing the restaurant at the same venue, and reading it Richard and I quickly realised, with a bit of a thrill, that the reviewer had visited on the same evening as our wedding. The references to the unseasonal heat, for a start – it had been stupidly hot for October and the best man had 'joked' it was a good omen that we would have a 'steamy' marriage. The wedding had apparently only added to the charm of the place for the *Telegraph* man, but embedded in the review was a caustic reference to a 'very *un*romantic argument' he'd overheard storming on the terrace just below his open window. Well, that argument was me and Ben.

He gave me the usual bullshit about marrying the mistress and creating a vacancy. I said that was very unoriginal of him and why couldn't he just be happy for me and if he really felt that way, I wished he hadn't bothered to come at all. He stormed off, but not before throwing up in the potted flowers. The next morning, I went downstairs early and walked out onto the terrace. Ben had checked out and a handful of birds were pecking enthusiastically at the remains of his vomit.

Ben and I reconnected when I was pregnant – he'd been genuinely pleased for me, and came to see us shortly after the birth, though I haven't seen him since. But there are some friends you can just call, any time. I am banking on this and I'm nervous dialling his number, partly because he hasn't replied to my earlier, garbled message. But he doesn't let me down.

'Sal!' he cries. 'God, yes, yes, let's meet. I've no car just now … Can you get the train down here? Just name your day. Can't wait to see you, hon.'

And just like that, I feel for the first time in weeks that I have something to look forward to.

Social services ring to tell me they want to interview me, separately from Richard. Richard had warned me this would happen, from all his research. Mary comes to the house when he is out at work. He'd said they would try to take us apart; I'd said he was paranoid.

'You keep a lovely tidy house,' Mary comments as she drifts behind me into the kitchen. She says it pleasantly enough, but my mind is on overdrive: is that a criticism? Is our home not child-friendly enough?

'Well, I try to keep busy,' I say, gesturing with a couple of mugs.

She shakes her head and says, 'Water will be fine for me.'

'Shall we go through to the front?'

Once we've settled in the lounge, she takes out her files.

'I just wanted a chat,' she says, 'about the post-natal depression.'

'Well, I was never diagnosed—'

'But you were prescribed anti-depressants.'

'Yes, but I … I never took them,' I murmur. 'Even Richard doesn't know about that.'

'He wouldn't approve?'

'It's not that. He … didn't like, doesn't like, lots of outside intervention, I suppose.' As soon as I say it I regret it. I don't know how I am supposed to *be*: guarded, or honest? To what degree? What are the right answers? Does Mary have them, there, in that bloody folder of hers?

'So you never talked to him about the visit … *visits* … you made to the doctor, reporting your low mood.'

'Well, conversations between a patient and their GP are supposed to be confidential,' I snap. She ignores this.

'Do you keep many secrets from your husband, Sally?'

'No, I—'

'Would you say you're afraid of him?'

'Certainly not.'

'Would you describe him as a violent man?'

'No, I wouldn't.'

'But he does have a conviction, doesn't he? For violence?'

I feel like a contestant in a quiz show I can't win. *For God's sake*, I want to shout, *you obviously know where you're going with this, just say what you want to say and leave. Why ask me questions when you already know the answers?*

'You'd have to ask him about that,' I say, but she looks at me pointedly. 'Yes, yes, he does. From a long time ago.'

It was before I met him and I don't know much about it; only that he has a scar on his shoulder as a result. He'd stepped in to stop a fight, he told me: big guy picking on much smaller guy, that kind of thing. The altercation turned into a brawl and in the chaos someone broke a bottle and Richard was glassed; but because he'd thrown a punch that had broken the other guy's jaw, it was him who'd been charged with assault. He was lucky it wasn't GBH, he said.

'I'll do that, thank you,' Mary says. 'He's never been violent with you? With the children?'

'Of course not.'

'Does he have a temper?' I hesitate.

Mary raises her eyebrows.

'Well, I suppose so. But doesn't everyone?'

I can't believe I just said that aloud.

As soon as we were 'officially' a couple, Richard booked us a holiday. We were to have five days in Marrakech. There was some grumbling from Zoe along the lines of 'If you're going to take time off work, maybe you should take your *daughter* somewhere', but even that couldn't dampen my excitement. He'd booked a boutique riad, far fancier than anything I'd been able to afford on my meagre student and post-grad incomes.

On what was supposed to be a relaxing mini-break, I saw Richard's temper for the first time.

I loved Marrakech. It was so different to anywhere I'd been before. We spent our first evening in the Jemaa el-Fnaa, a vast open square buzzing with snake charmers, fortune tellers and acrobats, overlooked by the minaret of the Koutoubia Mosque. It would have been like stepping back in time were it not for the occasional groups of teenagers whizzing by on mopeds. I insisted we ate at the open-air market rather than at one of the restaurants that lined the square, because I couldn't bear to move inside and away from the thrilling atmosphere. The charcoal-filled smoke and the musical calls of the stallholders were just too enticing. 'The food here will be cheaper and better than in a restaurant,' I told Richard as we sat down at a trestle table, and when he pulled a face I said, 'If you really want to splash the cash, you can take me home in a horse and carriage.'

He laughed then and eventually admitted that he enjoyed the lamb tagine. And when full darkness fell, he did hail us a carriage and we rode out of town, the shape of the Atlas Mountains a forbidding backdrop, and resolved to go back to the same spot the next morning and explore the souks.

We'd been warned the souks were labyrinthine and it was easy to get lost, but Richard didn't appear concerned. This was one of the reasons I'd fallen for him: his absolute confidence and ease in any situation. The morning was hot and we were grateful for the shade afforded by the canopied alleys, broken only by the occasional sun-drenched square where children played football and men in long robes rode by on ancient bicycles.

With hindsight, Richard was irritable from the start, muttering about the mosquito bites he'd accrued the previous evening, which were causing him periodically to scratch the back of his neck or bend to rub at his ankles with such force I thought it must hurt to do it.

As I'd anticipated, having read every Marrakech guidebook I could get my hands on in the weeks running up to the trip, the stallholders and craftsmen were persistent and highly vocal in their efforts to get us to view and sample their wares. Despite those early signs of discomfort, Richard at first took their haranguing in good humour, engaging in easy banter, even asking to be taught Arabic swear-words, laughing and shaking hands and then moving on. He even teased one guy, who was trying to get us to go to his hammam – 'the best in all of Marrakech' – by insisting that *he* visit *us* at home in England and try our bath out for size.

I loved looking at all the stalls and shops, although I sensed Richard didn't want me to actually buy anything. If I lingered in one place for more than a couple of minutes, he would swoop in, take my arm and steer me away. I was enchanted by wicker baskets, earthenware pots, hookahs, brightly coloured slippers and sandals. He kept reminding me we didn't have much space in our cases. 'Well, then, let's buy something that isn't for taking home,' I said, stopping at a stall displaying mountains of dates, apricots, figs and almonds. Crates filled with huge lemons and pomegranates were stacked as high as me. I sampled and then bought a paper bag filled with sugar-covered almonds, which left a caramel taste on my tongue.

The morning wore on and Richard was making noises about lunch. He was a creature of habit where food was concerned, fanatical about his three meals a day. My stomach was full of the nuts I'd been grazing on, but I agreed we'd make our way out of the souks.

Within minutes it became apparent we were lost. There was no order to the streets and alleys; they made no sense. We tried to go back the way we'd come, but nothing looked familiar. We found ourselves in a heavily shaded area with an overpowering smell. I looked down to see animal hides stretched out on the pavement. 'The tanneries,' I murmured, fumbling with the souk map we'd picked up at the hotel.

'Forget the map,' Richard muttered, pushing it out of my hand. 'It's useless.'

'Hey!' I bent to pick up the folded paper; at that moment a crowd of men surrounded us, offering to take us on a tour of the tanneries, for a small fee. They were met with Richard's exasperated 'No, thank you', which then rose to a shouted 'No! I said no!'

I turned to him, as the men slunk away. 'All right, calm down, will you? There's no need to be rude to people.'

'Isn't there? I'm getting a bit sick of the constant harassment.' His face was red; he ran his hand through his hair. 'I just want to get the hell out of here.'

A Moroccan boy, maybe nine or ten years old, was watching us, with a toothy smile. He was barefoot and his clothes had the faded look of having been washed over and over.

'You want help?' he asked; his voice had a musical, light quality. 'You want out of the souks, yes?' Richard rolled his eyes but I smiled at the boy.

'Yes, please. Back to the square? Jemaa el-Fnaa?' The boy nodded enthusiastically. I turned to Richard and whispered, 'I read about this. One of these young guides can show you out of the souks in minutes. We just give him a few dirham and we're out. OK?'

Sure enough, the boy led us back through the souks at astonishing speed, ducking and weaving through the crowds, occasionally glancing over his shoulder to make sure we were following. Before too long the alleyways widened, light streamed in and miraculously, we were at the entrance to the square.

'Thank you.' I smiled at the boy. 'Merci.' He smiled back and held out his hand. Richard peeled off a few notes, probably the equivalent of about £3, and pressed it into his palm. The boy looked at it, then back at Richard.

'Is not enough,' he said. 'You give me more.'

'What?' Richard's eyes flashed.

'Not enough.' The child shrugged, his hand still outstretched.

'Richard, give him a couple more quid and let's get out of here,' I said.

He turned on me. 'What? No way!' Then, turning back to the boy, he exploded. 'How dare you? Who do you think you are? Get out of here!'

I looked at him; his fists were clenched and his eyes were blazing. I'd never seen anything like it. I touched his arm lightly and he pushed my hand away. I swallowed.

'Bastard,' the boy spat, shoving the notes into his pocket. 'You pay more.'

'No fucking way, you little shit.' Richard's hand was on the boy's shoulder now and again I put a hand on his arm, firmer this time; again he shoved me, roughly, away. 'When I was your age I wouldn't have dared speak to an adult like that, and if I had …'

'Richard!' My shout broke his flow, and in the moment he turned back towards me, the boy shook out of his grip and ran away back into the souks, a trail of yelled Arabic expletives hanging in the air behind him.

Later, sitting in a café, Richard said he was sorry, that he didn't know what came over him. He said he was stressed; he hated Marrakech; he was tired of getting ripped off.

'I thought you were going to hit him,' I said quietly.

He said he'd never do that, he was just a kid and he'd never hit a kid, but I wasn't so sure. I sipped my mint tea in silence, but everything tasted wrong; Richard hated it here, and even being here with me didn't change that, and I knew with a sick feeling in my stomach that the whole trip was ruined.

'I'm sorry if I scared you,' Richard said. I nodded and said it was OK, but it wasn't.

* * *

Richard calls to say he will be late home. I tell him that's all right, take the dinner off the heat. When he finally gets back, it's growing dark and we launch straight into our daily review of our situation. This is our new normal. He reports some tenuous legal loophole he, or his solicitor, has uncovered. It doesn't sound quite involving enough to have kept him out until nearly ten o'clock, but my head is full of the conversation with Mary and I haven't the mental space to question him.

'How did you get on today?' he eventually asks.

'Not good,' I say. 'They're trying to paint me as depressive, you as violent.'

He frowns.

'Well, what did you say?'

'I didn't drop you in it, if that's what you mean,' I snap, too quickly, because the truth is I'm terrified that I did. 'But they've got both our histories, obviously. They'll draw their own conclusions, won't they?'

He exhales, a long, slow breath, and then he reaches for me. This is Richard's go-to solution – physical closeness – but it isn't mine. The only person I want close to me is my baby.

'I'm tired,' I say, and push him away.

Chapter Ten

Martha

I tell them I'm going to the library. Really I'm going to the pub, with Del, Pip and Lyns.

'Revision time,' Del says cheerily, somehow balancing four drinks in her little hands and delivering them to the table.

'It's so shit,' Pip groans. 'I'm going to fail everything, I just know it. But what's the point? Everyone says your GCSE results don't actually make any difference to your life. So you can do all this work, and it gets you nowhere anyway.'

'Yeah, that's why it's not worth bothering.' Lynsey brings the drink to her lips and grimaces; she doesn't even like vodka, I don't know why she insists on ordering it.

'Well, that's not true, is it?' I say, suddenly irritable. 'Of course they make a difference, especially if you want to go to college or something.'

'You'd better run along home then, hadn't you?' Pip snaps.

'You don't even need to study, M.' Del smiles. 'You're super clever anyway.'

'I don't know about that,' I mumble. 'My mock results were crap.' Dad had totally bawled me out on those; said he expected more from me, because yeah, I was supposed to be clever. These days, I doubt he even cares what happens in the exams. It was obvious on that stupid London trip that he had no clue.

After Ol was born, Dad still called me his 'number one girl', to which I'd reply 'I'm your only girl'. He'd smile and go back to Ol. After all, he was a baby and needed him more. There wasn't enough of him to go around and I was supposed to be a good girl, which means suck it up and get on with it. And now it's even worse. I might as well spend my time in the pub with people who don't care about their future. Well, apart from Del; for all her bravado, I know her well enough to know that at home she has a carefully planned-out revision timetable, and heaps of textbooks at her little desk where she sits up late most nights.

'Ooh, look who's over there,' Lynsey coos suddenly. 'Your friend.' I glance over to the pool table and see Brendan, his jeans slung low on his hips, watching us. When he sees me looking he winks. Del frowns.

'Be careful there,' she says.

'Why?' I turn to look at her, but she has caught the eye of one of the art-college boys at the bar and is gathering up her bag.

'Hold it there,' she says. 'I'm off to score.' It occurs to me that while almost everyone we know who uses drugs buys from Brendan, Del doesn't. I wonder what she knows.

I want to talk to her more, but this will probably be the last I see of her all evening.

At home, I overhear Dad on the phone. He mustn't realise I'm back, because he's come upstairs and is standing right outside my bedroom door. It's obvious he's telling someone what's happened to Ol. I throw my magazine onto the bed and tiptoe across my room, willing the floorboards not to creak.

'The thing is, I can't say I was with you, obviously. So I'm a suspect. But if I do say I was with you, well, I'm kind of screwed ... Didn't you hear me? My son has broken his arm. Of course it's fucking serious ... No, I'm not asking you for anything. Just wanted to let you know why I haven't ... Oh, right then. Fine. Sorry, I thought you'd give a shit ... Yes, sorry, sorry, it's been pretty stressful here.' Suddenly his voice rises, making me jump. 'Stop calling him "my kid". His name is Oliver. He has a name, for fuck's sake.' Then his footsteps stomp away and, as he moves down the hall, I hear him make a frustrated, wild sound, not quite a shout. Like an animal. It makes me shiver.

I am becoming friends with him. With Brendan. At least, I think so. He invites me to his house after school 'to watch a film'.

'Are you coming?' Del asks, shrugging on her coat. It's an automatic question because I almost always say 'yes' and we walk home together, running over the day's events. But this time I tell her, as casually as I can, that I'm going to Brendan's.

'O-kay,' she says slowly, narrowing her eyes.

'What?'

'You should watch yourself, hon.'

'What do you mean?'

She shrugs. 'I've heard things about him. Not good things.'

'Like what?' I ask but even as I do, I know there's not much she can say to me that will stop me from going. But I also know it must be serious to bother Del. It can't be the drugs, for example; she's hardly one to judge on that front.

'He's a bit handy with his fists, apparently,' she says. This isn't exactly news; Brendan has been known to fight kids from other schools when they dare walk down one of 'his' streets. It's a bit like a small-scale turf war, kind of pathetic but a lot of the kids find it exciting when the chant of 'Fight!' ripples through the corridors and classrooms.

'He's hardly likely to hit me, is he?' I say, but I'm aware my voice sounds small.

'Probably not,' she concedes, but looks at me closely for a moment. 'Like I say, just be careful, OK?' She turns and as the second home-time bell rings she jogs to catch up with a group of other girls, double doors swinging behind her.

There aren't many areas in Farnham that my dad would describe as 'out of bounds'. I mean, it's just not that sort of place. When we lived in London, Dad was very clear about where I could and couldn't go, on my own I mean. He used to say, 'Even in the best bits of town, you're never more than a few hundred yards away from a scumbag.' He was probably right.

I have the feeling as we walk towards Brendan's house that Dad wouldn't want me in this neighbourhood. It's hard to describe why it's different from where we live. The houses are boxy and squat, not tall and smart like the houses on our road. Everything looks kind of old and tired. People sit at bus stops, smoking, and stop talking when we walk by. Just after a block of flats, Brendan turns abruptly onto a driveway, squeezing past a caravan that's missing a wheel. It tilts towards the fence and its windows are thick with dust. For a mad moment I wonder if that's where he lives.

He sees me looking and laughs, saying, 'That's just where I get sent when I've been naughty.' Then he tugs keys out of his pocket and unlocks the front door to the actual house. We go straight up the stairs, followed by a skinny Jack Russell on whom Brendan slams his bedroom door. He has a massive TV and a floor-to-ceiling bookcase full of DVDs. 'Wow,' I say, tilting my head to look at the titles and noting they are organised in alphabetical order.

'Drink? Smoke?'

I turn around and watch as he opens a packet of cigarettes and falls back onto the bed, eyebrows raised in my direction.

'The thing is, it's totally unfair,' he is saying, stroking my shoulder. We are lying on the bed, a few unwatched DVDs scattered at our feet. My heart is racing on account of the fact he's just kissed me. He kissed me! Brendan Lowe kissed *me*. He did it all casual as well, like we'd done it loads of times before, he just turned to me and gave me a little kiss on the nose, and then on the mouth, and then there was full-blown snogging and the whole time a crazy loud voice in my head was going 'Woah!' When he stopped I had to gasp because I'd been holding my breath the entire time. He laughed at that.

And now he's in the middle of a rant against the criminalisation of drugs. It isn't something I've ever given much thought, but the way he puts it, it makes sense. 'It's just wrong,' he's saying. 'It's making criminals out of people who just want to have a good time, people who aren't harming anyone. And you know why, don't you?'

'Why?' I whisper, wanting to sit up and look at him, but not wanting to lose my place lying on his chest.

'The government. They want everyone miserable. Miserable and afraid. Then we'll keep voting them in. Can't have people on drugs, thinking differently.'

'I suppose that makes sense,' I say.

'They shouldn't be going after the users, anyway,' he says. 'They should go after the dealers.'

This makes me laugh, I can't help it.

'Aren't *you* a dealer?' My eyes flick around the room and land on the expensive telly. Everyone knows Brendan's mum is on benefits. No one knows about his dad, who seems to come and go.

'No! Not like them,' he says, and he sounds offended, and I open my mouth to try to apologise, but he keeps talking, and holds me a bit closer, so he can't be too bothered. 'I'm more of a … supplier.' His cheek is so close to mine that I can actually feel the grin spreading across his face. I wonder if it would be OK to kiss him again.

'There aren't many people I trust,' he is saying, his voice suddenly low. 'Do you know what I mean?'

I nod; I do know, I really do.

'I feel the same,' I say.

'I'm in a bit of trouble,' he says, and although his voice is casual, somehow I can tell it's taking a lot for him to open up like this.

'What is it?'

'They're watching me,' he says. 'The police, the social, all that. The *establishment*. You know? I need to lay low for a while. But it's not fair on my customers, is it? They've done nothing wrong.' He lets out a sigh. 'I hate letting them down.'

'What do you need?' I ask suddenly, twisting my neck to try to see his face. 'Can I help?'

'It's not much, really. I need … a delivery person. Just for a while. Wow, Martha, it would be really great if you could help out.'

For a few minutes I think this is it, this is my chance to move up a circle, to *really* be part of the in crowd. To totally deserve Del's friendship and to get respect from tons of others. Man, life would be easier. And Brendan really seems to like me, and I want to help him, I really do.

But … but … but …

The voice in my head telling me that what he's asking is a bad idea is just too loud. Most annoyingly of all, it sounds a lot like my dad's voice. And I know what Sally would say: that if Brendan really liked me, it wouldn't matter if I said no to him on this. He'd understand. And if he didn't, he wasn't worth bothering with. *Jesus.* When did I start thinking, let alone caring, about what Sally would say?

'Well?' he is murmuring into my hair. I pull myself free from his snake-like arms and sit up.

'Yeah, look, the thing is, I'd like to help, but … I just don't think I can.' It comes out in a rush and my face is burning.

He smiles such a wide smile it lights up his whole face and I'm just feeling a warmth kindling in me when he says, 'Oh, I'm sorry, Martha. You've misunderstood me. I don't think you get it. You seem to think you have a *choice* in this. Guess what? You don't.'

My stomach drops. It's weird; I've never seen that before, when someone's words are so out of step with their face. I just stare at him. I really can't think what he's getting at.

'You see, I've got this –' he's waving his mobile phone '– and thanks to this, I think you'll do exactly as you're told.'

I zone out. My mother tried to use hypnosis on me, more than once, with varying degrees of success. She did cure my arachnophobia, which she insisted on calling 'creature phobia', because she said fervently she really didn't want me to be afraid of anything. I'm not, I said, only spiders.

She did it by getting me to imagine a film playing backwards.

I try to do the same, now, with that night at our house, in the den, the night before they took Ol. I try to rewind my life back to then, try to replay it to see what I've missed.

Brendan's breath too close to my face, his hand in my hair.

His laugh.

A cold laugh, and the fire went out.

Now he's explaining that he's going to 'make me famous' on mysluttygirlfriend.com.

The smile goes rigid on my face.

'But … I'm not your girlfriend,' I say, because, stupidly, this is the first thought I have.

'Of course not. But they don't know that, do they?'

'Who's they?'

'The people who look at the site.' He grins. 'It'll only take me a few seconds to upload the photos, and boom! You'll be famous. Hey, maybe you'd *like* me to do it?' He holds up his phone and shows me a stream of photos. Girls in all sorts of positions. I feel suddenly cold.

'But you don't have any pictures like that. Of me.'

'Oh, Martha. Poor Martha.' He takes the phone away and with a press and a swipe, there they are.

Filling the screen, my face. My eyes, closed. My mouth, slack and open. And shoved into my mouth, I mean it is partly hidden by his hand, but it is unmistakably *it*.

Crazy thoughts come into my head, like, *But I haven't done that. That can't be the first time I did that, I thought it would be different. Like with a boyfriend. He's not my boyfriend.* I feel stupid. I feel sick. The idea of anyone seeing these pictures …

'I'll do it,' I say, my voice tiny. 'I'll do whatever you want.'

What he wants is for me to just deliver a few packages, he says.

'I'll do it. Now delete the pictures.'

'You've got to be joking. These babies are my insurance policy.'

I get out of Brendan's house as quickly as I can, and it's weird because he's all fake-friendly, and even kisses me when I leave. I walk home, my head in a whirl. What have I done? What am I going to do? When I get back, Dad and Sally are bent over the laptop, heads close together like conspirators. I shout a quick 'hello' but all I can think is that I have to get upstairs. I feel myself being pulled to my room, my bed, the little box in the bottom of my wardrobe, the bathroom, and peace. Sounds nice, huh?

The wardrobe was my present when Ol was born. That might seem an odd gift, but up until then all I'd had at Dad's house was a clothes rail. I knew it annoyed him; he said it made the room look untidy, and I didn't like looking at my stuff hanging there either, empty of arms and legs, a pathetic collection of lumberjack shirts and T-shirts and school uniform. The new wardrobe fitted in well with the style of the house: it was an antique, French apparently, and had been painted off-white and deliberately 'distressed', the paint chipped and flaked to show hints of dark wood underneath. It matched the house but it didn't match the rest of my bedroom furniture, which was the standard-issue flat pack pine you can get cheap and at short notice. I loved the wardrobe.

In the bottom, towards the back, I keep a shoebox. In the shoebox, I keep blades, pins, scissors, bandages, plasters and surgical tape.

Zoe does meditation, self-hypnosis, all that kind of crap. She put in a rare phone call last weekend to me to tell me I should try mindfulness; it would help me with 'exam pressure'. I was amazed.

'I thought you said I shouldn't worry about them, since exams are a meaningless badge for the bourgeois elite, or a social construct, or something,' I muttered. My mother says everything is a social construct: love, capitalism, fucking toilet rolls. 'Should I be worried, or not?' I was bored and felt like irritating her.

'There clearly *is* some underlying anxiety there, M, however much you try to suppress it,' she crowed. 'I'm only trying to help.'

I put the phone down.

Here are the things that *actually* help me:

Cider.

Cigarettes.

My friends.

Cutting.

Before I discovered that I could do this, I was pretty angry. That's a gigantic understatement, actually: I was fucking furious. The weird thing was, I didn't even know why. And I wasn't angry in a cool, rebellious way, I was angry in an ugly way I didn't want anyone to see. So I started doing stuff, to let it out, in ways people couldn't see. I'd dig my fingernails into the palms of my hands. I would grit my teeth. Once I did that so hard I chipped a tooth.

I ignore it when Dad calls out something about dinner, already feeling calmer with every stair I climb and count, each step one closer to my goal.

It started with scissors. I had scissors I used for cutting my hair, well, my fringe, anyway. When you're fifteen and living with your dad, haircuts aren't something he thinks to arrange for you, or ask if you'd like, or offer to pay for. Sally has tried the matey 'let's go to the hairdresser's together, girls' time' approach but I always put her off, and besides, since she had Ol, she's kind of let herself go where grooming is concerned, if you know what I mean.

The scissors made little scratches in my skin. I tried to draw perfect parallel lines on my arms, and when I was concentrating on that, nothing else could get in. It was like the world around me was on pause. I fantasised about cutting out parts of me. The 'baby fat' that my mother said would disappear once I hit my teens lingered around my arms and my tummy. I wondered if I could sculpt myself, imagined taking a chisel and knocking away the bits I didn't like.

The scissors weren't very sharp and I started to wonder what more a razor blade would do. It was weird because I'd always been kind of scared of knives. I am the 'world's slowest sous chef', my dad always says, because I'm so careful chopping vegetables. I've always been terrified of having an accident.

But the cutting is different; it's controlled. It's like art, and I'm good at art. Zoe once showed me an old picture of Richey Edwards from the Manic Street Preachers, '4 Real' carved into his arm, his eyes cast down. I was mesmerised by it. I bought all their early albums and pored over his lyrics like poetry.

I take out my box, head to the bathroom, lock the door and get started.

Chapter Eleven

Sally

Another week, another addition to the report on Oliver's safety. Quotes from anonymous 'friends'.

I once said: 'I made him, I can do what I want with him.' I'd thought it a funny joke. I can remember the comment but not the company, mentally scanning faces in my head for that of my Judas. It had to be one of the mums, didn't it?

It was clearly a joke, I remember laughing as I'd said it.

The report also tells me that I once said I felt like throwing him out of the window when he wouldn't stop crying. I'd said it was a good job babies started smiling at six weeks as that's about the point you start considering sending them back. Then they smile at you and you're hooked: 'Evolution's way of making sure you keep your baby!' I'd laughed then too, apparently.

That one may smile, and smile, and be a villain.

Yet another 'friend' has commented that I'd 'probably' had post-natal depression. *Thanks for that.* As far as I know none of my friends are medically qualified. I am, but this seems irrelevant. My work have been contacted and asked how drunk I was 'that night'. The answer, of course, is 'very'. They were asked whether they believed I had a problem with alcohol. Had I ever missed work due to a hangover, for example? The answer to these questions was 'no', but that doesn't seem to matter; the mere fact of them having been asked leaves a huge dark cloud in the air. And the doctor at the hospital reported smelling alcohol on me when we brought Ollie in. There are no such damning indictments of Richard. Of course there aren't. He hardly spends any time with Oliver, to know or feel any of these things to be able to joke about them.

Every time we visit our son, social services generate a 'contact report'. Imagine being watched in your every interaction with your child, knowing that notes, and judgements, are being made. Imagine all your insecurities about your ability as a mother being confirmed and lined up to form a case against you.

Do I play with him too much, or not enough? I'm criticised for getting Ollie's toys out and lining them up for him, instead of letting him 'explore and discover freely' and 'instigate his own play'. Subtext: I'm controlling. Never mind the fact *he has an arm in plaster and I was trying to help him*. So the next time, I leave him to it and this is also recorded. I am unsure to just what degree I am supposed to let him explore on his own, and I stop him from pulling a heavy ornament down onto himself, but 'only just in time to prevent injury', the next report says. Subtext: I'm (dangerously) disinterested.

I'm overly fussy about cleanliness because I change him twice in one hour and am 'fastidious' about wiping him. History of OCD duly noted. If I'd left him in a soiled nappy, presumably I'd be negligent.

I cuddle him too much on some occasions (I'm smothering him), not enough on others (I'm cold). My parenting 'style' is recorded as inconsistent, erratic.

I want to stop reading the reports, because it seems I literally can't win, and in fact Richard has told me to stop reading them, but I can't, of course. Like an actor hungry for reviews, good or bad, I can't stop. And the more I read, the less I trust my own version of myself and the more I start to think that maybe they are right.

You can be as qualified as you like, can read all the books you like, but you can still fail to recognise depression when it reaches up and slaps you across the face.

I thought I had flu.

I still can't accept it, not really. Whisper it: *post-natal depression*. Is that what I had? It will form part of the judgment for or against me, I suppose, so I ought to decide pretty quickly.

So here is what happened the day I realised something was wrong. I thought I had flu because it started with shivering. And aches, aches in my bones that made me need to lie down, want to lie still, and get close to the ground. So I did. Perfectly flat and motionless, afraid to move. That was the day I first went to see the GP. The second time, I was prescribed the anti-depressants that I never took.

I'd been tired, but this was different. I'd been tired since the day Ollie was born, an exhaustion that had never quite caught up with itself, although there was one day it almost did. Ollie was just two weeks old, my mum was visiting for a few days and Richard had gone to work. Mum left me to sleep until 11am. I slept, and slept, so that when I woke I wasn't sure where I was, or even, for a moment, who I was. But I knew there was something wrong with the sky. I looked out of the window, from my bed, and saw that the sun was too high, the day too old.

Cold-fingered panic crawled over my scalp and I shouted 'Ollie!', as though he could respond to his name, and then 'Mum?', but I found my voice was too quiet, my throat dehydrated from too much sleep. I pulled on a dressing gown (Richard's, I realised only when Mum looked at me and laughed) and headed down to the lounge to find Mum cradling Ollie, who was sucking from a bottle, an expression of pure bliss on his face.

That was the beginning of the end, breastfeeding-wise, although I persevered for a few more weeks, alternating with bottles until my breasts dried up. And any benefit I gained from that heavenly sleep was cancelled out by a dark covering of guilt.

I've found an article online, in a healthcare journal, about unexplained fractures in infants. Unlike Richard's collection of emotional accounts from the point of view of wronged parents, this is a medical paper, devoid of sentiment, and its tone is cool and objective. I find this soothing. The date of the child protection conference is circled on the calendar on the wall, the way I used to circle play dates and baby clinic check-ups.

I've printed off the whole thing, which is several pages long, and I have it in a pile on the kitchen table. I'm summarising it in the way I used to do when I was revising, making notes on a small pad, underlining and circling important points as I go. Most of my notes have 'NO' next to them as I rule out the possible causes of Ollie's injury, one by one.

Osteogenesis imperfecta. Type I?

Metabolic bone disease of prematurity. NO (born just 1 week early).

Cole-Carpenter Syndrome. NO.

Idiopathic juvenile osteoporosis. No?

Of course, even an objective, scientific writer has to mention that statistically speaking, the majority of fractures in infants are non-accidental.

I'm staring at the notes, at the papers, willing something I haven't yet seen to jump off the page, when the doorbell rings. On the way down the hall I try to shake the words and data out of my mind, which is so fogged up I don't know if I can reset to normal mode and have a conversation. I'm not expecting anyone, so hopefully whoever it is can be sent away with minimum fuss.

I open the door to Julia, her head positioned in a perfect tilt of concern.

'Hi,' she says.

'Hi.' Panic floods through me; I always feel like this with unexpected visitors. It's worse when I know them, but even the postman, dropping off a parcel, can send me into spasms of worry: is he looking behind me, at the house? Are there cobwebs? Is he looking at me, hair rumpled as though having just taken a nap, and is he judging me?

'So I just thought I'd swing by, see how you are,' she's saying, apparently unperturbed that she's still standing in the porch.

She looks genuine enough. I sigh and open the door wider, letting her in and leading her down the hall to the kitchen, while she witters about the weather.

I don't have many female friends. The few I had at university have crept back in over recent years, courtesy of Facebook, but I don't trust their shiny, instagrammed lives. I never trusted girls, in fact. Always feared their judgement more than that of men. They seemed harder to please.

I felt from early on in life that most girls were superior to me, and I felt it hard.

Basically I didn't even want to be a girl, if I couldn't be one of the best ones, if I couldn't be an 'in' girl.

Julia looks like she'd be an 'in' girl, although without really trying. She has normal curves, normal flaws, but somehow always seems happy in her own skin. She'll happily leave the house without make-up, for example, which would make me break out in a sweat.

'Where's Henry?' I ask her as I automatically fill the kettle and take two mugs from the cupboard. Julia likes her tea.

'I left him with my mum for an hour. Popped to the shops, which was weird without him fussing the whole time. Oh –' she stops herself '– sorry, Sally.' She looks down.

'It's OK.' I sigh. 'Don't worry. At one time I'd have been glad of a break, too.' I try to smile, but then I remember the social services report. I look away. *Keep your guard up, Sally.*

Julia is looking at the pile of papers on the table. I pick them up and move them away as I set her tea down in front of her.

'Why did you come?' I ask quietly.

'Oh, Sally. I just thought you might need a friend.'

'I don't know what that means,' I say, sitting opposite her and putting my head in my hands.

I thought I had friends, back when I was ill, but they were ghosts and shadows. I didn't want to go out much, and soon didn't need to, because I was sucked into an online world where there were other girls like me. When I started to get well, though, they dissolved. And when I look back, I suppose they weren't really friends, because they were working at keeping me in the same sick place as them. I'm constantly amazed by the ways we can damage each other, under the guise of support.

And because I had my baby young – well, relatively young, compared to most educated, professional women – I lost most of the real-life friends I made at school and uni. I think that was the reason, anyway. It seemed to be. For a while I became consumed with the mad sense that Richard had 'trapped' me.

And then these new women came along, the other mothers, friends made just by virtue of having a baby, therefore friends that I maybe don't deserve at all.

'I'm here for you,' Julia says. 'That's all it means. As much or as little as you like.'

'Thanks,' I say, but I'm not sure if I mean it, and when she reaches for my hand I pull away, pretending to brush something off my lap. It's a nice idea, this friendship thing, but aside from Ben, I don't know who I can or should trust.

Chapter Twelve

Richard

Martha comes in, slams the door behind her and runs upstairs. This is standard behaviour, these days. 'Dinner?' I call, and as usual she answers that she will 'get some later'. I look at Sally, next to me on the sofa; she shrugs.

'She's a teenager,' she says.

'I get that. I just can't seem to do anything right.'

'She's fifteen, you're her dad, of course you can't. Leave her to it. Honestly.'

'Well, the supportive parent bit didn't work,' I acknowledge, thinking of the disastrous London trip, 'so maybe you're right and I should back off.'

We turn our attention back to what we're doing. We are sitting together in the way we've sat so many times before while choosing a holiday, or a bathroom suite, theatre tickets or garden furniture. Laptop on the coffee table in front of us where we can both see it, a drink on either side: bottled beer for me, fruit tea for Sally. I haven't seen her drink alcohol since the night Ol went to hospital. I'm not complaining;

she's an emotional drinker and we could probably do without that.

While on the other occasions we might have been excited, each click of the mouse revealing a new possible option to be considered, discussed, maybe argued over in a good-natured sort of way, now we aren't looking for anything to buy or book or enjoy. We are looking for possible diagnoses for our son, that would make the alternative – that one of us has caused him harm – less likely, even impossible. Because if that alternative were true, how could we sit together, look at each other? But the questions are there, unsaid. Whereas before we might have touched shoulders, rested a hand on the other's knee, now we are brittle, arms tense, voices lowered.

'There must be something we're missing,' I mutter. 'Isn't there someone you know at your old work who could help? Can you go in?' I don't expect much of a response – she's been kind of reluctant up to now, I don't know why – but to my surprise she says, 'I'll go tomorrow. I'm not getting anywhere sitting around here, am I?'

I smile, and try to hug her, but she wriggles away. I can feel the life we had falling apart, and the worst of it is knowing that it's my fault.

We men do get a bit of a raw deal. Even biologically the odds are stacked against us. We don't have a whole lot to do with bringing babies into the world, do we? Our role is minimal, as I've been reminded by both my wives. Zoe was pretty open about her view of me as basically a sperm donor; she's older than me and made it clear she thought I was her 'last chance' of having a child. And even with Sally, who came at things in a much more romantic way and tried to involve me, in the early days at least, I ended up feeling a bit of a spare part. I mean, women have even got the means to feed the baby – how can men match that? I was kind of relieved when Sally quit breastfeeding, although I know she was upset. But at least I could give Ol a bottle, even though she'd watch me, her eyes hawk-like. I didn't see how I could do it wrong, but she must have thought I could.

Roll back further though, to when Sally was pregnant, and I suppose I did balls it up when she asked me if I'd swap places with her, if it were possible. She was in the late stages, swollen ankles, heartburn, all that jazz, and above all she was *terrified* about the birth. But she didn't want to hear any of my experiences from Martha being born; I'd learned that. It was like she wanted to pretend I'd never done any of it before. Which was kind of hurtful to be honest. If anyone tries to act like your child doesn't exist, that's the most hurtful thing in the world.

Anyway, she asked me would I swap with her if I could and 'do the labour, do the birth'. I said 'Hell, no!' and she scowled, and then cried. I put it down to hormones at the time but I guess I can see now that she felt unsupported or something. But since it's a rhetorical question, I didn't really see the issue. I thought I was being honest. I lost track of when that stopped being a good thing.

Next we watch a video. The charity I found, which supports parents whose children have been taken into care, gave it to us. They've been supportive but it's depressing how busy they are. Sally makes fun of me for calling it a video. She says I'm 'so eighties'. We almost laugh; almost forget.

The film brings with it waves of guilt, and fear. Guilt for the families in worse positions than ours, parents who have lost their children and have no hope of their being returned. Then fear, because we aren't through this yet. We look at each other as the credits roll behind some sombre music, and unsaid between us, the question: What if Ol gets adopted?

So now we slink off to bed in our shame and our fear. Neither of us sleeps, but we don't talk to each other either. I get up and open the blinds so I can lie and watch the rain, first rain in weeks, great sheets of it blowing sideways down the road.

This distance between us was there before all this happened. For months I've been going to bed every night in the knowledge my wife doesn't like me very much.

If she knew what I've done, she'd hate me.

Chapter Thirteen

Sally

I've come to hospital, to my hospital, to look for help. But somehow I find myself on the ward, my old ward. The first girl I see is nine or ten, sitting up in bed and chatting to a couple I presume to be her parents, and looks like any other child apart from the tubes and wires emanating from her hand, her stomach, and under her sheets. I have to stop myself from slipping into my old role, with my familiar script: 'Hi, I'm from Pharmacy. I'm just going to take your chart for a few minutes.' I don't look like medical staff, wearing jeans, hoodie, trainers. I might not be working but it feels good to be here. So I just smile at the girl and her parents and walk up and down the corridor, popping my head around doors from time to time, dispensing smiles and gentle 'Hello's as though they themselves are some kind of medicine.

A woman falls into step beside me and takes my arm; it's Cathy, one of the senior nurses. We had a good relationship while I was working here; I look at her and smile.

'Let's go for a coffee,' she says gently, and we walk to the staff canteen, through the corridors I know so well.

Richard always said he hated hospitals. 'It's the smell,' he would say. 'How can you stand it?' I've never really noticed it, I suppose I got used to it, but suddenly I know what he means. It isn't a bad smell, not exactly, but it is unlike anything else. Maybe that was unsettling to him. The air is full of it now, as we walk, something thick and unidentifiable, the combination, I suppose, of infection and disinfection, fighting each other. As we near the restaurant it is overlaid with the smells of cooking: roasting meat, steaming vegetables. I put a hand to my mouth, afraid I might gag.

'Are you OK?' Cathy asks.

'I'm all right.'

'Let's get a seat,' and within a couple of minutes she is sitting facing me, two cups on the table between us. I want to make small talk, the way we used to, gossip about some TV programme or other, moan about the weather, compare weekend plans, but I grapple for the words and find they aren't there.

'I'm sorry for what you're going through,' she says, her eyes kind. So she knows; everyone knows, I suppose. I think back to all the reports, the questions my bosses and colleagues have been asked. The invitations to frame me, to blame me.

'Thank you,' I whisper.

'What's the latest?' She takes a sip of her coffee.

'Well.' I find my voice and go into mechanical mode. 'Oliver is staying with his grandparents while ... while they carry out the investigation. I miss him.'

'I'm sure.' We sit in silence for a few minutes, but it isn't uncomfortable, and I feel my breathing start to slow down. I hadn't realised it had been fast.

'Thank you,' I say again. She leans over the table slightly.

'Why didn't you bring Oliver here, that night?'

'I don't know ... Richard said he'd tried ringing both hospitals, before I even woke up, to see who had the shorter waiting time in A&E.'

'They wouldn't commit to anything over the phone.'

'No, of course not. Anyway he decided Frimley would be quicker to get to – I wasn't convinced – and quieter. Maybe it's because Ollie was born there so it seemed right to him, somehow.'

Ollie was born in Frimley Park because that was what Richard chose, having researched maternity departments thoroughly. In the hours after the birth, when Richard had gone home 'to freshen up' (I wasn't sure how *un*fresh he could be at this point, compared to me), I felt a bit sad that had we been at the Royal Surrey, there would have been a stream of visitors to my bed. I suppose it gave me more time alone with my boy, but the odd friendly face wouldn't have gone amiss.

'Maybe he didn't want ... oh, never mind.' She shakes her head as though trying to get rid of an unwelcome thought.

'What?'

'I don't know. Maybe he felt you should keep it separate from your friends here, for some reason.' It's comforting to hear the word 'friends', even though I mostly think of them as 'colleagues'. I touch her hand and smile. 'Sorry,' she says, 'I didn't mean to offend you. I hope I've not spoken out of turn.'

'Don't worry. I think stuff like that myself. I've a head full of conspiracy theories at the moment. That's what you do, don't you, when the reality is too much to take in? Come up with alternatives – however incredible, at least they're better than the horrible reality.'

'What can we do to help?' she asks, and I start to say 'nothing', but then I remember the real reason I am here, and I speak decisively. It isn't just Richard who can take action, make things happen. I have to step up, too.

'I need ... we need ... a second opinion, or something. Anything. I just want someone who knows about this kind of thing, really knows about it, to help us. To take a look at the X-rays, the scans ... to give us a different viewpoint, if there is one.' Cathy nods.

'I might know someone,' she says, then she looks at me closely and adds, 'Sally, what do *you* think happened?'

And I'm cast back to that night, to my drunken fumbling with the lock, stumbling through the door, being woken from a thick sleep, confronted by Oliver's tear-stained face. The high-pitched shrieks he made. And the dreams I've had, re-running those scenes, but in the dream version Ollie can speak, his baby lips moving to form perfect, clear words, incongruous coming from his tiny head, but unmistakeable.

This is what happened. This is why I'm in pain. This is who hurt me. And then I wake up.

'I don't know,' I say. 'I've a couple of theories. He caught his arm in the bars of the cot, maybe? He's a restless sleeper.'

'Would it break, though?'

'I don't know. Maybe, if there's something else, some reason we don't know of, why his bones are weak or something. But there's nothing obvious, or I think it would have been picked up earlier. That's why I need some help.' I sigh. 'The hospital, the social services, the police –' I see Cathy balk a little at the word *police*, but she makes a good effort to disguise it '– they all seem very happy to jump to the obvious conclusion that he was hurt deliberately. But it's not the obvious conclusion, not to us.'

'I know someone,' she says, 'a paediatric pathologist. He might be able to help. He's worked on this kind of case. He doesn't work here, which is probably a good thing. You want someone who can appear as neutral as possible, I suppose.' She reaches into her pocket, pulls out a pen and starts to scribble on a napkin. 'This is him. You can get the number from his website, I expect.' I look at it, and the upside-down name. Daniel Stone. She's right; I don't know him. Another stranger being drawn into our lives. We both drain our coffees and as she hands me the number she touches my hand again. 'Good luck, Sally.'

So now I have a name, a possible lifeline, and yet I can't bring myself to take it. I sit in the car, the napkin in my hand, and I'm utterly paralysed.

It's like that urge you sometimes get to fling yourself in front of a tube train, or off the top of a high building. Doesn't everyone get that?

It is teetering on the edge, feeling alive and exposed and scared and safe and wired all at the same time.

I am tempted to let go.

Madness has soft, welcoming arms.

If you're surrounded by choking thorns, why wouldn't you want to escape into a cool, still lake, let your head go under, block out the sounds and the light?

Back when I was ill as a teenager, there were times that were pretty glorious (of course, my parents would say it was hell. For them). It was the perfect balance, for me: I was utterly in control and at the same time utterly free of responsibility.

They pampered me and tiptoed around me and did whatever I wanted. They were so terrified of my illness; to them it was a sleeping, rabid dog they didn't dare wake.

I was serene.

There's a high that comes with starvation. It's one of the reasons it's so hard to come back from.

I feel again just like when I was seventeen, like actually what if I just opted out? I don't want to deal with any of this. I don't want to 'fight', to 'be strong', or to 'be brave' – I want someone else to do and be those things for me, because I'm not up to it, just like I'm not up to being a mother, or even a wife, or much of anything, really.

It's like there are clouds over me, or cancers at the edge of my brain. In the centre of my head there is light, and normal thought, and at the edges the dual monsters of anorexia and depression just waiting to encroach on the healthy brain and consume it.

I want to go home and get under the duvet and not speak to anyone. I want to close my eyes and hug myself and not think about any of it.

Social workers and parents and police and doctors and so-called 'friends' and Richard with his fucking laptop, the incessant tap-tap-tap on the keys as though the answers are in there somewhere, and Martha with her terminal fucking indifference.

I want them all to fuck off and leave me alone and stop demanding things of me.

I want out.

The trouble is, the only thing I want more is Ollie. Ollie back in his cot, back in my arms.

So I know opting out is not, well … an option.

I will put on the front, the face, that is required. I will do what is necessary.

And inside I'll be crumbling, but an old voice is already telling me that I have ways of coping with that.

Missing him is now just part of who I am. I figure if I can make myself smaller, maybe the pain at the centre of me will get smaller, too.

Chapter Fourteen

Richard

I'm at work when Sally calls me and asks me to come home.

'I feel like I'm losing it,' she says. 'I'm struggling.'

'I'm coming,' I say, grabbing my coat. All the way back, the strangest thoughts pass through my head, almost as though they belong to someone else. Like: if she breaks down and I keep it together, does that mean she loves him more? That's what people are thinking; I know they are. If I hear 'Well, it must be hard on the mother' one more time, I'll swing for someone, I swear.

I get home and open the front door onto what immediately feels like an empty house. I half-jog from room to room, calling her name, and am met with silence. From the kitchen window I see a shape at the far end of the lawn.

We have an apple tree at the bottom of our garden and I find Sally sitting on the grass, picking at the tiny white petals that have fallen there. In her lap is a small pile of them, like snow.

She doesn't stir when I move towards her. She looks a fright: no make-up, hair hanging limp and unbrushed around her face. I notice for the first time that she has lost weight in the last few weeks. I think about the meals I've seen left untouched on her plate.

'What are you doing, Sally?'

'I'm trying to tidy up the garden.' She looks up at me and says seriously, 'Do you think I could vacuum it?'

I sit down next to her and put my arms around her shoulders and squeeze. Because I still love her, I really do. I pick up some blossom and cast it gently into her lap.

'I'll help you,' I say.

We'd been seeing each other over a year, and I'd already left Zoe, before Sally told me about the problems she'd had as a teenager. The years of anorexia and the 'bit of OCD', which sounded like 'a lot of' to me.

Suddenly things I'd noticed about her started to make sense: the way she picked at food and never seemed really to enjoy it, although she could list the ingredients of any given dish and talk to you about its nutritional value or otherwise with massive enthusiasm. The way she couldn't rest until certain tasks were complete, especially in the house. I realised I'd been seeing the hangover, the shadow, from her illness. She told me about the family therapy when she was seventeen. Sally's dad had been trying without success to put a stop to her habits: repetitive hand washing and persistent shaking out of her clothing and bed sheets. The therapist was adamant her father should leave her be. Sally described a long altercation between the two men at the end of which the therapist, usually quiet and patient, had actually interrupted her father and insisted, 'I think you need to understand. These habits. At the moment, they are what's keeping her alive.'

That's why, on the lawn, I don't shout at her, however much part of me wants to, or say she is crazy. That's why I sit with her. *She needs this*, I tell myself.

And she needs you, you shit.

Chapter Fifteen

Martha

Dad and Sally drag me to Grandma's, 'to see my brother', even though I'm not that bothered. Seeing as Dad has warned me, in that super-serious way he has, to 'be careful' what I say to social services, I'm overjoyed to see that Mary woman there and I don't dare open my mouth.

I mean, it's all right, I suppose, seeing Ol. But Dad seems to expect me to show some kind of maternal feelings, which is odd when you think about it, considering how totally paranoid he is about me getting pregnant. He's spent years warning me off boys. I guess as a kid I played with dolls. I had one baby doll in particular that I loved, which in itself is a bit weird, giving little girls plastic babies as though to say 'Get used to this, this is going to be your role'. But I don't *get* real babies, and especially not this one. Oliver cries for no reason. Oh, I know he has a broken arm so that makes me sound really harsh, but it's nothing new, these huge tantrums out of nowhere. I wish *I* could shout and scream and have everyone just coo over *me* as a result.

Maybe because of the baby doll – Lucy, I called her – Dad assumed that when Ol came along I'd be a 'little mother' figure, or something. Poor old Dad, he must look at all the women in his life and despair, because none of us has a fucking clue about babies. Dad makes a big show of sitting Oliver on my lap, and I try to play with him, but of course he starts screaming, which just makes me feel a bit of a dick. I just want to put him back on the floor and get out of here. I stare at him. It's the first time I've seen him since that night. It's weird; it's not been that long but he's grown, for sure. Sally is being attentive-but-not-too-much. She is way tense; you can tell by the way her eyes keep flicking over to Mary. And to Grandma, for that matter. I sometimes wonder if I'd have bonded better with Ol if he wasn't Sally's, if he was my full brother; but then, the only thing more disgusting than Dad and Sally having a baby is the idea of Dad and Zoe doing it.

Grandma loves me. She calls me her princess and she spoils me, always. I am happy to let her. She gestures to me to follow her into the kitchen, gets me to help her put biscuits on plates, fill the milk jug, that kind of thing. She looks at me with those eyes that always remind me of a bird's.

'Are you OK?' she asks.

'Yep,' I say. 'I just can't really be bothered with all of this.' She chuckles.

'You don't miss him? Your brother?'

I resist the temptation to say my usual '*half*-brother'; it does get tiring.

'Miss the constant whining? Not really.'

'And your dad and Sally ... are they all right?'

I shrug.

'Hard to say,' I say, but I know that when we get back to our house there will be a row; there always is, right after they've seen Ol. It's like seeing him makes them feel worse, not better. Grandma starts rummaging in her handbag, which always sits on the counter in her kitchen, and pulls out her purse. I make my usual show of pretending I don't want to take her money; she kisses me on the cheek, as always, and presses a tenner into my hand.

'Now come on,' she says, 'let's get back in there and keep an eye on them all.'

Del always tells me that places have souls. If that's true, our house has lost its soul. I realise that since Ol went, everything is a little bit worse.

Dad and Sally's relationship is in meltdown, although they are trying to hide it, or they don't even see it themselves. And it's so weird because for ages I hated that they were together but now, with everything falling apart and ruined, I'd actually like to hear them laughing together again.

I know they are hiding things from me, which is ironic since I am keeping stuff from them (especially Sally). They keep going quiet when I walk in the room. It's dumb, really, because, after all, I am the only one of the three of us who was actually in the house the whole night Ol got hurt. But I don't say that out loud, obviously, and I don't even like thinking it because it makes me feel kind of responsible, and also (mainly) because I was there but not there. In the house, but not really *there*, since I was stoned and everything. And that thought makes me panic, so I push it back down and accept my new position on the fringes. Ha! New position? Who am I kidding? I've been on the edge ever since Sally turned up, and even more so after Ol. So I keep my head down.

I decide to speak to Del about what's happening with Ol. I mean, she'll work it out soon enough when she comes over to our place and it doesn't totally hum, and it's quiet and all that.

Plus, I have to tell her because I was totally called out by Mrs Jarrett today, and Del saw. It was after Geography. Mrs Jarrett, who's our form teacher and also does PSE, which Del calls 'Psych Ed' but is really a bit of a nothing subject, just a fancy way of telling you to be nice to each other, took me to one side to tell me she'd heard 'what was happening at home'. I must've looked at her blankly (oh, I do that apparently; I've been told, most memorably in black and white in last year's school report. 'Martha's blank expression can communicate the effect of disinterest.' *Really?*) because she went on, 'I'm sorry about your brother.'

'Half-brother,' I mumbled and then, as though I was confused by her concern, as if to say it wasn't a big deal or anything, I added, 'He's not dead or anything.'

She looked a bit startled and then she said I could always check in with the school counsellor, if I wanted to. When did all schools get frigging counsellors? I've talked about this with Zoe, who trained as a counsellor at some point, and she thinks it's a *marvellous* idea. Well of course she does, presumably because it might save *her* from actually doing any parenting, which she clearly views as a massive pain in the ass.

Anyway, this kind of bullshit has happened to me once before, when Dad and Zoe divorced. Mrs Jarrett got hold of me then as well and said she was 'surprised' and 'a bit alarmed' that Dad had told her about the break-up (which by then was old news, so much so I think Sally was up the duff) at parents' evening, and why hadn't I mentioned it? I said I guessed I didn't talk about private stuff much. Not with teachers, anyway.

Anyway so all this is how I find myself cross-legged on the swings with Del. If I'm going to do confession, it may as well be with my best friend.

I tell Del that Dad went out, and I was on my own (I miss out the bit about Brendan). I tell her about them taking Ol to hospital and coming home without him.

She clicks her teeth and says, 'Man, they really take babies off of people, just like that?'

I shrug. 'I guess.'

'But they didn't suspect anything *before* this happened?'

I shake my head, but I don't know. I never thought of that before. We sit in silence for a bit and then she says something really weird. She says, 'It seems to me you have to really love a child to hurt it.'

I look at her. Del does this; she says things that make the exact opposite of sense, but if you wait it out, sometimes she says more stuff that makes you see what she means. I wait.

'I mean,' she says eventually, 'you gotta have strong feelings towards anyone to hurt them. Cos who can rile you up the most? The people you love the most.'

'I get that,' I say slowly, 'but some people who hurt kids must hate them.'

'Sure,' she says. She's unwrapping a sweet she's retrieved from the bottom of her bag. 'But I bet there are not so many of those. I bet most people who hurt kids love the bones of them.' I unfold my legs and let my feet touch the ground, then I use them to bounce off and I'm airborne, head back, watching the sky move as the swing carries me.

'I don't have any strong feelings about Oliver either way,' I say into the wind. 'I'm indifferent to him.' Eventually, using my heels as brakes, I stop the swing and turn to look at Del, who is chewing thoughtfully on her sweet.

'OK,' she says. But I'm not sure she's convinced. She starts to swing, but stops abruptly after a couple of arcs. 'Hang on,' she says. 'Brendan Lowe was at your house, right?'

'What?'

'Brendan was at your house. You smoked weed with him, you said ... when was that? Not the same night? The night Ol got hurt?'

I stare at her. 'Yes, it was. But—'

She gives me that look, eyebrows way up in her forehead, as if to say, 'You haven't thought of this? *Really?*'

'What are you saying?' I'm starting to feel sick. 'You're not seriously suggesting Brendan went upstairs, into Ol's room, and broke his arm?'

'I told you he's bad news.'

'Yeah, but ... come on. A baby. And, why? Why would he do that?'

Del shrugs. It's maddening when she does that; she says something outrageous, then just shrugs. I'm starting to feel a bit irritated, but at the back of that, sicker and sicker.

'I don't know,' she says, 'it was just a thought. If he was there, I don't think you can rule him out.'

'Oh, I don't think ...' I'm trying desperately to remember whether he left the room at any point. I don't think he did. But then, I don't remember ... the other stuff that happened, either.

'Look, M, I know he's your friend, but—'

'He's not my friend,' I snap. 'I don't know what he is.'

Del looks at me closely. 'Is there something you've not told me? You can tell me anything, you know that, right?'

'I know. It's fine, I just don't want to talk about *him*, OK?'

'OK. If you say so. And if you've had a bust-up with him, I can't say I'm sorry.' She starts swinging again and the conversation is over.

I haven't heard anything from Brendan. It has been a few days and I'm beginning to wonder if I imagined that weird evening in his house, if I got the wrong end of the stick or something. Maybe he was joking. He can't be the villain Del has painted him to be, can he? And I know he's been violent but that's in fights with other lads; I'm sure he wouldn't hurt a baby. Would he? But the pictures were real; I still have them in my head, the face that was mine but not mine, twisted and slack-mouthed. I've been obsessively checking the Internet on my phone, but found nothing. Not that I would need to look; if he does carry out his threat I'll hear about it almost instantly.

Everything is instant. Instant messaging, instant access to information. Dad loves to give me the whole 'When I was your age, all I had was a Sega Megadrive' speech. I don't even know what a Sega Megadrive is, but it sounds lame. And most of the time I think, wow, how would we cope without the Internet, smart phones, iPads, all of that. But sometimes I just want the world to slow down. I sit with my back to the bathroom door, leaning against it, the blade poised over my arm. I will do the fat part of the forearm, up near the elbow. You can get everything online; even advice on how to cut yourself safely. It's thanks to one of those websites that I've put together a decent first-aid kit. I know the outer part of my arm is safer than the inner arm, less chance of hitting an artery. I stare at it, at the hairs and freckles, and I wonder if it will be enough, if it will work. Because this being 'safe' is hard, something is drawing me towards the inside part where the skin is paper-thin and paler, its network of blue lines seeming to demand that I trace them with a knife, a scalpel. Like a razor-sharp pencil. Like art. I stare at it. I feel light-headed and I have not even started.

I flip my arm back over, back to the fleshy part, too fleshy, and I sink the blade into the skin. Slowly, I move it back, draw a perfect line. Blood rises to the surface and I press the sides of the cut to help it spill out. The sound of Dad and Sally sniping at each other downstairs recedes, and I sink into peace.

A bit later, a bit lightheaded, I bounce into the kitchen just as they start banging on about the missed calls on Sally's phone from that night. Something drops inside me and my shoulders automatically twist themselves into knots. I move more slowly, almost tiptoeing, as though trying to escape detection.

'I didn't call you,' Dad is saying, 'but the point is, you didn't answer. Why not?'

'No, the point is, the phone didn't ring me all by itself, did it?' She throws a pointed look at me.

'Too busy flirting with your *workmates*.' Dad says 'workmates' like it's a dirty word; Sally ignores it although she looks ready to spit.

'I can show you the missed calls – look.' She holds her mobile up to his face and he catches her wrist.

There is something about that I don't like so before I have the chance to really think about it I hear myself blurt out, 'OK, OK, it was me.' I look at Dad, '*Stop*. I rang you, Sally.'

'Why?'

'I don't remember.' I shrug and Sally looks at me incredulously, but the thing is, it's true. The next thing I know their voices are getting louder and I can't even work out what is being said, the way they are talking over each other, and they look ready to swing for each other, so without knowing what is going to come out of my mouth I shout, 'Stop having a go at him! He wasn't even here!'

Shit. I didn't mean to tell her. Obviously.

He'd said to me, 'Daddy just has to pop out for an hour. You'll be OK, won't you, sweetheart?': a question that was more of a statement and didn't really invite any answer other than 'Yes, sure'. He always called himself 'Daddy' – in the third person – when he felt guilty about something ('Daddy's really sorry, sweetheart' is something I've heard more times than I like to remember), but he hadn't done anything bad to me, so I couldn't understand it.

So I agreed, of course. After I gave him the Calpol, Ol finally stopped with his ridiculous screaming. You had to admire the kid's stamina, even while you felt like screaming yourself and possibly throwing him against a wall. But he was asleep and his red face looked cute now it was all still and smooth.

Then Brendan came round and everything is fuzzy from then on. But I know at some point after he left, Ol woke up and started again, even more angry-sounding than before. I panicked and tried to call Dad. His phone was switched off, so I called Sally. Twice or three times, I don't remember. I must have made the calls inside the pockets of time when I felt briefly normal, little pinpricks of light dotted through the paranoid haze. Then I was overtaken again by the voice that said if she answered it wouldn't be good, and I hung up.

Everything goes kind of still, everyone staring at each other, Sally looking *really* angry but weirdly not all that surprised. They start doing that horrible arguing-but-not-properly-arguing thing, you know like when people just speak in really low, unnaturally calm voices but you can just tell they are boiling underneath. I back out of the room in that way I've seen people do in films, when the other character has a gun and they're keeping their eye on it (as if, y'know, if I can *see* the weapon it can't harm me).

When I get back to my bedroom, I notice my phone is flashing. I lie on the bed and pick it up, expecting a message from Del.

It's from Brendan.

I hope you're ready, it says, *your new job starts tomorrow.*

Chapter Sixteen

Sally

'Stop having a go at him! He wasn't even here!'

I try to keep my voice calm and gentle when I ask, 'Where was he?', but Martha just shakes her head, shrugs, and any response would be irrelevant, anyway, because I know.

I know in an instant that there is another woman. The distance between us, punctuated by acts of kindness that I can see now were motivated by guilt. The tailing off of the attempts at initiating sex, and the weird distant look on his face when he did. The odd working hours.

I also know I have to do two things, now. I have to find proof; and I have to keep it to myself for as long as it takes to get Ollie back.

I ask Richard of course, but in a half-hearted way because I know he will lie; I say, 'Where were you, then?', and 'How come you never mentioned this before, when I asked?', and he answers, 'I had business to attend to.' Just like that, stiff as a board. He isn't even trying to be convincing. Martha starts to back out of the door.

'Who the fuck talks like that?' I demand. 'Who says, "I had business to attend to", to anyone, never mind their wife?' But I'm not shouting. It's pointless, and I learned long ago not to fan the flames of Richard's temper with my own.

It seems crazy given how Richard and I started, but I've always trusted him. I knew first-hand that he was capable of cheating, but I believed him when he told me it was because I was so special. His marriage to Zoe was over, had been a mistake from the start, in fact; they'd only married (in an uncharacteristic nod to conventionality from Zoe) because she was pregnant with Martha. I'd sympathised and admired him for having done 'the right thing', even though all along his heart had told him that he didn't truly love her. I'd seen him as self-sacrificing and decent, if misguided.

'And we were happy, for a bit,' he'd admitted, 'but then I met you and I knew what happiness really could be, and what I'd been missing all that time.'

I hadn't pushed him, had been a good little mistress, let him choose 'the right time'. I knew he would come to me eventually because I believed in the idea of happiness he sold me. It was so powerful. It felt like our right.

I didn't think he would do the same to me.

I know he is a flirt, of course. I know he likes – loves – women. I've actually always liked the way he could put my female friends, even my mum, at total ease with his easy compliments, his interest in their lives. Even confident, composed Julia often blushes when he speaks to her. He has a megawatt smile and is the kind of guy who always makes sure your glass is full, and says things like 'That's so brilliant, wow, well done', in response to news of the smallest achievement. I've been proud he'd chosen to be with me, even more so because he chose it in the face of adversity, in the face of causing hurt to others and being criticised by his friends and family. I knew he'd look after Martha financially, and Zoe come to that; it wasn't like he was abandoning them. He'd just fallen in love and he couldn't help it.

I believed in all of it.

He even made me think that the very facts of him having been a 'lad', a 'player', in his early days and having been unfaithful before made him less likely to stray from me.

'I've done my playing around,' he'd say. 'You don't want to marry some young virgin who's never lived. Eventually they'll start to wonder what else is out there. I *know* what's out there, and I know there's nothing better than this.'

But now he's found something better.

And I look at myself and I can't blame him.

Every couple has their origin story. It's hard when everyone knows yours began when there was already somebody on the pages. I would have loved to be able to tell people about our first 'date', because it was wonderful.

When I graduated, Richard called me to say he wanted to take me out for the day, to celebrate. I thought it was a bit odd; he was my boss, after all.

'We'll do a proper London day,' he said. 'Museum, art gallery, whatever. Fancy lunch. Walk around the park.

Theatre. Madame bloody Tussauds, if you want. Anything. Everything. What do you say?'

I laughed. 'It sounds great,' I said. 'But not sure I can afford it. I'm skint.' I immediately regretted this; did it sound like I was complaining he didn't pay me enough? If it did, he seemed unconcerned.

'It's my treat,' he said, and when I hesitated, added, 'Course, you can pay me back when you get your first job and enormous pay packet. If you must.'

I tell myself I was just an innocent graduate, with no wiles or agenda, but was I? I spent a long time getting ready, even picking out my nicest underwear, although I felt foolish and embarrassed doing it. He was my boss; at best, he was a friend, and he was *married*. Of course nothing was going to happen between us. And I certainly wouldn't instigate it. And yet the idea of spending a whole day with him, just the two of us, made my stomach tilt with a mix of excitement and nerves. The fact he wanted to spend a whole day with me, the fact that this successful, handsome, urbane man, this extremely busy man, would spare a day for me, was … intoxicating. So I put on the thong and the balcony bra, and studied myself in the mirror wearing them, and I reasoned to myself that it was just to make myself feel good. That there was no way he would see the underwear, of course not, it was just a confidence booster for me. Nothing wrong with that.

We met at Charing Cross, with a brief peck on the cheek among the throngs of people, and we started our 'date' (which we would continually, self-consciously, refer to as a 'non-date' throughout) at the National Portrait Gallery. I was nervous; I knew nothing about art. Richard struck me as someone who knew something about everything. And of course, although I was trying not to think about this, he was married to an artist.

We moved from room to room, whispering in that reverent way people do in art galleries and museums. I was overwhelmed: to me, everything was beautiful and brilliant, and I had no idea how any of it had been achieved. I'm a scientist: painting and sculpture and photography are, to me, as mysterious as the heavens. Every now and then I stole a glance at him, watched his profile as he peered at the portraits, his head tilted slightly to the side. He had the look of a 1940s movie star: a Cary Grant or a young Gregory Peck. His face was timeless. Someone should paint *him*, I thought.

Standing in front of *Elizabeth, Queen of Bohemia*, I said in a low voice, 'What do you think of this one?' I let my eyes absorb the tones of gold and cream, the intricate details of her embroidered gown, her wig a rusty halo, her hands like those of a porcelain doll. Her eyes looked back at me, fixed, blank.

Richard stood back, studied it, his face crumpled in concentration. He leaned forward, seemed to scan the painting for clues. Then he leaned back again and let out a thoughtful sigh.

'Well,' he said finally, 'she's no oil painting.'

I burst out laughing, he took my arm, and in tacit agreement we hurried to the café, where we ordered coffees and Richard pulled a book out of the deep pocket of his coat: *The Bluffer's Guide to Art*.

We did have the long lunch but we never made it to the theatre. We made it to bed instead, in a hotel with a view of the river and the London skyline. He placed £300 in cash on the reception desk like it was loose change. I sort of hated myself for being impressed by money, but once we were in the suite I felt I was in a world I'd never dreamed of being a part of. I'd never before stayed in a hotel room that was on two floors. It was basically a flat. I could have lived there, and if he'd asked me, I would have.

I don't know how he managed to stay away all night; I didn't ask. I didn't want to think about it. But we woke up in the morning, the blinds open, the sun streaming in and the whole of the city laid out before us. Seeing and unseen, four storeys up from the river and the bustle of unsuspecting people.

I slept with him in his house, only the once. I'm not proud of that. He said he felt guilty, but that he just couldn't keep his hands off me. I made him weak, he said. We fell out of the bed. I wonder now if he wanted to finish on the floor so he wouldn't have to bother changing the sheets before Zoe got back from wherever she was. I wonder if he took me to the National Portrait Gallery that first day because he'd been there with her, and he thought the little things he'd picked up from her about art might impress me. I wonder, now, lots of things about the man I live with and love.

I try to tell myself it isn't the cheating that hurts most, it's the lie.

Then I realise that this is bollocks. It is the cheating. It's the knowledge of them touching, her body undoubtedly better, tighter, firmer than mine, his sighs, his excitement, elicited by her and not me. Did he hold her afterwards? Did he talk about me, tell her how I didn't pay him enough attention, what a nag I was, did he make her laugh with boring domestic anecdotes? Or did he not mention me at all? Did he slip his wedding ring off, airbrush me out of existence? Which was the worst betrayal? Has he used the same lines he used on me: 'I just can't help myself'; 'You're intoxicating'; 'It's like I'm addicted to you'; and on, and on.

Oh my God, the wedding ring. He lost it a few months ago, it disappeared and then re-appeared a few days later. Wow. Was that when it started?

I see it every time I close my eyes: their bodies together. I wake every day with a sick feeling in my stomach. Eating is moving from difficult to impossible, every morsel like lead in my mouth, taking an eternity to chew. Nothing can fill this hollowness, anyway.

But of course, the lie has its own implications. If Richard was out for most of the evening, he couldn't have hurt Ollie, could he? Along with the detonated bomb that is his affair, fling, whatever it was or is, comes another explosion: the realisation that all along I've been wanting to blame him for us losing Ollie. And now I can't. Where does that leave me? Is self-protection going to lead me to point the finger at Martha, who, however selfish or spiteful she sometimes seems, is just a kid herself?

And look how desperate Richard was to keep this other woman from me: he'd rather put himself in the firing line for his son's injury than be found out. He could have used her as an alibi, but he didn't. What does this mean? That he wanted to preserve our marriage, or just that he's a spineless coward?

I try all the classic ways to get my evidence. The phone, of course. His text message inbox is clean. I should have known. When I was The Other Woman, he used to say at the end of frantic text conversations, 'I just hate having to erase you'. I thumb through his contacts and write down the numbers next to every female name. I also note any names I don't recognise, male or female, any initials or acronyms. He might have given her a code name.

I go through his pockets for receipts: inconclusive. Smell his shirts for perfume – old school! Even check his collars for lipstick – again, inconclusive.

In the end it is the good old-fashioned post that catches him out. He always leaves the house early and I usually pile his letters up on the sideboard for when he gets home. It has never, never before occurred to me to open any of them, and it gives me a horrible twinge of guilt to do so now. A bank statement, and an itemised mobile phone bill. Easy. The large cash withdrawals from ATMs in towns he hasn't mentioned visiting. The same number appearing again and again, text messages and phone calls, middle of the night, first thing in the morning (I remember with a pang the time when he used to text me at 7am every day without fail,

'Good morning beautiful' or sometimes just kisses. When had that stopped?)

The phone records from the night Ollie got hurt: a string of texts, shortly after I'd left the house. A short call, a long blank period, and a last text at 1am.

I take the recurring number from the bill and cross-match it against my list with a phonebook entry: J.

It's disappointingly mundane, really. It would have been more satisfying to catch them, if not 'at it' exactly, then huddled over a drink in some pub somewhere, hands clasped together under the table. The way we used to. But does anyone find out that way, any more? No: we find out in our homes, following the electronic traces everyone leaves behind. It's easy.

Mary calls to re-schedule the child protection conference. Our 'high priority' case has been put back ten days, with twenty-four hours' notice. This means ten more days without Ollie (because in some part of my mind I've been imagining that after that meeting everything would be resolved and they would just give him right back to me – how naïve I've been), ten more days not knowing what comes next.

I have ten days to prepare myself to walk into the most important event in my family's life, carrying the knowledge that my husband has a lover.

Ben greets me at the station (he comes in, meets me at the ticket barrier, rather than waiting in the car park. I find that strangely touching), and the first thing he says is, 'Hey, where's the little man?' He'd assumed I would bring him, of course. Oliver has after all been more or less welded to my hip for ten months. And I hadn't said otherwise on the phone. I look at Ben and burst into tears.

I've travelled to Portsmouth to see him because he said he had no car 'just now' (I can't remember him ever having a car), plus I just needed to get out of Farnham. But all the same, I'm relieved we aren't going to his place; he'd admitted on the phone that it was 'small, and kinda scuzzy. They call it a studio, but actually it's a bedsit. You know the sort of place'. I knew, but I couldn't imagine living in one now, nearing thirty. But Ben is different; he is the eternal student – quite literally, as after a couple of years trying to get work and never settling on anything, he'd gone down to Portsmouth Uni to do a PhD. He was vague about how long it would take to finish. I wondered how he managed to live, but he assured me he was all right. 'I don't need much,' he said, and for a moment I thought about only having the possessions – and the people – to fit into one room, and in a strange way I envied him.

We cross the street from the station and duck into the first café we see. Ben doesn't ask me what I want – old friends don't need to – but silently brings me tea and gestures to the sugar with questioning eyebrows. I shake my head.

'Tell me everything,' he says.

I've come across cases of suspected abuse in my work, of course. Sick kids can have shitty parents too. We never get involved, though, just pass them on to the department that deals with those things. And now I find that I, we, are one of those cases, and I'm ashamed at how I've judged those mothers.

'You must be at an advantage, compared to some people in that situation,' Ben muses. 'I mean, your medical knowledge and all that. You must be … well, credible.'

'Oh, I know what all the possible causes are. We're up to our ears in research. Osteogenesis imperfecta – brittle bones. Surely would have been picked up sooner. Some congenital defect but, again, I think that would have been caught. My personal theory is it was an accident; he caught his arm in between the bars of the cot or something. He's such a wriggler.' I smile automatically at the picture in my mind of Ollie, at all sorts of odd angles in bed, blankets kicked off. 'But that's not enough for social services, who keep coming back to the fact that in the majority of cases like this, the injury is non-accidental.' I take a gulp of tea then add, 'Can't believe I've just referred to us as a "case". This is what happens. It's so alien.'

'Are you talking to Richard about all of this?' I look for the tell-tale frown line that often appears between Ben's eyebrows when he mentions my husband's name, but it doesn't seem to be there. Maybe he's had Botox.

'A bit.' I sigh. 'Not really. I don't know. There's this … distance between us. He's obsessing over the legal stuff, getting the right representation although no one's mentioned court as such, you know … he's just all about finding a solution.'

'Well, that's natural, right?'

'Of course. So then I feel guilty and totally inadequate because it's like he's doing all the work and I'm just … immobilised.' Wow, it feels better to be saying these things aloud. 'Immobilised with grief.'

'But Sally,' Ben says gently, 'he's not dead.'

'No, but he's hurt.' My voice cracks on the word. 'And I shouldn't have let it happen.' The flicker of a frown passes over Ben's face and I start to feel sick. Does he think … ? 'Oh, not you as well,' I say. 'Not you of all people. Please.'

'Ssh,' he says, his hand on mine. 'It's OK, Sally. You know I'm here for you, whatever.'

And in an instant I know I'm going to cry, and I really don't want to cry in public, but the feeling comes as though from my gut, choking me, making it hard to breathe, impossible to swallow it back down. It should be a loud sob, but I fix my lips shut tight, and just let the water tip out of my eyes and splash onto the tablecloth.

'You hear about these cases, don't you, of kids being taken off their parents, and you just assume—' He stops himself and, looking down at his cup, says, 'Sorry.'

'It's all right.' I sigh. 'I know. You assume the parents have done something wrong. No smoke without fire and all that. I used to think like that too.'

'There was one I heard about … social workers took a toddler away from his home because when they visited there was dog shit on the bedroom carpet. At first I thought well, quite right, what kind of home are they running where there's shit all over the place, and that's not safe for a little kid, and anyway there must be other stuff going on, and all that. Quite right they took the lad away.

'Then I spoke to this friend of mine, she's a single mum, right, and she was like "well, maybe they were just having a really bad day, you don't know how long the shit was there, and maybe the dog was sick", and so on, and I realised I was pretty quick to judge. I mean, shit happens.' He chuckles awkwardly at his own pun. 'Doesn't mean they weren't good parents. Y'know?'

I feel a momentary, surprising, pang of envy over the mention of this 'friend', this single mum, while I wonder just how close they are. But I push it aside and I smile at Ben because I know he is trying to make me feel better. I put my hand over his.

'Thanks,' I say.

I didn't plan to tell Ben about Richard and 'J'. I didn't plan to tell anyone, not yet. In fact I am doing all I can to imagine it isn't real. So I don't know why, when he walks me back to the station, the horrible reality of it, so far pressed down, comes bubbling up inside me and I end up blurting it out to him as we stand under the station clock.

'What?' he says, which is the proper response, really.

I shrug.

'Yes, he's shagging someone. Or, he's been shagging someone.'

'You're sure?'

'99%.'

'Does he know you know?'

'No. Well, he might suspect, now. He's deleted his call history and all that. He hasn't come up with a very plausible excuse about where he was that night. He's made very little effort to convince me it was all innocent.'

'God, Sally.'

'It's all right.' But it isn't, of course, and my eyes are filling with tears again; I look upwards. Someone once told me you can't cry if you look upwards. It's physically impossible. I've never tested it before but it doesn't seem to be true. 'My train is here,' I say just as the announcement comes over the tannoy.

'Don't go,' he says, taking my arm. 'Get the next one.' I can't look at his face, at the concern there, the love.

'I have to go.'

'Sally, this ... this changes things.'

'No, it doesn't. What does it change? No, what I have to do is ignore it, and get on with getting Ollie back.'

'You can't—'

'No, all right, I can't ignore it,' I snap at him and feel immediately sorry for it, 'but I can put it aside, for now. I have to. I haven't the energy for this now as well as everything else. I'll deal with Richard later.' Ben looks doubtful. 'I *promise*.'

Apparently a person has been hit by a train between Havant and Haslemere. I'm sitting at a table with a newspaper spread in front of me, not really looking at the words, and it has taken me a few minutes to realise we aren't going anywhere. An announcement advises us to get out and stretch our legs. I scan the platform but Ben has gone. News of ever-extending delays is flashing on every screen, and the station is packed with miserable commuters. They always say it so dispassionately, don't they: 'A person was hit by a train'. As if it was the easiest thing in the world to be hit by a train, as though trains were inclined to just pop up out of nowhere and run you over while you were going innocently about your business. 'A person has been hit by a train,' they say, as though it was an accident. But everyone in the station knows it won't have been an accident, and all everyone cares about is the fact they'll be late home.

Despite having a bellyful of hot drinks from my afternoon with Ben, I duck into Starbucks, because really, what else is there to do? I sit at a high stool looking out onto the platform, nursing a latte that I don't really want.

I hear the boy's voice before I see him. He is insistent, repetitive, monotone, so his cries blend in with the general coffee shop hubbub to begin with. But as he becomes more high-pitched and urgent the word he is saying, over and over, becomes clear: 'Mummy. Mummy. Mum-mee!'

I glance around. He is older than Ollie, and walking – well, he is standing, next to his pushchair, holding on to one of its handles and shaking it with every 'ee' of 'Mummee'. In the pushchair is a dummy and a battered cloth rabbit that may have once been white.

A woman, presumably the boy's mother, sits on another high stool and talks loudly into her mobile. She is using a stream of expletives to describe a 'bitch' who has wronged her in some indecipherable way, and keeps saying 'I know, *right*?' in a weird, transatlantic-type accent. The only attention she pays her son is to occasionally bat his hands away as he tries, unsuccessfully, to claw his way up her jeans.

'I don't know why people have children if they're going to just *ignore* them.' It is out of my mouth before I can stop it.

'I beg your pardon?' The words are oddly formal, coming from a woman who's just been swearing down the phone. Her heavily lined eyes glitter. 'I'll call you back,' she mutters into the handset and places it on the counter, standing up and moving towards me. Her son is still tugging at her clothes, although he's fallen silent; I stare at him rather than look at her.

'I don't see how it's any of your business, you stuck-up cow.'

I want to scream that it is my business, because I work with families whose kids are sick and even dying and they'd give anything to hear 'Mummy' and would never ignore it, and because my son who is only just forming the word has been taken from me and it is unfair and unbearable.

But I say, 'It isn't. It isn't my business.' I leave the café, swept up into the whoosh of people, everyone moving and shoving because the train has, at last, arrived.

It's dark when I get home and the smell of roast chicken and the murmur of the radio are coming from the back of the house. I walk into the kitchen where Richard is peeling vegetables and Martha is sitting at the breakfast bar. Neither of them looks at me.

'Where have you been?' Richard murmurs.

'I went to see Julia,' I lie. I don't know why, but I don't want him to know I've seen Ben. *Oh, we can both have secrets, Richard.*

'It's late,' he says. 'You could have let me know.'

'What's the point?' I find myself saying. 'What is there for me to come home for, anyway?' Richard puts the knife down and looks at me, his eyes glinting.

'Oh, I don't know – me?' He picks the knife up again and waves it around, saying again, more loudly but somehow less convincingly, 'Me? Us?'

Martha, apparently indifferent, slowly turns the pages of a gossip magazine, fiddles with her phone and replaces her earphones.

Chapter Seventeen

Richard

We get ready in silence. I try to hug Sally, touch her hand, but she keeps slipping out of my grasp. She smiles at me as she does, as if to placate me, as if to say, 'Just not now, hey?', but the smile doesn't reach her eyes.

'Sal, I know you're worried about today,' I say, as I pat my pockets down, checking for the eighteenth time that I have my phone, wallet, keys, 'but … there isn't anything else bothering you, is there?' I feel a bit of a dick asking; as if all *this* isn't enough. I think (hope) that is exactly what she'll reply. But she doesn't. She stares at me. Her eyes stay on me when I pick up my folder, where I've been saving all my notes, and I start rifling through the printed case studies, the radiologist report, all the information and details I know off by heart. There is such a long pause before she answers that I assume nothing is coming, and this is how I end up speaking over her,

'Well, since you ask—' she says in a brittle voice.

'The main thing is that we present a united front today,' I say at the same time. She draws a deep breath.

'I couldn't agree more, Richard.'

We smile at each other, but they are the kind of smiles you see between people who accidentally catch each other's eye on the tube.

I've been thinking about just that, this united front thing, for ages and I keep thinking about it as we get into the car. I am driving and Sally is staring out of the passenger window, her head turned away from me. I look at her hair and notice it has got longer than usual. There is a space between us, it was there before this business with Ol, but I know it is growing. Worse than that, it is becoming more than space; it's solidifying. It is beginning to look like a wall.

I know that it's my fault, of course.

I just hope the people at the conference won't see it.

We are met by Mary as soon as we walk into the local authority building, which looks inside just as you imagine such buildings to look. Nondescript. Mary fits in there: she is also neutral and bland-looking, but it's still oddly comforting to see a familiar face. She shakes our hands.

'I'm going to introduce you to the chairperson,' she explains as we fall into step beside her, walking briskly down the corridor. 'Her name is Verity. She's very experienced. Her role is to facilitate the meeting, take notes and so on, then she'll draw everyone's comments together and sum up. OK?' We both nod.

Verity is waiting for us in the conference room. There are lots of empty chairs and a huge file on the table. She is younger than Mary and well put-together, smartly dressed, neatly tied-back hair, but just short of attractive. I don't know what it is; her eyes are too far apart, her nose a bit wide at the bridge. A six out of ten. I immediately chide myself for assessing her that way: maybe it's nerves, or habit, I don't know. I try to concentrate on what she's saying.

'The key thing is, try not to speak over anyone, or get upset.' She looks at Sally when she says this, but is unable to catch her eye; Sally is staring out of the window. 'You'll get your opportunity to contribute, don't worry. It's my job to make sure everyone's voices are heard.' She pauses, studying our faces. 'Can I get you anything before we bring the others in? Water?'

'Yes please, water,' I murmur, looking around the room. I still can't quite believe we are here.

'This kind of thing just doesn't happen to people like us,' I had said to Sally when we were sitting in the kitchen, a couple of weeks before; she was holding the letter that confirmed the CPC had been put back. She'd been especially irritable all day.

'People like us? What does that mean?'

'You know ... respectable people.'

'What, you think people who drive nice cars and join wine clubs don't hurt their children?'

'I'm not saying that. But – a *child protection conference*. Seems like that's for ... I don't know, druggies and wasters.'

'And poor people.'

'Come on, you know what I mean.'

'Not people like us.'

'What are you getting so worked up about?'

'You're such a fucking hypocrite. You make out you're all working class, up the proletariat and all that bollocks, but you're a total social climber. You're the biggest snob there is.'

'Why are you having such a go at me? What exactly have I done?'

'I'm sure if you thought about it for long enough, you could put your finger on it.'

I had wavered then, had wondered whether to try to touch her, rub her shoulders, make a vague apology, but instead I had taken the coward's route and left the room with a muttered, 'Forget it, there's no talking to you when you're like this.'

Now, everyone does get to say their piece, under Verity's watchful lead. It's surreal: kind of like a business meeting, but the business is our son, and as much as everyone is at pains to emphasise their concern for his welfare, I can't shake my unease at having him treated as a 'case'.

A representative from the hospital takes out the X-rays and outlines what we already know about the injury. Torus fracture, usually the result of twisting the limb. A policeman makes some general comments about 'these kinds of instances'. Mary summarises the known facts of what happened, and reads out the sections of the report in which people we know have talked about the way we were with Ol. Some of these observations are more complimentary than others. She describes the supervised visits, summarises her contact reports and describes how upset Ol tends to get. I want to say, *of course he's upset, he's confused, he misses us,* but I do as I've been told and keep my mouth shut.

We'd agreed in advance that when it came to our turn, I would speak first, then Sally. We were going to keep it brief: I would run through all my notes, present the 'second opinions' we'd gathered, try to keep things clear and factual. Sally was going to make a kind of 'impact statement', talk about how important it was for us to all be together while Ol was so young, and how much we missed him, of course.

I do my bit; it's straightforward enough. Our 'evidence' looks a bit paltry, so far, despite our efforts. I talk about the full skeletal survey Ol had and the fact that no other injuries were found. I'm still not sure this is a good thing, it could go either way: it says we haven't hurt him before, but it also makes a congenital defect look less likely. I tell them Sally has her meeting coming up with the pathologist, Stone. We're pleading for time, really.

When it's her turn she just mumbles something like 'I agree with everything my husband has said', and stares at the table. I put my hand on her arm and hiss: 'Is that *it*?', and she does an overly dramatic flinch, almost a shudder. Then she turns and looks directly at Mary and whispers, 'Please give me my baby back. I need him.' She blinks as though trying not to cry, and won't look at me.

I shiver. I've heard her say so many times 'I need my baby back', but this is the first time it's sounded like an act.

In the summing-up, things get really odd.

Verity says she is going to summarise our strengths as a family, before moving on to the concerns. It's on the word 'strengths' that Sally makes the noise. It could have passed as a cough – in fact she almost immediately tries to pass it off as such, looking around as though she's forgotten where she was for a moment, saying 'Oh! Excuse me' – but it isn't a cough; it is a cross between a long 'Humph!' and a hysterical laugh.

I wonder what it means, but I think I have an idea. My stomach starts to churn.

Sally barely says anything else for the rest of the meeting, but her brief outburst lingers in the room like an echo. I see the eyes of everyone in that room narrow slightly when they look at her.

The decision is made that Ol is still classed as 'at risk' and we will continue to have supervised visits, with a review meeting in three months' time. They say they'll consider all the information I've brought to the table, but I can't help feeling they are humouring me. Three months!

'His cast comes off next week,' I say stupidly, as though losing the cast will take away all evidence of what had happened to him and therefore mean it hadn't happened at all. I realise I've been seeing that moment as the deadline, the point at which everything would change, but they aren't done with us.

'Three months,' Verity says, closing her ring binder and getting up to show us the door.

In the car, I lose it. I start the engine and then switch it off again, and bang my hand on the steering wheel. Sally jumps.

'What was the meek little woman act all about, then?'

'What are you talking about?'

'Were you trying to make me look bad in there, or what?'

'Oh, no. No, Richard. You can do that all on your own.'

And that's when I know for sure that she knows.

People will laugh at this but I think I'm a romantic.

I love falling in love. I fall in love often, and hard (no pun intended). And each time feels better and higher than the last, like getting a hit of a stronger, purer drug.

I fell in love with Zoe, well, sort of. See even now, I know I'm qualifying it, retrofitting it because it doesn't suit the story, trying to make it less than it was, but I suppose I must have felt it. Then I fell in love with Sally, who totally eclipsed Zoe. Then there was Jenna.

When I admit how I met Jenna, it sounds pretty pathetic. She is a barista. When I told my mate Darren about her, he asked, as he always does, 'What does she do?' When I answered he thought I said 'barrister'. I laughed, and said, 'God no.' It just came out, and I felt pretty bad so I immediately added that she was an actress, too. He didn't need to know how successful or otherwise, and when he asked, 'Has she been in anything I might have seen?', I answered pointedly, 'When's the last time you were in a theatre, Darren?', and that shut him up pretty sharpish.

Anyway, she's a barista, in a top-notch café I happen to like a lot, so I would see her every day. She's gorgeous – obviously that's the first thing I noticed about her – but she had this toughness that I liked. She had a potty mouth, too. She made me laugh.

She had some sort of Spanish heritage, and when I found this out (it was pretty obvious anyway, something about her, dark hair in a messy ponytail, and her skin, not tanned exactly but I don't know, it had a Mediterranean quality to it, she was the kind of pale olive that looked like she *should* be darker, if that makes sense), I used to tee her off by saying 'Hola!' every morning, and she'd roll her eyes at me and put her hand on her hip. She progressed from giving me the scripted polite good mornings to saying 'oh, not *you* again' to saying nothing at all, just glowering at me with those flashing eyes. But eventually one day, when I said 'Hola!', she laughed. I think that was the start of it.

She knew me by name by then – 'I'm supposed to ask your fucking name now when I take your order,' she said one day, Sharpie pen poised over paper cup like a scalpel (she was familiar enough with me to swear at me anyway, a treat she reserved only for regulars) – and after the laugh, the laugh that changed everything, it was only a short step to a couple of sentences, scraps of conversation, and on one unusually quiet morning she leaned over the counter and talked to me for a full five minutes, occasionally chewing the end of a pencil, and she touched my arm as she got up to go, and that day I went back into the café after work and asked her out.

We went to one of those pubs, in a village just outside town, with a nice beer garden and a stream running by. The kind of place where they didn't have table numbers but gave you a painted wooden spoon when you ordered food.

'Tell me a bit about yourself,' I said, once we were settled. I'd ordered a small wine, she asked for a pint, and there was one of those moments when the barman handed us each the wrong drinks, and Jenna had scowled at him. I liked her for that. 'Tell me what you're passionate about,' I said.

'Nothing,' she said, and took a drink. 'I'm bored.'

'Oh, wow – sorry. And we've only just got here!'

'Not with you, cretin. I'm bored with life. Terminally bored.' As though to emphasise this, she stretched and yawned. When she raised her arms her T-shirt lifted up over her ribs and I found myself staring at her taut stomach.

'Well, that's a shame. Bored at … what? Twenty-five?'

'I'm thirty.'

'Crikey,' I said, genuinely surprised, and immediately hating myself for saying the word 'crikey', because she looked at me with an expression close to pity. 'You really look a lot younger than that. You're older than my wife.'

'You usually take out girls who are younger than her, right?'

'Sorry. I didn't mean … well, I don't take girls out, as a rule.'

'Of course you don't.'

'Hey—'

'Oh, please,' she said, waving her hand as though batting away an insect, 'I'm not judging. But I'd rather not be given the whole "I don't usually do this kind of thing" line, thanks.'

Wow. This was moving fast. OK, I wasn't being totally honest with the innocent married man act, but I also wasn't used to facing a woman with quite such unblinking eyes and such a direct way of talking. I shifted in my seat.

'What about you?' I said, deciding to try to change tack. 'Do you usually do this kind of thing?'

Jenna took a sip of her pint.

'Yes,' she said. 'In fact I only ever sleep with married men.' Her eyes were set on me, steady; I wasn't sure if she was joking.

'But we're not sleeping together,' I pointed out.

'Not yet.'

Later I had just pulled onto the drive when Jenna sent me a message: *I'm thinking about you.*

I replied: *What are you doing?*

I'm touching myself.

My dick twitched in my pants.

I was desperate to get back to her. Pictured her in her house, flat, room, fucking caravan for all I knew, wherever the hell she lived, pictured her with her hand down her knickers and all I wanted, every single cell and fibre and hair of me wanted to get back, back to where she was, or get back to an hour ago, watching her across that beer garden table. Given that chance, instead of sitting still and polite, I would put my hands on her, up her skirt. All I could see when I closed my eyes was those olive-coloured, bare legs crossing and uncrossing, the glimpses of thigh, the skin shiny and soft. I would have cut off my own hand in that instant if you'd told me that right before I did, I could be back at that table with it thrust up her skirt.

Things moved pretty quickly from that point. Once the pretence is down, which usually takes a while (God knows it took ages with Sally), once it's obvious, it's out in the open, that you're going to have sex; it just becomes about when and where and how often. Jenna was by turns frantic – sending me crazily dirty messages – and cool – sometimes I didn't hear from her at all for days on end.

Until today at the CPC, there was only one occasion when I thought I might get found out. I lost my wedding ring. Sally was really mad about it.

'Well, why did you take it off?'

'I didn't take it off; it fell off.'

'Where?'

'If I knew where, it wouldn't be lost, would it?'

'But you had it on when you went out?'

'Of course I did. What a stupid question.'

'Don't call me stupid.'

'I didn't say you were stupid, I said it was a stupid question.'

And on, and on.

And the next night I went back to Jenna's.

'You left this here,' she said, holding the ring between her thumb and forefinger, gingerly, as though it might contaminate her.

'Well, I can't take it back now, or she'll know I didn't lose it in the pub.'

'Why did you take it off?'

'Don't you start!'

'You know, you don't just become unmarried because you take off the ring.'

'More's the pity.'

'Spare me, please.' She threw the ring onto the table, where it did a couple of spins and came to rest, both of us looking at it. 'And don't leave any of your things here again.'

I took the ring and put it back on, and went back home. Sally murmured, 'You got it back, then.' I said it had been found in the pub toilets. She didn't challenge me any further. I should have known at that point that things wouldn't end well.

Chapter Eighteen

Sally

We are back from the CPC, having driven most of the way in silence, and we're going through the usual motions a couple does when they get back to their house: taking off coats and shoes, putting the kettle on. I lean on the counter, my head feeling so heavy I want to just lay it there and never lift it again.

'Three more months,' I whisper. 'How can they even do that? How is this fair?'

'It isn't,' Richard says, his voice trembling, 'but we can't just roll over. We have to keep fighting. See what your Stone guy has to say, keep up the research, go along with all their tests and profiling and observations and don't give them a single thing to criticise us for. Surely, *surely*, they'll have to concede at some point that it might have been an accident.' We stare at each other. He corrects himself. '*Must* have been an accident.'

'They'll try to break us up. They want one of us to blame the other.'

'I know.'

'That would make it a lot easier for them.'

'I know,' he says again, then takes a deep breath and adds in a voice I can tell he is trying to keep controlled. 'But you know, you did a good impression in that room of not liking me very much.'

I look at him. He looks tired, sad. For a minute I want to hug him. I want to be able to forget, to ignore, everything I know. The betrayal, the lies. I want to erase it all and for us to feel like a team, because he's right, he's been right all along, working together, *being* together, is the way to get our baby back.

But I can't hold it in. I'm crumbling inside and I feel like if I keep pretending I'll disappear completely.

'I know,' I say eventually.

'Know what?' he says, and I think, *oh, please don't do this*. Is this how it's going to be? This dance, this game? I sigh and play along.

'I know about *her*.'

'I've no idea what you're on about.' But like even the best poker player, he has a tell, a giveaway that his more experienced adversaries can spot. The back of his hand, swept across his top lip, either wiping away microscopic beads of sweat or trying to brush off the lie.

'OK, I'll spell it out. I know you've been shagging someone.'

'Where have you got that from?' His voice is cool but his eyes are flickering around the room.

'Come on, Richard, I'm too tired for this,' I mutter. 'Let's not waste time. Don't insult my intelligence. I *know*.'

'And *how* exactly do you "know" this thing that you think you know?' He's moved from total faked innocence to indignation pretty quickly. I know what that means. He is on the rack. I remember him saying to me, about Zoe, when she'd found some clue to our affair and confronted him, 'I made her feel bad about snooping on me ... in the end *she* apologised to *me*.' He'd seemed almost proud; it had made me feel uneasy but I'd ignored it, pushed it to one side as you do with the less pleasant parts of the person your stupid heart has chosen to love.

And here in the present, I am the wronged wife and we carry on with the dance.

When the admission finally comes, it's a bit like when someone dies after a terminal illness: you know it's coming, it's going to happen no question, but when it does, it's still a shock. It just goes to show how strong, and how illogical, hope is.

I must have been hoping that however big the pile of evidence (literally a pile: papers on papers were his undoing), my suspicions would be proven wrong, a huge mistake, because when Richard finally, quietly, says, 'OK,' followed by a load of other stuff I don't listen to ('OK, but it's not what you think ... OK, but hear me out ... OK, but it's only a recent thing'), I only hear the 'OK' and everything that one word means causes a huge crushing fist to close around my heart. Or possibly my windpipe, because I am suddenly finding it very difficult to breathe.

A sound like a gasp comes out of me.

'Sal.' He looks at me closely. 'Are you all right?'

'Do NOT do that. Don't give me the concern, now.' I am desperate to take the hand he is holding out, to fold myself into his arms, but of course it would all be pretend, everything is tainted, and he'll never hold me again without me thinking about him holding her. 'Tell me about her.'

'What?'

'Come on, tell me. How long? How old is she? Where did you do it? When? Is that who you've been texting at night?'

'Sally, I don't think it's a good—'

'No!' I scream. 'You don't get to hold out now. You don't get the control. You have to tell me. You owe me that much.' And he does as I ask, and as soon as he does, I am sorry. She's thirty. She works in a café. And she's an *actress*. For fuck's sake. It's not serious, no, not yet. Not yet! He really likes her. He's sorry. He *couldn't help himself*. There are no answers he can give me that could make anything better. It's like rubbing grit into an open wound.

It really does feel like someone has died.

'Do you love her?' I eventually say in a small voice. I expect him to immediately say, 'Of course not,' but the pause he leaves says everything. The pause *is* everything. Tears come. They sit in my eyes and I keep my eyelids wide open in the wild belief that as long as they don't actually fall down my cheeks, I can be strong, I won't break. Everything in front of me blurs and wobbles.

'I'd better go,' he says, and I don't argue.

I sit on the stairs and cry. What else is there to do?

Oliver is gone.

Richard is gone. To *her*, I assume.

What do I have left, now?

Chapter Nineteen

Martha

I listen to her, crying on the stairs. I don't come out of my room.

The slamming door of a different house, yet it sounds just the same as last time. I wonder why I am never enough to keep him.

He fought to have me here, that's what he said, to be with him, and now he is gone, again. Left me alone, with her.

How could he do that to me?

It's easy. My 'job'. Brown paper packages. A memory surfaces of me and Zoe, in rare mother-daughter time, cuddled on the sofa in the London house, watching *The Sound of Music*. She said it was her favourite film. It seemed out of step with everything else I knew about her. I said, 'I thought your favourite film was *Cinema Paradiso*.' She said yes, it was, but *The Sound of Music* was a guilty pleasure, just like the popcorn and fizzy drinks she'd laid out before pressing play. She said she'd watched it twenty-six times as a girl. She turned the main lights off but in the glow from the screen I could just about see her mouthing the words. White nightdresses twirled and windows were closed against the thunderstorm. Brown paper packages. My favourite things.

I don't think this was what Julie Andrews had in mind.

Brendan gives me the addresses; I look them up on my iPhone, get on my bike and am gone. The parcels are small enough to put in my coat pocket, or even in my bra. I don't ask what's in them and he doesn't tell me. I know, though, of course. Sometimes – rarely – there is a message, like the time he gave me two brown envelopes that had been stuffed, folded in on themselves and wrapped around and around with tape. The smaller one was to be handed over with the words 'this one's complementary'. I practised the line all the way there. It seemed like something a waiter in a posh restaurant might say. The guy laughed when I said it.

The houses aren't what I expected, not for the most part anyway. I'd imagined that drug addicts ('users,' Brendan repeatedly corrects me, 'drug *users*') lived in scummy bedsits or crowded flats. Or in doorways, to be honest. But of course most of Brendan's 'customers' are kids like us, and live at home with their parents. Therefore I have to observe strict timings, to coincide with when those parents are out. One corner house, in a cul-de-sac, has a pear tree in the front garden.

I tell myself it isn't that bad, really. It just becomes something I do, like homework or hanging out with Del. I make room for it in my day and I get on with it. But I still get a feeling like I'm going to be sick every time my phone beeps, just in case it's him with one of his messages: 'Another job. Tonight.' And after each one I'll come home and hurry to the bathroom and cut, and wash, everything away. And I really am peaceful then because straight after a 'job' I am the furthest I can be from the next one. Then my hours and days are a slide downwards, towards the next message, the next delivery, the next fast cycle home, empty-handed and wild with relief.

Of course, I'm never completely empty-handed: I have to collect money too, and give it to Brendan, who counts it in front of me, twice. Rolls of notes he flicks through his fingers and then separates into meticulous piles. Then he'll shove each pile into a different pocket: jeans, front and back; jacket. He saw me watching him do this once, and smirked.

'Cost of goods, overheads, profits,' he said, punctuating each word with a pat of the pocket. 'You have to be sensible with your money, little one. I'm MD of my own business here, you know.'

He doesn't pay me, of course. My payment is my new-found school status – it has been noted that I am Brendan Lowe's Year Eleven pet – and of course, the promise of not being hideously shamed on the internet.

I've asked him when it will stop. He said, 'Oh, little one, you've only just started.'

I've started cutting my feet. I was worried someone might notice the marks on my arms, or the fact I always wear long sleeves, even when it's hot, and anyway, I like the way it feels when my feet start to heal. Especially in the creases on the underside of my toes. It itches like crazy, the skin grows back thick and hard and white. I try to wait as long as possible before scratching them and when I do, it's bliss, the most overwhelming feeling of relief. One day I walked home from town, wearing flip-flops, and every step was tingling agony. I desperately wanted to stop, sit down on the pavement and scratch, but I made myself walk on.

When I got home the itching had subsided. I scratched and scratched anyway, desperate to get the feeling back, and the next thing I knew I was sobbing because I knew I'd missed the moment, I'd ruined everything. I scratched so hard that the cut re-opened and there was blood in my fingernails but I couldn't stop. I held my foot twisted up into my lap and let blood fall onto my skirt, but I still felt nothing, so I went into the bathroom and cut my arms, my stomach.

I thought Sally was onto me, once. She sliced into her finger while chopping mushrooms (she'd been staring out the window, which she is doing a lot of these days) – she made a real song and dance about it, too – and went to the cupboard looking for plasters. She emptied the box onto the worktop and frowned.

'We've gone through a lot of these lately,' she murmured, and looked at me. As usual, I ignored her, and left the room without saying anything.

Sally is going slowly, quietly mad. Her tidiness obsession obviously extends to the fridge because it is getting emptier by the day. She's stopped bothering to cook. She never sits down; she just flits from room to room, moving things, cleaning them or throwing them away. She doesn't speak really, except to herself. I want to ask her if Dad is coming back, but I am afraid of the answer. What a weird way to end up: just the two of us, when we don't even really like each other.

I could ask Dad directly what's going on; he has sent me a few texts, but I can't bring myself to reply. I could go back to Zoe's, but how would that work? What about school? It crosses my mind that in London I could escape Brendan, but would it really be that easy? There's no escape from the Internet, after all. And more to the point, my mother is basically a nightmare. Possibly madder than Sally. And she didn't want me before, so why would she want me now?

I was always closer to my dad than my mum, at least, before Sally and Oliver happened. People always said we were alike: same way of speaking, of walking. Dad used to say he wanted us to have a good relationship, he wanted to do a better job than his own dad had, which seemed weird as I've always thought Granddad was pretty cool.

So when Dad left (the first time, I mean, when he left Zoe), I was pretty gutted and couldn't understand why he would leave me (for a while, anyway, again until Sally came along and they took me in – perhaps I should be grateful to her for that – never thought of that before). He said he didn't have the time to give me, because of work and that. But it was a load of crap. He had time for other women, after all. He must have thought I was a total fucking idiot if he thought I didn't know about them.

I am sitting on the sofa, absent-mindedly scratching my feet, the thickening skin on my toes and heels.

'Does no one else in this house think to do this?' Sally is muttering; she's been walking around pulling flowers from vases and shoving them, head first, into a bin bag. I get up and peer into the bag.

'They looked OK to me—' I begin.

'They're dead,' she says flatly, and leaves the room.

Like I say: I think she's going a bit mad. But even this weird set-up is better than going back to Zoe's. At least here I'm pretty much left alone.

Chapter Twenty

Richard

My first thought is to go to Jenna. My second is that I shouldn't just turn up, so I text her.

Are you home? x

Nothing. I drive a little closer to her flat and park up.

I'm a couple of streets away. Fancy a visitor? Xx

I sit in the car for what seems like a long time. It starts to rain, fat droplets bouncing off the windscreen. My phone doesn't beep or vibrate, but I keep checking it anyway. I am surprised and, in a weird way, disappointed not to hear from Sally. I've been expecting a stream of vitriol, as she surely isn't done with me yet. This is why I need Jenna: as a kind of human shield.

But beyond the tapping of rain on glass, there is just silence.

I re-start the engine and drive.

I could have a fresh start with Jenna. I've messed things up with Sally; even if she'd never found out, I know now that from the first time I kissed Jenna I crossed a line and created a block, a boulder, in our marriage. Even if Sally couldn't see it, she'd have known it was there. It wasn't fair to expect her to have to feel her way around this invisible barrier any time she wanted to get close to me. And as for me, I would be carrying a secret, and I know from experience that that just wears you down after a while.

But of course leaving, and maybe being with someone else, means leaving my kids. Well, Ol, anyway. Martha is practically grown up, after all, and hopefully she would come with me. I can't see her wanting to stay with Sally or go back to Zoe. It's not exactly ideal to cast myself as the least awful of three poor options, but I think that's how she'll see it. We were close when she was younger, and I'm sure we can be again. I just need to work on it a little harder. I know that.

Ol is trickier. Obviously I never thought I wouldn't be there for him every single day, and I never planned any of this. Or, let's be honest, never planned to get found out, anyway. Being forced to be apart from Ol these last weeks has been awful. In a messed-up way the circumstances have made it easier, because I've busied myself, with research, with the business of getting him back. And I've been full of righteous indignation, which can carry you a long way, like adrenaline. But I won't have any of that when I'm just the cheating louse who left, will I?

It crosses my mind that I could fight for custody of Ol. I bat the thought away hurriedly; there's a knot of something like fear in my stomach at the idea of it. But it keeps coming back, because since he's been gone, my visions of him and me together have morphed from the cliché football-in-the-park stuff (the domain of the weekend dad), to the more involved scenes of school runs, dinners cooked and cleaned up together, homework pored over, stories shared. If – *when* – we get him back, I don't want to lose any of that, regardless of what's gone on between me and Sally. And I shouldn't have to. Should I?

The strange thing is, I always thought if anything, it would be Sally who would cheat on *me*. It would be crazily out of character, mind: she's not perfect – who is? – but she's honest and decent. She hates lies. Zoe wouldn't agree, probably nor would Martha, but look, she didn't screw anyone over. I did. Everyone always likes to blame the woman. Especially women. Women blame women. So much for the sisterhood.

Sally hates this, too; she says it's patronising to men. She says she hates the 'narrative' of men not being able to help themselves, like you put a pretty girl in front of them and what are they supposed to do but succumb – she says this is insulting.

And here our views part ways. I want to tell her it's good of her to see it like that but it's not patronising or insulting; a hell of a lot of men really are shallow, vain, dick-led gits. Myself included. But I never tell her.

Anyway, I digress. I thought it might be Sally who'd stray partly because she's younger than me. Ten years might not have seemed like much when we met, but as time goes on it seems like a wider gap. It felt like more than ten years when, a couple of years after we met, we did a 5k charity run together and she beat me. 'You've been chicked, mate,' my so-called 'friend' Darren, who is a bit of an arsehole, kept saying. 'I'd never beat you over a longer distance,' Sally said, but she was beaming; the flush in her cheeks was pride while the flush in mine was exertion and sweat. Ten years, I thought. She'll be fitter for longer, and eventually she'll overtake me on all the distances.

Sally did that thing women often do: she said she wanted to know everything. She laughed when I told her Jenna was an actress; not just laughed … scoffed.

'You never used to be like that,' I said. 'Dismissive. Cold. You've a cruel streak, do you know that?'

'How do you know what I'm like when a husband cheats on me? Oh, wait, you wouldn't know, because it hasn't happened before. Has it?'

I replied with, 'Of course not,' unanticipated bitterness in my voice.

She looked at me closely, then said, with a note of curiosity, 'What is it? Did you expect me to be *kind* about her?'

I told her I had no excuse for what I'd done, but that I thought I was actually a romantic.

'You're not a romantic,' she said. 'You just think with your dick. What's romantic about that?'

'I want movie love. *Brief Encounter. Notting Hill.*'

'Oh my God!' she screamed. 'That's fiction! It doesn't exist, that's the whole point! If that's what you're looking for, you are never going to be happy.'

'Fine. I accept that.'

'No. No. *I* don't bloody well accept that. I won't.' That was Sally. Not for the first time, she was refusing to give up on me.

I don't consider the possibility of being alone. In my head, it is Sally or Jenna. And since my relationship with Sally is effectively ruined, that leaves Jenna as the only option. That might sound stupid. It's like, I don't know, baking (not that I've done much of that, bar a few gingerbread men when Martha was little). You make a cake and it comes out wrong; what do you do? You can try and cover it with icing, but it's still bitter and crumbling underneath. No, I will bake a new cake. Far easier.

And Jenna is great: young and fit, and just difficult enough that I know I will keep finding her interesting and not get bored. I could easily convince myself that I love her.

It's only now I'm wondering if she feels the same about me.

Jenna's car is there. She has an old red Fiesta, with fluffy dice (presumably ironic) hanging from the rear-view mirror. There is a half-empty pack of Marlboro Lights on the passenger seat, various empty plastic bottles in the footwell, and a fashion magazine on the parcel shelf. The exterior of the car is thick with dirt, not the one-off kind that shows you've been driving in muddy countryside, but great streaks of everyday dust. The rain is making shiny circles in it. I pull up alongside it. So she is at home.

I look up at the windows to her flat. It's mostly in darkness but there is a low light coming from her bedroom. Maybe candles? I glance at the car clock. 12.30am. A thought passes across my mind – who is she lighting candles for at this time of night? – but I push it aside.

I get out of my car, walk to the main doors, and press the intercom.

No answer.

I push the button again, hold my finger there, and listen to the insistent buzz. If she's asleep, I reason, I ought to wake her up; what with the lit candles and everything.

When there is still no answer a cold feeling starts to creep over my scalp and down the back of my neck.

I stand back from the building and try to pitch my voice so that somehow she will hear me but I won't disturb her neighbours. What comes out is a hoarse croak, loud in the darkness.

'Jenna!' My voice sounds like it belongs to someone else, weirdly high-pitched and desperate, 'Jenna, are you OK?'

I move towards the intercom again but not before I see a light flick on in the ground floor flat and a woman's face appearing through the curtains, flinging me a filthy look. 'What the—?' the face starts to mouth, but I turn away.

Just then there is the creak of a window being opened and I look up. There she is, her hair piled high on her head and her face make-up free apart from her eyeliner tattoo.

'Bloody hell, Richard,' she hisses, 'what do you think you're doing?'

I'm wrong-footed for a moment, literally; I stumble a bit into the communal flowerbeds as I lean back to look at her properly.

'Can I come up?' I say in a pointless attempt at a shouty whisper. To my surprise and abject disappointment, she says 'no' quite firmly, closes the window and disappears from view.

I sit in the car, my face in my hands. What to do now? Find a hotel, I suppose. But the prospect of a hotel bed without her in it is crushingly lonely. I'm now convinced she has someone else up there, and my stomach churns at the thought. I have an image of her in that candlelight, straddling some faceless guy, younger and fitter than me, and I shake my head to try to get rid of it. What the hell have I done?

Just as I'm about to turn the key in the ignition, there is a loud tap on the driver's window, which is spattered now with rain. I hold down the button to open it and Jenna's furious face comes into view.

It's only the second time I've been to Jenna's flat. The first time, I hung around her shop until she finished and offered her a lift back. Sally and I had been arguing and I was in no mood to go home.

'It's not far.' She frowned. 'I usually walk.'

'Come on, I won't stay long. Just—'

'A cup of coffee?' She gave the espresso machine one last rudimentary polish and, throwing her tea towel on the counter with a grimace, picked up her keys.

'Not necessarily.' I tried a winning smile.

'I don't normally take my friends home.'

'Is that what I am? A friend?'

'Would you prefer the term fuck buddy?'

I balked; I'd hoped I was a bit more than that.

'Friend will do fine,' I said, and she didn't reply, but she did walk with me to the car.

Jenna's flat tries hard to be an apartment but is just a flat. It's a few years old and has the mass-produced look of these kinds of places: magnolia walls, fawn carpet, basic kitchen and bathroom suites, spotlights. The finish is nowhere near what you'd find in one of my developments. It might have looked impressive when it was first done, but these places soon look run down. Especially if they aren't looked after, which this one definitely isn't, I thought, on my first visit. There were marks on the doorframes and light switches, as though they'd never been wiped. It had an 'open-plan living room', which means that the kitchen was really just a wall in the lounge. I hated those. The cupboards had a gloss finish but were grubby; I touched the fake-steel handle of one to get out a glass, and felt grime on my fingers. The bin was overflowing and there was a stale smell. For someone who took great care of her appearance, she didn't seem to bother much with her home. I didn't say anything, but I couldn't quite relax.

We never went there again. Jenna didn't mind, she'd seemed uncomfortable the whole time anyway, like she couldn't wait for me to leave. Maybe she *was* conscious that it was a bit of a mess. From then on we met in hotels. Once, she came to my office. Sometimes we fucked in the car. She seemed to like that.

This time, there is a nicer smell about the place. Must be the candles. Vanilla, and something else, almost too sweet, but not quite. And another fragrance behind it, spicy and enticing. I realise as she shuts the door behind us that it is coming from her.

'You smell nice,' I say, trying to nuzzle her neck.

'I was having a bath,' she replies, pulling away and walking down the hall. I notice she pulls her bedroom door closed as she passes. I follow her into the kitchen / dining / living room. 'What are you doing here, Richard?' She opens the freezer and takes out a bottle of vodka. She waves it at me; I shake my head.

'I've left Sally,' I say.

Jenna looks at me, narrows her eyes.

'Left, or been kicked out?'

I think about it for a minute.

'Left,' I say, surprise in my voice.

'Why?'

'What do you mean, why?'

'Why on earth would you leave?'

'She found out about us.' I try to ignore the look that passes across Jenna's face when I say the word *us*. I know she doesn't like 'relationship labels' and that kind of thing; I am always careful what I say. But now is the time to move things along, surely.

'That doesn't answer my question.' She takes a gulp of the vodka, neat, and doesn't flinch. 'Why would you leave?'

Because everything is ruined, I say silently. *Because I want to bake a new cake.* My thoughts aren't making sense, even to me. How can I explain them to Jenna? Why am I afraid that if I do, she will just pity me?

'She knows,' I say again, as though that explains everything. Jenna shrugs.

'She'll get over it, I expect.'

'It's not about that—'

'Why did you come here, Richard?' she asks again.

I suddenly feel very foolish.

'To tell you … to tell you I'd left. And to see if …' I tail off, look at my feet.

'You should have come here to break it off with me,' she says. 'You've got it all wrong.'

'But … I think I love you,' I say. The words hang in the air, and then she laughs.

We sit down with the bottle of vodka between us. She tells me she doesn't 'do' relationships. I realise she's said this before and I've chosen not to properly hear it, thought maybe it was a defence mechanism or something. But she means it, and it's crushing. She tells me it's been 'a lot of fun', as though we've just had a day out together at a fairground. She likes sleeping with married men, she says (her use of the plural is not lost on me), because they don't demand anything of her. And here I am, looking like I might start making demands. She tells me as soon as the wives find out she always backs off.

I ask her if I can stay, and we do the back-and-forth routine of her saying it's not a good idea, me pleading, until eventually she tugs a duvet and pillow out of the airing cupboard and throws them onto the sofa. The bedding smells stale.

'Just this once,' she says, 'and no creeping into my room in the middle of the night.'

'The thought hadn't occurred to me,' I lie.

'It's over, Richard, and I'm not going to change my mind. Tomorrow you should get up and go home to your wife.'

Chapter Twenty-One

Sally

'It's Sally. Richard's wife.'

I hadn't really expected to hear myself speak. I don't even know why I've phoned her, why I've been phoning her for days. I'd kept her number when I found it on Richard's phone and saved it into my own under 'TB' (for, unimaginatively, 'The Bitch'). I just wanted to hear her voice, to hear if there was a clue in there to what was so special about her, what was worth risking everything. But all I'd heard up to now was 'Hello?' at first light, almost musical, and eventually sharper, exasperated. Even the exasperation didn't give me any satisfaction, but I'd carried on anyway. Call after call, withholding my number, listening to her voice, then hanging up.

I ask her some questions to which I already know the answers – When? Where? How long? – and she answers carefully. Her voice feels 'put on', the kind of voice a telephone insurance salesman might use with a reluctant customer. Overly calm, measured. Every word properly placed. Rehearsed, even. She keeps using my name, in phrases like 'The thing is, Sally,' and every time she does it I wanted to scream, *Don't! Don't say my name. You don't know me.*

I'm tempted to go into the coffee shop where she works, which she has foolishly named. The idea that I could see her, bring her out of my imaginings and into existence, is frightening yet intoxicating.

But I won't because I already know how she will look, how she will be. She will be young, of course, and pretty; poised; better than me in every way. Because the person I see in the mirror is so ruined, how could she be anything else?

I'm about to hang up, about to apologise, even, for disturbing her day, for inconveniencing her, when a sudden urge rises up in me and I bark, 'You can't take my son, you know.'

There is a pause, and then she laughs. She laughs and in that moment I hate her more than I have ever hated anyone.

'I don't even want your husband, Sally. Why the hell would I want your kid?'

I wonder later what had compelled me to say it and I realise that it's the vision of him with her (or even some other, as yet faceless, woman) and Oliver. Acting as a family.

This will be the reality, if not soon, then one day, if we split up. Assuming we get Oliver back, of course.

I think about Zoe, and Martha, and whether there was the same crippling fear there, when I tipped up. When it was me who was the interloper in a marriage. I wonder if that's why Zoe sometimes seems distant from her daughter.

Maybe she can't bear to share her. Maybe only having half of your child is so awful it's easier to back away.

I've finally got my meeting with Cathy's contact, the paediatric pathologist. Daniel Stone. He'd listened on the phone, so intently that I had to check a few times that he was still there. He said he'd help if he could, said he'd worked on a few similar cases in the family courts. I said I hoped it wouldn't get that far. He didn't respond.

He offered to meet me in Farnham, but I said I needed to get out of the house, out of the town, and would come to him.

For all I've been fanatical about keeping the house neat, I realise I've neglected the car. I get in it and am hit by a musty smell and the faint odour of rotting fruit. I find a banana skin under the passenger seat and recall peeling it and passing its insides back to Ollie, who was crying in the back. That banana had bought me five minutes of silence the last time my son was in the car. That silence that had seemed so important is now deafening.

I drive over the Hog's Back with the windows open, the Surrey Hills creeping into my vision from my left. The morning mists are lifting and it looks like it will become a clear day; I have to flip the visor down to keep the sun from dazzling me.

Richard is imprinted on the landscape for me. I realise our shared history is also a shared geography. Every turn recalls a picnic, a pub lunch, a long walk on the Downs, in the more carefree days before we had our baby. Innocent motorway signs bring tears to my eyes, as they prompt memories of places we've been, days out we've shared. I wonder wildly if I will have to leave the country to escape these constant reminders of him, of us.

We all review the past through the filter of what's happened since. That's why it's important to live in the present.

I wish I could remember properly all the lovely things Richard said to me, at the start. All of our past now exists through the filter of where we are now, and the filter is muddy.

But as I drive these roads, only happy memories present themselves, none of the arguments, none of the shit.

I like knowing the names of things, like being able to label and classify (and in my job, treat and hopefully make better).

I sat on a riverbank with Richard, not long after we got together, the kind of overgrown English riverbank with billowing grass and bursts of colour. The only sounds were the rushing water and riotous birds. I told him I could name all the flowers.

'So can I,' he said, plucking a blue forget-me-not (Myosotis scorpioides, I could have told him) and turning it over in his hand.

'Can you really?' I smiled.

'Sure,' he said. 'This one's Eric, this one's Bruce …' Pluck, pluck, one stem after another, and I slapped his shoulder and he threw the blooms in the water and wrestled me into the grass. 'Come on, what are their *Latin* names,' I whispered. 'That's easy,' he said, his words punctuated with kisses to my shoulders and neck, 'Ericus Majoralis. Brucius Azaelia.' Later there would be midge bites and windburn and a sleepless night in a blown-about tent. Things were simple, then.

Something about the name Daniel Stone has led me to expect a much younger man; he sounded the dashing sort, it seemed like the name of a leading man in one of those TV dramas about spooks. I could not have been more wrong. He is mid-fifties, with a bushy, salt-and-pepper beard. He opens the door of his cottage and greets me like an old friend.

There aren't many paediatric pathologists in the country, or even the world. They are in short supply, Stone tells me, as he makes coffee with the help of an ancient-looking machine that is so loud he has to almost shout to be heard over it. He says his field is a specialism that not many are drawn to, as it can be quite emotionally challenging, what with most of his work being done with cadavers. He says all this in a matter-of-fact way. I murmur my understanding; in my line of work, the vast majority of children get well, but I have seen my share of dead babies and traumatised families.

He leads me into an office room lined with bookshelves, sits down and looks at me over his glasses. On his desk are printouts of everything I've sent him.

'The problem you've got is, X-rays are generally accepted as the main medical evidence for injury.' I nod; I know this. 'Has Oliver ever had his Vitamin D levels measured?'

'No. I mean, not that I know of. Should he have?'

'It's not routinely done, but there are odd cases where … you've heard of rickets?'

'Of course.' I resist the temptation to remind Stone I'm a healthcare professional, too. This has happened a lot, bizarrely, since Oliver was born. It's as though my new role as a mum negates my old life when I had a career, and opinions that were important to people. I used to mind, when it first started happening; I mind less now. All I mind about now is getting Ollie back home. I admit that rickets had crossed my mind as a possibility but I'd rejected it as just too unlikely.

'Were you anaemic during your pregnancy?'

'Yes! Very. I was on iron tablets for a long time after the birth, too.'

'Then Oliver might have had a Vitamin D deficiency even since before birth. There's some evidence this can weaken bones and lead to small fractures. It's not watertight, but I'd say it's the best chance you've got. Was he breastfed?'

'Yes. Only for a while.' The old guilt, the reluctance to admit I haven't been the 'perfect' mother, snakes into my thoughts. 'Why do you ask?'

'Vitamin D deficiency is most common in infants solely breastfed and it's rare in formula-fed babies.' He frowns. 'That's not to say it isn't a possibility. It's just rare.'

'OK. What do we do?'

'I suggest we get a blood sample from Oliver and have it tested ASAP. It might already be too late. Any deficiency he had might have corrected itself by now.'

'But … he's not living with us. I can't get him to you.'

'We'll find a way. But it will have to be above board, Sally. You'll have to get social services permission. I can't write you a witness report unless it's all kosher.'

'I understand. I'll speak to Mary.'

I drive back feeling I have, at last, a thread of something to hold onto. A chance. I have to focus on this now, not Richard. Which is fine right up until I get back home.

I'm beginning to regret being the one who stayed in the house. It had seemed right and fair – *you're the one who cheated, you can leave, you're not taking my home,* all of that – but Richard has now found himself a one-bedroom flat on a short-term let, and so he is free. I am stuck in this place with the shadows of what are increasingly looking like ludicrous dreams.

It's getting hot and I've started sleeping with the windows open. Staying on my side of the bed, Richard's side of the duvet smooth and unrumpled. A fly buzzes around the bedroom. Flies beat their wings around 200 times per second. The sound it makes may as well be a pneumatic drill. Maybe I can sleep through it, I tell myself, and am reminded in the same instant of how only white noise would settle Ollie in that awful phase of wakefulness he had at around six months. I would squeeze him into the by then too-small pram and rock it and park it by the dishwasher or washing machine, set to a long cycle, empty, in the middle of the night.

But I can't sleep through the fly, find myself willing it dead, wishing I could capture a spider and set it onto it. I think of the spider I watched crawl across my books earlier today, back and forth along the shelf like a caged bear.

Tomorrow I will buy fly spray and enjoy watching the little bastard shrivel and die, and then I will go to bed in silence.

I call Mary's mobile and she picks up on the second ring.

'Mary, it's Sally Townsend,' I say. 'I need a favour. Please.' There is a beat before she replies.

'I don't know about favours but I'll help if I can. What is it?'

'I think I might know how Ollie broke his arm.'

'I'm listening.'

'I need one thing ... a blood test.' She doesn't say anything; I wait. She hasn't said no, which has to be good. 'I went to see someone ... a specialist. I think he can help us find some answers. Please, Mary, can we just get a blood sample from Ollie? We need to look at his ... at his Vitamin D.' She sighs.

'I suppose we can arrange that.'

'Really? Because that would be amazing, because—'

'Sally,' she interrupts, 'how sure are you that this is the answer? Really?'

'I don't know, Mary. I have to try, but I don't know anything for sure.'

'He can have the test. Cynthia can take him to the clinic,' she says, 'and I'll go too.'

'Can't I go? I took him for all of his vaccinations ...' I tail off, beset by memories of his red face and confused wails at two months, three months, four months, him wriggling in my arms as the nurse approached with the needle and me whispering in his ears. 'I know how to calm him down.'

'It's procedure,' says Mary. 'It's outside of your normal visiting schedule.' And then, with a little more warmth, 'We'll get the bloods, Sally, and we'll send the results to your man for him to look at.'

'Thank you.'

'Naturally, we don't officially need Richard's permission as well for this, but I'm assuming he knows?' I pause. I won't tell Richard until we get the results.

'Of course,' I say. 'Of course he does.'

I'd never imagined that my only son's first birthday party would be held anywhere but in our home, nor that it would be attended by two people from social services.

I hadn't expected either, obviously, that Richard and I would be separated. But we've agreed he will be at the party, of course. And we will be civil, for Ollie's sake.

Ben comes up the night before. I am grateful for the company, and the help. He said he'd make cupcakes; now he stands in the doorway with a bag of flour and a packet of butter, grinning. 'You got eggs?'

'Of course! Come in.'

Martha is staying at Del's, so she's said. I wouldn't have thought it possible for us to be more distant from each other, but since her dad left, I barely see her. I don't have the energy to chase her down; she is fifteen, after all. If she wants to be treated like an adult, fine. I have other things to think about.

'*Please* try and remember that tomorrow is your brother's birthday,' I call out as she stomps down the hall.

'*Half* brother,' she corrects, slamming the door behind her.

After the cake baking, the kitchen dusted with white powder and the entrails of eggs drying to a crust on the worktops, we go into the garden so Ben can have a cigarette. Ben is the least committed smoker I've ever met – he smokes maybe two or three Marlboro Lights a day – but he does so with great flourish and enjoyment.

'I knew as soon as you told me he was an Aries there'd be trouble,' he muses, flicking ash into the jam jar I've brought out for the purpose.

'The stars were right, as always,' I say gravely. He looks up at the sky.

'Remember at uni, when we used to lie on the grass outside Halls and look at the stars? Can you believe that's, like, ten years ago?' I shake my head. Ben has barely changed, though: the same haircut, fringe flopping into his eyes, the same tight jeans and battered Converse, the same ring on his right hand.

'You couldn't bake then,' I observe.

'This is true –' he takes a leisurely drag on his cigarette '– but I made a mean tuna bake.'

'Ugh!' I laugh. 'A tin of tomato soup, a tin of tuna, and a load of over-cooked pasta.'

'And black pepper,' he says, mock indignant, 'and grated cheese.'

'All of it blue-and-white stripe.'

'Ah, yes, Tesco Value. The staple student diet.'

'Those were the days.' We sit in smiling silence for a while, the shared memories like an arm around us.

'You know, of course,' he goes on, 'that I loved you madly, back then.'

I nod; he's told me this before, although never at the time. Spots of rain start to fall and I look up at the sky.

'Let's go inside,' I say. 'I'll make your bed up.'

The sofa bed is a ridiculous contraption, requiring extreme strength and some kind of engineering degree to manipulate it into something you can sleep on. I considered giving Ben Martha's bed but I'm sure she would see someone else in her room as a gross invasion of privacy. And Ben assured me he'd be happy in the lounge. 'So if I can't sleep,' he'd said, 'I can just whack the TV on.' By the time we've made up the bed we are both red-faced with the effort.

I throw the spare bedding onto it, we look at each other, laugh and launch ourselves onto the duvet. Ben takes my hand, threading his fingers through mine, and I don't stop him.

My loneliness is all confused; the insides of me are chanting *I miss him, I miss him*, but I don't know if I just miss Ollie, or Richard, or both. I only know I am aching.

'Ben . . .' I begin, but I can't find the words. My breathing sounds too fast and too loud in my ears.

'The thing is, I've loved you so long and so hopelessly, the feelings are still there, but they're ... impotent. For want of a better word,' he adds with an awkward laugh.

'I'm sure you're not impotent.' I lean closer to him, moving my hand onto his leg. 'Love me again, Ben. Please.'

'I never stopped, you idiot. I just ... put it away.'

Could I do that, I wonder, thinking of Richard. Always thinking of Richard. Could I just put my feelings away?

Then he is kissing me and it feels all wrong. We kissed once at uni, of course, in the first year, pissed on white cider and touching each other up on the dance floor. Then we'd stumbled back to Halls and he'd passed out on the floor of my room. Nothing else happened and then we became best friends. In fact, I'd forgotten about it until now, the press of his lips bringing it back.

I feel like I am outside myself, watching. I remember those final weeks of university, a mix of celebration and trepidation, the sense of being on the edge of something. Pints of cider and black and urgent tongues down throats. A 'last chance' air everywhere. But I had already mentally moved away, I was in love with a married man by then and everyone else was in his shadow, so I watched from the side-lines and waited for his call.

It was always Richard.

'It's no good, Ben,' I say, pulling away. 'I'd be using you.'

'Er ... Sal? Please don't think me a typical single-minded man but, at this point in proceedings, I'm quite happy to be used.'

'At this point in proceedings' is such a *Ben* thing to say I can't help smiling.

'You'd be sorry tomorrow,' I say.

'I think I'll be sorry tomorrow either way.' He sighs, leaning back on the bed and straightening his clothes. I do the same; when had he unhooked my bra? 'At least my way I would have got laid.'

I play-punch him on the arm and we both laugh, the last vestiges of any sexual tension disappearing into the air like cigarette smoke.

'Cup of tea?' I say. 'It's not Tesco Value, I promise.'

In the morning, Richard knocks on the front door, as a guest would. I suppose that's what he is, now. I look at his shape through the glass. A few paces behind me, in the hall, Ben loiters. From upstairs I can hear tinny music from Martha's room.

'Your dad's here,' I call. Once I hear the radio flick over to silence, followed by Martha's footsteps on the landing, I open the door.

'Hi,' I say, moving aside to let him in. He is dressed smartly – expensive jeans, stripy shirt – but he hasn't shaved. His eyes look tired.

'You look nice,' we both say at once. Ben coughs.

'Hi, Ben.' Richard steps forward and holds out his hand; for a minute I think Ben isn't going to take it, but he does. 'Good to see you again.' This is Richard's stock, polite phrase, usually delivered when he means the very opposite, but he accompanies it with the broad smile that disarms most people. Most people, but not Ben, who grimaces.

By now Martha is in the hall and, to my surprise, throws her arms around Richard.

'Hello, sweetheart,' he mumbles into her hair.

I retreat into the kitchen, but they follow me, an awkward trio.

'The place looks great,' Richard says, gesturing towards the breakfast room. I was up early and I've dressed everything with a pirate theme: there is a pirate ship piñata, a tablecloth decorated with Jolly Rogers and parrots, a huge 'Happy 1st Birthday' sign and a cake in the shape of a treasure chest, chocolate coins cascading from it.

'Well, Ben helped me with it,' I say. 'And I thought as it's nice out, we can have most of the party in the garden.' I point outside where I've set up the garden table with citronella candles and jugs of Pimms for the grown-ups, and scattered toys across the lawn for the children (not that there are many coming). I've hung red and blue bunting all around the garden fence.

'When is the birthday boy getting here?' Richard's voice is light but his words a reminder, just as the unplayed-with toys are a reminder: *he's not here, he's not here. He should be here.*

'Any time now.' I try to smile. 'Mary's bringing him. And your mum and dad, of course. They're quite the quartet these days.'

It took some persuading to have the party at our house, as the default position had seemed to be to hold it at Cynthia's. I had to plead with social services. I was helped, I think, by the expression on Cynthia's face when I pointed out that there'd be lots of other babies – I could see her eyes moving in her head, the smile fixed on her face, as she calculated the degree of mess and inconvenience a whole clutch of one-year-olds could inflict. Unless they are related to her, Cynthia is not actually a fan of young children. In the end Mary – her newest friend – relented. It doesn't sit easily with me to be grateful to Mary, but it seems like I now have a couple of reasons.

As always when I see Oliver, my heart leaps in my chest. I'd asked Cynthia to dress him in a cute Star Wars T-shirt I'd bought him, and denim shorts, but he is wearing trousers I've never seen before and a striped shirt, not dissimilar to the one Richard is wearing, which grates, to be honest. Almost immediately Ollie gets through the door, they are posing for photographs, with everyone making cracks about 'mini me'. The shirt is fastened right up to the top; I walk over and undo the first button.

'He spilt breakfast on the other thing,' Cynthia says airily. 'But this is much smarter, anyway.'

Mary has brought a colleague along. A young guy with a sheepish expression.

One of you not enough, Mary? Felt you had to tag team? So you can keep an eye on both of us in case we decide to throw our son around? I glance at Richard and hope he can read my look: *Act normal. Don't give them anything. Please. A normal family on a special day.*

And within a few minutes the remainder of the guests have arrived and I don't have time to think, and I can't do anything but behave as though everything *is* normal.

Social services asked us to keep the numbers small but even at that, some people are notable by their absence: Julia and Melinda are here, with their husbands and kids, but not Esme. My mum has come, but not my dad. None of my old friends are here, except Ben, of course.

Ben has brought Oliver a beautiful, hand-painted, wooden train. It is exactly the kind of gift people without children buy. People with children know that they only want to play with plastic crap. Even though I know the train will end up as an ornament, I love it and give Ben a warm kiss on the cheek.

'I hope everything is OK between us,' I whisper before pulling away.

'Of course,' Ben replies. 'Always.'

Richard gestures for me to come over. I realise he's been watching. With an apologetic smile at Ben I go to him.

'Be careful there,' Richard says.

'What?'

'You know what I mean.'

'He's helping me.'

'I bet he is.'

'What's that supposed to mean?'

'Oh, come on.'

'Not everyone has an agenda, you know.'

'Everyone has an agenda.'

'Not everyone's like you.'

'You're still my wife.'

'Ha!' I turn from him and fix a frozen smile to my face for the benefit of Mary and her pubescent sidekick.

Julia comes over to me. 'Esme sends her love,' she says, quaffing Pimms, her baby trying to clamber up her calves. For an insane second I hate her for having a name that begins with J. J, the single letter that cast my already shaky life out to sea. I am thrown back into the moment of seeing it in Richard's phone and I feel panic rise like a hot bubble in my chest.

'She sends her love but she's not here.'

'She had something else on,' she says. Then, in a lower voice. 'Actually, I think she just feels a bit ... odd about things.'

'Oh, *she* feels odd? Poor Esme!'

Julia rubs my arm in what I suppose is meant to be a supportive way, and I resist the temptation to shake her off. I try to smile and change the subject. 'Hey, Henry looks like he's trying to walk already!'

'Yes, the little bugger. He's never still.'

'How was his birthday?' If there was a party, I wasn't invited. Henry was born a few days before Oliver. I remember at the time, Julia sent a text to the rest of us in the group, assuring us that labour 'wasn't that bad, really!'

'Oh, it was lovely, thanks. I mean, you know, quiet. But they don't really understand what's going on at this age, do they?' She gives a forced laugh. I suppose there was a party, then. I start to zone out a little, gazing down the garden at where Ollie is tumbling around on the grass, his dad tickling him, Mary hovering nearby. I click back into the conversation when Julia says she has written a letter for Henry to mark the occasion, and she plans to write him one every year and give them to him when he turns eighteen.

'Well, that's a nice idea,' I say tightly. 'I might do the same. But maybe I'll start when Ollie's two.' *You know, assuming he's back and assuming I'm not in prison or something.*

I try to spend as much time as possible playing with Ollie, but at the same time I'm distracted, hyper-vigilant, my eyes flickering over the guests and trying to keep watch on all of them at once. People have fallen into couples. Martha and her friend Del, in the corner of the garden, smoking and failing to disguise it. Melinda and Richard. Julia and Ben, who look bemused. Mel and Julia's husbands, talking about football, the universal language of men thrown together by their wives. My mother and Cynthia. *Oh, God*. My mother and Cynthia, talking. This never ends well.

I lift Ollie onto my hip. Now that he's had the cast off, his grip is back to its usual super-strength and he clings to me. I edge over to where the two women are deep in conversation. Thankfully, the main topic of Mum's chat seems to be the traffic; unbelievably bad for a Sunday, apparently. My parents live in St Albans, a good hour around the M25. Cynthia is half-listening, a look of distaste on her face. She makes little secret of the fact that she has no idea why anyone would voluntarily live north of London.

Despite the apparently innocuous conversation, they both fall silent as I get near. My mother gives a tight smile.

'How's my lovely grandson, then?' she coos. 'Look how big you're getting, darling.' For a horrified moment I think she means me (it wouldn't be that surprising), then I realise she is holding her hands out to Ollie, who is wriggling and clinging to me even more tightly. 'You must be looking after him well, Cynthia.'

'Oh, we're doing our best.' Richard's mother smiles.

I happen on Richard and Bruce, Julia's husband, looking at dates on their phones to try to set up a game of golf 'for the dads'. *How dare he?* I know I said act normal, but this is bang out of order. I snap.

'No! *You* –' I point at Richard with a shaking finger '– have opted out of family life, let's be clear about that. You don't get to pick and choose. In fact, I think it's time you left.' Bruce, mouth slack with cartoonish shock, slopes away. I march into the house and Mary follows me.

I stand at the kitchen worktop and down an entire glass of wine, not pausing to consider what she might think about this. I remember the notes at the CPC: 'Mother absent on the evening of injury (intoxicated)'. I look at her.

'Do you want to tell me what's going on?' she says. I stare out of the window.

'This was a bad idea,' I murmur. 'I've had hardly any time with Ollie, there are all these people here ... I'm trying to be normal ... I don't know.' I wipe a hand over my face.

'And Richard?'

I flinch. 'Yes. Richard ...'

'What's going on between you?'

I don't know what makes me say it. Maybe because I look out of the window and see Richard refilling Julia's glass, his head cocked in that way of his, while she laughs and chatters and blushes. *I wish he would just* go. I look at Mary, who is waiting patiently for some definitive word from me, and then I lower my head and say, 'The truth is, nothing would surprise me, Mary. I'm not sure any more *what* he's capable of.'

Chapter Twenty-Two

Richard

Two days after the birthday party, Mary calls me and asks me in 'for a chat'. Well, actually she offers to come to the house, but since I don't technically live there any more, I make up some story that I will be passing their offices that afternoon anyway so will go to her.

'Look forward to seeing you, Mary,' I say, trying to keep the lightness in my voice that usually works with women.

'One o'clock,' she says, and puts the phone down.

She's a bit friendlier in person, but my guard is up. I'm always suspicious when they ask to see one of us on our own. She brings me a cup of tea.

'How are things?' she asks.

'Well, we miss Oliver, obviously.' I don't bother to disguise the irritation in my voice. 'He seems to be doing OK at my mum's though, thank God.' It's been forty-nine days, I want to say. Forty-nine days and nights with him not at home. Oh yes, Sally is not the only one who counts the days. She records them on the calendar in the kitchen, scratching through each date with a single line, like a prisoner marking time.

'Yes, we're pleased with the care he's getting there.' She leans forward. 'How are things at home?' I just stare at her; fold my arms. 'Between you and Sally?' She sits back again, with a look that says *I can out-do you; I can wait in silence all day*. Well, well, well, Mary, I think, underneath the old clothes and scruffy hair, there's steel in you.

She wins. 'It's a stressful time,' I say eventually.

'Yes, I understand,' she says smoothly. I feel my leg start to tremble; the corner of my eye twitches. There is rage building in my chest; I will it back down.

'I wanted to talk to you,' she goes on, looking down at the prop in her lap, a notebook with hardly anything in it. Flicks through its pointless pages, 'about Martha.'

OK, this is unexpected. Martha?

'What about her?' I ask.

'I'll get to the point.' *I wish you would*. 'Sally told us that you used to hit Martha, when she was a little girl.'

Everything goes still.

I didn't hit her often. And it was controlled. I always gave a warning. Consistency is the key thing, in my opinion. With parenting, it's all about follow through, and consistency. I would say, 'If you do that one more time, I'll smack you.' And if she did, I did. Simple.

Zoe was never interested; she always said discipline was my responsibility. She would be no good at it, she said.

When I met Sally, she had a different view of it all. And she sort of convinced me. It's not often someone changes my mind about things. Anyway, at that stage Martha was much older – I couldn't really put a ten-year-old over my knee – and much better behaved. So you could argue that what I'd been doing had worked. But I stopped anyway.

Then, I don't know why, when she was pregnant with Oliver, Sally started bringing it all up again. In a sort of panicky way, she'd say things out of the blue, like 'You're not going to hit this child, are you?' or, when she was feeling more bolshie, she'd say it as a statement – 'I won't let you hit my child' – with protective hands over her stomach. There it was already – '*my* child', excluding me. And everything she said seemed to come from some book she'd read. Those bloody parenting bibles.

In frustration, I'd said, 'For Christ's sake, Sally, you can't find out everything from a book. Like how to be a parent. You can't just read up on that.' It wasn't meant as a criticism, not really. But looking back, that might have been the beginning of the end for us. She carried on.

'Research now shows that the carrot works, but not the stick,' Sally had read aloud, giving me a pointed look.

'Sally told you this?' I ask Mary now.

'Yes.'

'Not Martha.'

'Not Martha. We could speak to her again, of course – I don't suppose she'd *lie* to us.' Mary narrows her eyes.

'Well, I did hit her, yes, once or twice, but you know, everyone used to smack their kids then. It wasn't frowned on like it is now.'

'You should have told us.'

'Why? There's a difference between tapping a toddler on the bottom and breaking a baby's arm.'

'Is there?'

'Of course there is.'

'Why do you think Martha never mentioned this to us herself?'

'I don't know.'

'Protective, is she? Would you say?'

'No more so than any daughter. Besides which, I don't suppose it's ever bothered her. I can't imagine why it would bother Sally.'

'No, it's interesting, isn't it? That she should bring it up now, I mean.'

'Is it?'

'Did your parents hit you, Richard?'

I flinch. It isn't something I ever talk about. I don't think it did me any harm. I just don't like to talk about it.

My mum never hit me – she made my dad do it. I think she liked making me wait until he got home; the anticipation of the slap around the legs was worse than the slap itself when it came, inevitably half-hearted and awkward.

I don't know why he went along with it.

I don't know why I hated him for it and not her.

'Sometimes,' I say. 'Like I said, it wasn't always frowned on.'

'No.' She is watching me closely; I shift in my seat. 'I suppose not.' At that moment the door opens and a man I've never seen before comes into the room, holding a sheaf of papers. He hands them, wordlessly, to Mary, and she scans the pages, frowning. After a few moments she looks up at me.

'It looks like you can go,' she says, 'for now. We'll be in touch.'

On the way back, I start to wonder what else Sally has told them about me. The times I've lost my temper. Am I their number one suspect, now? Is she deliberately trying to hurt me?

I think of the thing she said to me about them at the start: 'They're trying to paint me as depressive, you as violent.' It hadn't occurred to me, then, that either of us would try to embellish those particular paintings. Things were shaky between us but we were still a team, then. Or so I thought.

There are things I've held back, when they've asked me about Sally. Like the time, about three months before the night Ol broke his arm, she called me at work and said, 'Come home early, please.' In the background I'd heard screaming. Ol was sleeping really badly at that time, and we were trying 'controlled crying' at night times, but it was failing miserably. Mainly because Sally kept breaking, kept getting up and scooping him out of the cot, taking him downstairs. She would be gone for hours, rocking him in the pram, once even strapping him into the car and taking him on a long drive in an attempt to send him off.

So we'd decided she would try it at nap time, instead, to start with; it would be easier in the light of day, I'd said, you'll be calmer, more able to cope with the crying.

But when I got through the door she was sitting on the stairs, her face haunted, streaked with tears. She looked shattered. Oliver was still screaming, although it had taken me twenty minutes to get back from work. 'He won't stop,' she was chanting, 'he won't stop. I've got to get out of here, I can't stand it.'

I didn't say anything but strode past her, up the stairs and into Ol's room. He was sitting up in his cot, bedclothes and toys strewn around him. He was crying so wildly that he was gulping for air, his voice hoarse. There was the unmistakeable stench of shit in the air.

I picked him up and as I changed his nappy I checked him over, cast my eyes and traced my fingers over every inch of his skin. I don't know what I was expecting to find. I never admitted that to anyone.

I keep trying to call Jenna, send her loads of texts, and she keeps ignoring me. So I turn up at the café. It's busy, full of students and gossiping mums. I glance around to make sure none of Sally's friends are in that crowd. Jenna is behind the counter, shouting orders to a boy who looks barely out of school and is trying to keep up with shaking hands. I just want to see her; I assumed she would blank me, so I'm surprised when she looks at me and says, 'I'm glad you're here.'

I order my coffee – one of the other baristas serves me – and I take it to the furthest corner of the café and cradle it in my hands. Before too long she is walking towards me, that swing still in her hips, that half-smile on her face that has always driven me crazy. But as she sits down, the smile falls away.

'Richard,' she says.

'Listen,' I say, 'I know you don't want to see me, but—'

'No, you listen,' she says. 'Don't come back here. And you can do me another favour. Tell that sad cow of a wife of yours not to call me again.'

Chapter Twenty-Three

Sally

When I see Richard's number flash up on my phone, my stomach does that little flip, like it used to when we were first together. I don't know why he still has such an effect on me: despite everything, I still want to please him, impress him. Still want him to want me. I wonder why he's calling. I answer in as breezy a voice as I can muster.

He doesn't even say hello but launches right in. He's furious.

'What the hell do you think you're doing, calling her?' *Oh.* And just like that, my walls are back up.

'Calling who?' I might as well get a rise out of him.

'You know damn well. What are you playing at?'

'You've seen her, then.' *He's still seeing her.* My stomach churns.

'Don't do that. Don't turn this back onto me. You've no right—'

'I've every right to call whoever I like. Why shouldn't I speak to her? We've got something in common, after all.'

'Just leave her alone, OK?'

'Whatever you say. Is that all?'

'No, it's not, actually. What's with running to social services telling them I used to smack my daughter?'

'Oh, I thought they already knew,' I say innocently.

'No, you fucking didn't.'

'It's true, though, isn't it? And you wouldn't intentionally lie, would you? Not over something so important?'

'If this is the game we're playing,' he hisses, 'dropping each other in it, then I can play, too. I've got plenty of material.'

I hang up.

Richard has a temper; anyone can see that. When something isn't going his way, he turns it outwards. Not like some men who, I'm told, turn in on themselves like a leaf. Richard fizzes with energy, sometimes rage.

But he's never hit me. He never would. I once told him that was the one thing I wouldn't tolerate in our marriage. One strike and you're out. I wonder now if he read that as tacit permission to cheat.

And now a dark part of me fantasises about telling them that he did, that he hit me. How could they disprove it? They already know he hit Martha, and that he lied about it the first time they asked. If I tell them he hit me, surely they would believe it, the nightmare could end and I could get Ollie back. This is where the madness of not having him has led me.

And I don't even know which of them I mean when I say 'him'.

I won't do it, of course, but I'm thinking about it, which is frightening enough. I don't know myself any more.

Then Daniel Stone calls me with the blood test results. The tests have shown that Oliver has unusually low levels of Vitamin D. I say, 'That's good, right? For our case, I mean.'

'Yes and no.' He pauses. 'It was just the one fracture they found, wasn't it?'

'Yes, they scanned his whole body.'

'Hmm.'

'What is it?' I thought that was a good thing; if they'd found other injuries we would surely have been dragged through the courts by now, although that threat still hangs over us. I hear family courts are harrowing but it's hard to imagine how much worse it could be than this limbo.

'It's just, if his Vitamin D were to blame, if he had rickets or a condition like it, it's likely he'd have other breaks. Other issues with the bones that should have shown up on X-rays. Little cracks in the ribs, that kind of thing.'

'Nope, nothing that they found. So this isn't a good result for us after all?'

'It might help. A copy of the results has already gone to your woman in social services but I'll write you a report as well. The best I can do is conclude that there's no way we can be one-hundred per cent certain Oliver's injury was caused by ... I mean, was non-accidental.'

'Thank you.'

'I'll bring it over to you as soon as it's done. I hope it helps, Sally.'

I clean the house from top to bottom. I light candles. I put a curry on to slow-cook, and before long the kitchen is filled with aromas of cumin and ginger and cloves. It's the first time I've cooked in I don't know how long. I put on a little make-up. As I wait for Richard to arrive, I take deep breaths. I'm together, I'm handling things, coping, and I will show him. When I called him to tell him about the report, he'd answered using a tone of voice that told me he was still angry with me, but I'd stayed calm and said I had to see him, it was important. For Ollie. He'd softened, then.

'Something smells good.' He steps into the hall, bringing cool evening air with him.

I nod. 'Curry.' He looks at me as though he expects me to offer him some. He certainly looks hungry. He's lost weight. 'For me and Martha,' I add. And as I say it, I feel a pang as I realise it's been a long time since we've all sat down and eaten together.

'Where is Martha?'

'Oh, she's gone out. She's out a lot these days.' In fact, I don't know where she is. I get a creeping sense of dread – I've been leaving her to it, maybe too much – and I resolve to do better. I start to chew my nail then stop myself, putting my hand in my pocket. 'I suppose it's not the most fun place to be right now.' Then, more brightly, 'I expect she'll be back when she realises her belly's empty.'

'Thanks for looking after her.'

'Well, I've not much option, have I?'

'Please Sally, let's not fight.'

I sigh. 'No, you're right. Let's not. Come on in and sit down. I need to show you this.'

After outlining the Vitamin D findings, Daniel Stone has written a compelling concluding statement. In it, he says that when a child is injured, if there's no witnessed accident, you can't just conclude that the parents did it; there has to be a grey area.

'Let's hope the grey area is enough,' I'd said to him, and he'd assured me he would make the same statement in court, if it came to that.

'This has got to be good news,' Richard says now, the report in his hand.

'Well, not for Ollie,' I say, frowning. I've been thinking about this ever since I got the news: the weird irony of feeling pleased that there's something wrong with your child.

'Well, no,' he says hurriedly, 'that's not what I meant.'

'It's OK. I spoke to Stone about it, and a friend from the hospital, and they both said in some cases, low Vitamin D levels in babies can correct themselves, especially if they're formula-fed. At any rate, it seems it can be easily treated with medication. So he should be all right, soon enough.'

'OK. Good.'

'That's not all though. Daniel seems to think it would be better if Ollie had other fractures.'

'Funny, I got the impression social services hoped for that too, but for different reasons. Seems like regardless of whether they're for us or against us, people want Ol to be more hurt than he actually was. I can't get my head around it.' I look at Richard when he says 'us', look at the circles under his eyes. For a moment he feels like *my* Richard again; there is a throb inside me so hard, so violent I feel like it must be visible on the outside.

'Maybe we can persuade them to do another chest film,' I say. 'Sometimes little fractures on the ribs don't show up. If they find one now, it might help.'

'Sally—'

'Right then,' I say, looking away, 'I'll pass it onto Mary – let's see if this makes any difference.'

'We need to get it to them quick. Get it to them before they get us to court. Because if that happens …' He doesn't have to say any more. I've seen it too, on the news. The case of a family whose son was put up for adoption by the family courts before they could prove in the criminal courts that they hadn't hurt him. And now they can't get him back. Ever.

'We can't let him be adopted,' I whisper. Even the words seem so ludicrous; it's such a ridiculously unfair idea, I can barely say them aloud.

'I know,' he says, and after a few moments, 'You've done really well, Sally.'

'Yes,' I mutter, 'while one of us has been fucking someone else, one of us has been busy trying to get our son back.'

'Let's not fight,' he says again.

'I don't want to,' I say, 'but there's this massive anger in me that's got nowhere to go. I haven't been able to get mad at you. I've not had time, or energy, and even when I first found out, you were out the door so fast I didn't even get the chance to shout and scream at you. Which is what you deserved.'

'I know. I—'

'You went to her, I suppose?'

'What?'

'That night, that night you left. You went straight to her.' Of course, when I spoke to Jenna she made it clear that she wasn't interested, that the whole thing had blown over. But I'm not sure whether to believe her. It could be a bluff. I am so sensitive to being made a fool of I will watch for it everywhere, now. For all I know they could be shacked up together.

'Yes, I did,' he admits.

It hits me like a blow to the stomach; here I go again, asking questions when I know I won't like the answers.

'Why?'

'I didn't know where else to go.'

'Not that night, I mean the whole thing. Why?'

He shrugs. 'I don't know. Why does anyone? Company. Comfort. Excitement.'

'Sex.' He doesn't say anything. 'You could have had that here, with me. What was wrong with me?'

'There's nothing wrong with you.'

'Oh, there must be. Come on, let's have it.' Here I go, I think, chipping away, picking at the scab, but I can't stop. 'What was it? I was too fat, too saggy? You wanted a young, firm body? I was boring? Crap in bed? What?'

'You really want to know?'

'Yes! I really do.' I really don't.

'All right then.' His voice is cool but his hands are shaking. 'I wanted to have sex with someone who didn't turn away every time I tried to touch them, or said they were too tired or worst of all went through the motions looking as though they'd rather be anywhere else.'

'Oh, I'm sorry. Sorry I was too exhausted from birthing and looking after *your son* to be up for it every night.'

'Oh, here we go again. He's my son when it suits you, isn't he? Only most of the time, he's *your* son, and I'm pushed out, but when the conversation gets tough he's mine. Like I forced you to have him or something. Ha! Well, I've got news for you, he's *our* son and it's us who have to sort this whole mess out.'

'You think I don't know that? What do you think all this is for?' I point at the report. 'I will get him back and let me tell you, no one will take him away from me again.'

'What's that supposed to mean? Is that a threat?'

'Take it how you like, Richard. You're the one who doesn't want to be part of this family.'

'When did I say that?'

'You didn't say it. You decided it when you got into bed with that … that slag.'

'Don't call her that.'

'I'll call her what I want. What would you call her?'

He falls silent, stares at the floor. When he looks up, he says, 'It's over, anyway.'

'Oh, I'm sorry.'

'Sarcasm really doesn't suit you.'

'Well, it's not up to you any more what does and doesn't suit me,' I say. And it hits me: *it's over, it's really over*. Whether Jenna's still on the scene or not, it's over. I've always justified my affair with Richard by the fact that we'd stayed together and got married. Like we were meant to be, so the end justified the means. I don't know what it means if the end is no longer the end. If the justification for what we did no longer exists. What does that say about either of us?

We sit in silence for a while, both bristling. Eventually I say, 'Was it worth it, then? Just tell me that. If it's come to nothing, this … this thing you did. Was it so good that it was worth losing me? Losing us?'

He stares at me.

'Of course not.' He puts his head in his hands and I think for a minute he's going to cry, but Richard never cries. I don't know what I'll do if he does. I already desperately want to put my arms around him. 'Is that really it?' he says in a mumble. 'You won't give me another chance?'

'What, because you've been dumped?' I laugh, but it isn't funny.

'No. No, not because of that.'

I want to say all the things a strong woman would say: I don't need you; I won't be anyone's second choice; I deserve more. That was what Ben had told me. He'd warned me, he said Richard would try to come back.

'He'll want to get back with you because he feels guilty,' Ben had said. 'And you're worth more than that.'

'Am I?' I'd asked, and he'd said yes, yes, but all I could think was, how can I be worth more than the thing I want most in the world – my family, mended?

Now Richard says, 'I love you.'

I want to close my ears. I've seen the movies and TV dramas, watched this scene in other lives, fictional lives, but I still find myself acting out the clichés.

'Don't touch me,' I say when he tries to put his arm around me. But it's not because I'm disgusted, angry, repulsed by what he's done, although I am all of those things. It's because if he touches me I won't be able to let him go. And to hold onto him I have to forgive him. I don't know if I can do that.

'You should go,' I say.

'Yes. I'm sorry, Sal.'

I get up, smoothing imaginary creases out of my clothes, running the chant in my head – *you're worth more, you're worth more* – but I don't really believe it. I have to get him to leave, now, before I change my mind. I lead the way into the hall, then hesitate.

'Richard. Hang on, I'll put you some of the curry into Tupperware.'

'Thank you, Sal.' He catches my hand. 'Whatever happens … with us. We're still Ol's mum and dad. Let's hope what you've got here helps us get our boy back.'

Chapter Twenty-Four

Martha

I plan to just follow the usual script: say the person's name, get confirmation it's them, then say: this is for you. Hand over the package, take the money, leave. Usually the whole transaction takes seconds. It's one of the reasons I can persuade myself I'm not really doing anything.

But this lad, Paddy his name is, seems to want to chat. He leans against the doorframe, looking at me. He is kind of geeky-looking – tall and skinny, wearing a scruffy T-shirt of some band I've never heard of – and he has a nice smile.

'Why don't you come in?' he says.

'I don't think so,' I mumble, looking behind me. I'm still holding out the parcel; he hasn't taken it yet. Then I notice sounds coming from the rooms behind him: the TV, and voices. And the warmth that leaks out of the house and seems to touch me. I realise how cold I am. The rain is the kind that comes down in sheets, seems to fall so hard that it could break right through the roads and flagstones and drown the earth. I have my hood up but I'm still soaked.

My bike has a puncture so I've been walking my 'rounds'. I'm tired, and hungry.

'We're having pizza,' Paddy says brightly, and as he takes the package from my hand his fingers brush across mine. 'Seriously, come on in – you're freezing.' I shrug; where's the harm? Something in the chuckling voices from inside the house, and the way he said 'we', have relaxed me a bit. And he is telling the truth about the pizza – I can smell it. My stomach growls.

He closes the door behind me and leads me past the front room, which I can see at a glance is made up as a bedroom. Ah, it's a student house. There is washing hanging over every radiator: pants, socks, scrunched up T-shirts. Now that the door is shut, the smell of the food mingles with the slightly stale odour of laundry left too long or not dried properly. A boys' student house, I think to myself with a smile.

The back room is dark, the curtains all closed even though it's only early evening, the only lights coming from the TV and the half-ajar door to a tiny kitchen. There are three other guys; two on the battered sofa, one sprawled on the floor.

'Budge up, then,' Paddy says, giving the sofa a kick and causing one of the lads who is sitting there to spill the beer he's just brought to his mouth. 'We've had a delivery. Make room for Brendan's little helper.'

There is a snide tone to his voice that I didn't notice out on the doorstep, and the darkness in the room makes me uneasy, but I try to ignore it and squeeze onto the end of the couch. I'm still thinking about the hammering rain outside. It's warm in here, and I don't have to stay long.

I glance at the discarded pizza boxes on the carpet, now containing only crusts.

'Hmm,' says Paddy, 'sorry about that. Greedy bastards. Here.' He passes me a bottle of beer, and the smile I saw before is back.

The film, some action movie I have only been half-watching, finishes and one of the boys changes the DVD. 'This should be good,' he says, glancing at me.

The screen turns from black to washed-out colour. The camerawork is a little shaky as it pans around a room, it looks like a hotel room: a mirror, a desk, chair, a balcony. A bed.

'What's this, a home movie?' I laugh, but the laugh stops half way when the camera zooms in on the bed. A woman, dressed in high heels, bra, and tiny shorts, is sitting on the edge of the bed, her legs wide apart. She stares into the camera with vacant eyes as she slides her hand into her shorts.

'I'm not sure I want to watch this,' I mumble, but the boys ignore me. Apart from Paddy; he is watching me closely. On the screen, the girl wriggles out of her shorts; she is wearing nothing underneath. I stare at her fingernails; they are so *long*. Surely what she's doing would *hurt*? Apparently not; she is panting, her head thrown back. One of the lads turns up the volume and they all snigger. There is the sound of a door opening and closing and two men come into view at the edge of the picture.

'Look, I really need to go.' I can feel my face burning. Paddy kneels in front of me and puts his hands on my legs. I flinch.

'No, no you don't.' He smiles. 'Stay and watch the movie with us.'

I press my knees together, but he is slipping his palms between them, trying to push them apart. 'I bet you'll like it.'

'No, I don't want to.' I look around the room wildly, trying not to let my eyes land on the TV, and see that two of the other three are watching me and grinning. The one on the floor appears to be asleep. The guy who'd spilled his beer suddenly reaches over and grabs my breast, hard. 'Hey!' I shout. 'What do you think you're doing?' But my voice is shaking.

'Oh, come on,' he mutters. 'We know all about you. Don't pretend you're not up for it.' His other hand is idling around the crotch of his jeans. There are little beads of sweat on his forehead. I push his hand away and he brings it up to my head, takes hold of my hair.

'Yeah.' Paddy leers, and with one abrupt movement pushes my legs apart. 'Brendan's told us all about you.' The mention of Brendan's name makes something in me snap, and with a noise that is meant to be 'No' but just comes out as a scream, I lift the empty beer bottle in my left hand and smash it into the side of Paddy's head.

Then I jump up and run out of the house.

For some reason I run straight to Brendan's. I don't know what I'm expecting there but it's probably more than I would get at home. It isn't until I'm standing on his front path, hands on my knees, trying to catch my breath, that I realise Paddy didn't give me the money.

'Fuck,' I mutter aloud, but I've already rung the bell and suddenly Brendan is standing in the doorway, framed by light.

'What's up with you?' he drawls in a familiar voice, made slow by weed.

'They … they were …' I can't breathe properly, much less speak.

'You'd better come in.' He stands aside and I stagger into the hall. He doesn't ask me up to his room, just looks at me expectantly.

'Paddy and his … mates,' I gasp. 'That was a fucking nightmare.' I realise there are tears on my face. Brendan is just staring at me, his arms folded.

'Have you got the money?'

'What?'

'The. Money.' He says the words slowly as though talking to an idiot. 'Fuck's sake. Silly cow.'

'Well, no, but—'

'What did you say?'

'No, I haven't got the money.' I start to sob, hating myself for it.

'You haven't got. The. Money.'

'He didn't give it to me. I—' and before I can say anything else, a fist, Brendan's fist, flies into my jaw, knocking me backwards. Pain explodes upwards into my face, and my mouth fills up with blood.

Then the front door is opened and I'm pushed out onto the path.

'Come back when you've got the money.' The door slams and the hall light goes out.

Chapter Twenty-Five

Sally

Time, which was such a precious commodity when Ollie was at home, there never being quite enough of it, now stretches out around me like a vast lake. It doesn't take much to just look after yourself, as well as a teenager who's never there and won't let you look after her anyway.

I decide to do a Richard detox. Maybe if I'm not sitting looking at his stuff I will stop wanting him. I start in the bedroom; I can't throw his things out, I suppose he will be back for them, but I can contain them. I make a pile of his clothes and clear out one drawer to stuff them all into. I force it closed and sit against it for a while, as though to keep a fairy-tale monster caged. I rifle through the washing basket and, taking out all his things, tip them into a bin-bag and throw it into the bottom of the wardrobe.

Next are the pictures. I take down every photograph in the house that includes him, leaving out Martha's room, of course, although who knows, she might thank me if I did. It's hard to judge how she feels about him these days:

one minute, she seems indifferent; then at Ollie's party, she was all over him. Well, at least until Del got there. Her partner in crime. I smile for a moment, envying her that close female friendship. Then I stop smiling, and remember how, after the party, I heard her crying behind the door of her room. I feel sorry that I hadn't knocked and asked if she was OK, although she'd have almost certainly ignored me.

Richard says he didn't cheat on the kids, he cheated on me. Somehow that makes it worse, as though I've been singled out for my particular awfulness as a partner.

He says cheating doesn't *de facto* make you a bad parent. (I've never heard him say 'de facto' before and I wonder if it's one of *her* sayings.) But, doesn't it? Surely it makes you a bad parent if you cheat knowing it could rip your family apart? Never mind the fact that ours is already broken. If you choose to leave and be with someone else, and this means leaving your kids, for at least some of the time, this does make you a bad parent, surely?

I find myself wanting to fight, not just for Ollie, but for Martha, too. This takes me by surprise. I don't know whether it's just spite. Martha and I have hardly been the best of friends. Maybe I see myself in her, a bit. I can't go back and protect my teenage self, but I can protect Martha.

Into the kitchen, and I locate all the useless stuff in the cupboards that was only there for Richard: peanut butter, Branston Pickle, bloody Berocca. Things I hate. I sweep it all into the bin. All the while, I try to build a mantra in my head, a list of Richard's faults, of the times he's let me down. As if this most recent disappointment isn't enough.

Not long after we moved into the house, Richard arranged a dinner party. I was heavily pregnant, we were in the middle of decorating and the guests were all his friends, so I wasn't overjoyed, but I went along with it. In some ways I felt I'd 'dragged' him away from London, so I wanted to show willing by supporting his social life.

According to Richard, the 'perfect number' for a dinner party was eight. That was why I ended up meeting three other couples for the first time that night; with hormones playing havoc with my attention span, I wished I could ask them all to wear name badges, but suspected this idea wouldn't be well received.

Thankfully I'd got potted biographies and physical descriptions from Richard in advance; the latter were stunningly accurate, so I was able to greet each guest with a sincere 'Oh, you must be ... *whoever*', along with a glass of champagne and a plate of canapés.

First to the door, as Richard had predicted, were his accountant Jerry and his wife Hannah. Jerry was a round-faced, waistless sort of guy ('Like a weeble,' Richard had said, a bit unkindly, I thought) and his wife a shy brunette. Pat and Ali followed; they'd been Richard's neighbours in Notting Hill and I was most nervous about meeting them because, of course, they were friends with Zoe. 'Oh, so *this* is where you've run off to,' Ali cooed as soon as she came through the door, looking the house up and down as she took Richard in an overlong embrace. She air-kissed me but there was no warmth in it. She was the kind of woman who seemed perpetually to have her nose turned up and her eyes narrowed. In time I would learn that that was just the way she was, and not to be intimidated by it.

Richard often described himself as having 'acquaintances rather than friends', but his main actual friend, Darren, came along with a girlfriend who could only have been in her early twenties, judging by her unlined face and sparkly eyes. 'Don't go to too much trouble to remember her name,' Richard whispered to me when we were in the kitchen. 'Darren's bedroom has a revolving door. They never last more than a few weeks.' Temporary or not, she certainly seemed to garner attention from the men in the room. She was dressed with so much care that I felt immediately self-conscious in my simple tunic and 'skinny' maternity jeans (who knew there was such a thing?) I sneaked upstairs to put on some jewellery and lip gloss before we sat down.

I was a bit surprised Richard had invited Darren, who was a little rough around the edges, although as it turned out he got along with Jerry well enough. Darren had his own landscaping business and I think Jerry was angling to do his accounts for him, but Darren managed to rebuff the heavy hints he made in that direction.

By the time everyone had had a few drinks (except me of course, nursing soda water and leaving the table from time to time to check on the beef wellington), the party relaxed and everyone seemed to have found their roles, and their voices.

'So, Sally,' said Pat, who seemed amiable enough in contrast to his stuck-up wife, 'we hear you're a pharmacist.'

'That's right.' I smiled.

'Where?' asked Ali in a monotone, looking at her nails. 'Boots in town, is it? Handing out haemorrhoid cream to old ladies?'

I tried to smile.

'No, I work at the hospital,' I said. 'Children's cancer. And what do *you* do, Ali?' I knew very well that Ali didn't work, but lived a very nice life courtesy of Pat's career as a senior actuary.

She blinked and opened her mouth as if to say something.

'Sally's very highly qualified, actually,' Richard interjected, turning his head briefly from his conversation with Jerry's wife; I hadn't realised he was listening. I cast a grateful smile in his direction, but he went on, 'I mean, she's not a doctor, but she's pretty bright.'

Pat nodded quickly.

'Yes, well, it sounds very interesting, I have to say. Did you have to study long?'

'Four years,' I said. *Not a doctor?* What the hell was that supposed to mean?

'She only got a 2:1,' Richard was saying, filling up his own glass, 'but it's still a good degree.'

'*You* don't even have a degree, mate,' piped up Darren from across the table. I saw anger flash across Richard's eyes; most people would miss it but I caught it, there for an instant, then it disappeared.

'True enough,' he said smoothly, with a shrug. He patted my hand. 'I'm really proud of Sally.'

'Excuse me.' I got up. 'I'll go and get the dinner, if everyone's ready.' I was so distracted I tried to get the wellington out of the oven without wearing a glove; I let the dish fall with a clatter back onto the shelf; then stood at the sink, my burned hand under the cold water tap, wondering just *how* Richard had managed to simultaneously praise me and undermine me in one conversation. And more importantly, why?

After the party, he lost it with me. Accused me of flirting with Pat. Even now, when I think of it, I have to remind myself that I was heavily pregnant and what's more, totally in love with Richard. I was no more capable of flirting than I was of running a marathon.

But the flashes were there in his eyes again. The ones I'd seen in Morocco, and occasionally when he was cross with Martha, and actually, more times directed at me than I'd care to admit.

At one time I'd have argued. I'd have accused him of projection, he'd have accused me right back of using fancy words to try to make him feel stupid, because I was *always doing that*, and I'd say *what it means is,* you're *the one who was flirting, you're the cheat after all*, and the cyclical argument would go on and on. (I only ever brought up the cheating to wind him up, if I ever thought he would actually do it, do it to me, I wouldn't have been there.) But I didn't have the strength to fight him – the baby was pulling all the energy out of me – and I wouldn't find it again for a long time.

So I just said, 'Whatever, Richard,' and went to bed, leaving him to clear up and seethe on his own.

I decide to go for a run. I look out of the window; I could do four or five miles before it gets dark. I have no idea whether I can even run two miles; it's been a while. After having Ollie, running seemed like a luxury, a use of time I couldn't afford. Obviously when I was home with him all day, I couldn't leave him. And when Richard got home in the evenings, I always felt that if I suggested it, he would give me one of his looks and we'd get into the usual argument about him being at work all day, this was his time to relax, and on and on. It wasn't worth it. But I can run now; get a bit of the old me back. What else is there to do?

I pull on my trainers. It's raining by the time I leave the house, but I don't mind that. In fact I love running in the rain; it feels like you're fighting God and winning. And then getting into the house, feeling the water cool on your skin, not sure how much is rain and how much sweat, the tingling, the sheer physical feel of it. Enough to connect you to your body and disconnect you from your mind.

It's a bit like the high I used to get from starving myself. There's a certain satisfaction that comes from being full, of course, but it's nothing like the one you get from being empty. Hollowed out. You feel lighter, and the pain in your stomach, like the ache in your legs from running, just lets you know you are alive.

We live on a hill and I stand in front of the house, water already trickling down my nose, and look both ways. Left goes up, right goes down. I could start with the downhill, warm up my legs, build up to the climb. Or I could take the steep route, get my heart pumping right away, then enjoy the easy route back.

I turn left.

I am on the downhill, about half a mile from home, and I feel my mobile buzzing in the pocket of my running trousers. I slip a hand behind me, fumble for the zip, slow up my pace but don't stop.

I look at the number. It's Mary. I stop and pick up.

'Sally? Apologies for the lateness of the call,' she says.

'That's OK,' I gasp. I really am out of shape.

'Are you all right?'

'Yes … yes. I'm out running. Hold on.' I lean forward, then back, stretching and trying to get my breath. 'What is it?'

'I'm just calling to let you know we are dropping the case against you.' Just like that; so casual. I have to ask her to repeat the words.

'We're dropping the case,' she says again. 'That doesn't mean Oliver won't be still … of interest to us, but it does mean—'

'He's coming home? I get … I mean, we, we … we get him back?'

'Yes. He's coming home.'

When I get back in, the house is silent and in darkness. I'm used to that, these days. I'm not sure what I'm supposed to do, now: celebrate? Ollie is coming home, tomorrow. Just like that. Almost three months of being apart, and tomorrow he will be back. Tomorrow everything will be different and the nightmare will be over. I wander into the kitchen and open the fridge, the light washing over me. I look at the contents and think about the things I will buy, first thing in the morning, for Ollie. His favourite yogurts. Extra milk. Bananas. I allow myself a smile.

I pour a glass of wine and decide to have a bath. There is an unopened packet of tea lights in a drawer; I take them out, look around for some matches. When was the last time I had a candlelit bath with a glass of wine? Perhaps it will calm me down; I feel such an odd mix of elation, nerves, and sadness. Richard isn't here; things are right again, but not right. How can I be happy?

I switch on the landing light and climb the stairs. I notice immediately that the bathroom door is shut, which is unusual. Wedging the candles and matches under one arm to free up a hand, I take hold of the handle and push. It doesn't open; there is something on the other side, pushing the door back. A weight. I frown. I put my glass down.

With both hands on the handle I shoulder the door, and get it open enough to fit my head into the gap.

And that's when I see her.

Chapter Twenty-Six

Martha

Someone is shaking me, a gentle shaking though, kind of like rocking, it feels pretty nice. I can't see anything but I can hear a voice, although it seems far away. It's Sally.

'Shit, Martha. Wake up! What have you done? What have you done?' *Am I in trouble?* I wonder, but she doesn't sound mad, not exactly. I'm aware of cold tiles underneath me and I try to turn into myself, make myself small and warm. I open my eyes just a fraction and I can see white and red, white and red stripes. 'Santa Claus,' I whisper, and start to giggle. Then I feel a weird pulsing in my arm, and the hands on me have moved to my head, stroking the hair from my forehead. I open my eyes fully and then I see that the white is my skin and the red is blood, too much blood, and I start to scream.

Zoe told me the truth about Santa Claus as soon as I was old enough to ask. It was the Christmas after I turned six.

My mother is a big fan of telling children the truth. I think it's bullshit – you should let kids have their magic for as long as possible.

I was six and I cried for five whole days.

'We have to ring your father,' Sally is saying. 'We've got to get your dad here. Shit! I've no signal.' We are in hospital; I'm not sure how we got here. I look around A&E, at the shuffling drunk buying coffee from the machine, at a cyclist still wearing Lycra, his eyebrow patched up with plasters that ooze blood, at a woman rubbing her leg and moaning softly.

'No,' I manage. 'Not Dad. Please.'

'I'm getting a bit tired of taking my children to hospital in the middle of the night.' She gives a tired, small smile. I think of her coming here that night, with Ol, and how frightened she must have been.

'Sally,' I say, 'did you just call me your child?'

'Yes. Yes, I suppose I did.'

The Irish nurse who patches me up is kind. She's apologetic about referring me to the doctor, saying, 'I have to, you know.' I nod, and before she leaves the room, she says, 'Look after yourself now, Martha, won't you?' I feel tears spring up in my eyes.

The doctor is younger than I expected, and just good-looking enough to make me feel self-conscious about my sorry state. He has a faint accent and a Scandinavian-sounding name. He sits on the bed beside me instead of using the chair.

Somehow because we're both facing outwards, and not each other, it's easy to talk to him. I guess that's his technique.

'It was a mistake,' I say quietly.

'OK,' he says. But then he starts to ask me questions; too many questions, and the wrong ones, because they're not just about me, they're about home. About Dad and Sally. And I realise that our family file must have a sticker on it or something, that our family has a badge attached to it now, some kind of 'suspected abusers' red flag. And I feel suddenly protective, and that's how I end up telling him way more than I planned to. I tell him all about the cutting. It's kind of a relief. But I wonder whether any of this will get back to social services and cause any more trouble.

'It's just ... something I do,' I say miserably. 'It's nothing to do with them. They didn't know. They'd never hurt me.' I think about Sally, sitting out in that waiting room alone, where they'd insisted she stay even though she wanted to come with me. I picture her chewing her nails and looking at the clock.

'Martha, I want you to do two things for me after you leave here,' the doctor says. 'Would that be OK?' I nod slowly. 'One: be safe. Be careful. I don't want to see you here in this state again. What you did tonight was very, very dangerous.

'And the second thing. I'm going to give you some information before you leave. Support groups. Counselling. You're not on your own, you know. And you can get help.' He pauses, stands up and looks at me directly. 'Deal?'

I shrug. 'Deal,' I say. 'Can I go home now please?'

It's the early hours of the morning and still dark outside when we get home but neither of us seems to want to sleep. It's like time has turned upside down. Sally pulls a blanket off the back of the sofa and wraps me in it. It smells of vanilla.

'I thought these were just for show,' I say.

'The blankets?'

'Yes.'

'Is that how you feel here?' She is looking around, at the carefully folded blankets, the cushions, the rug. Everything in the room positioned beautifully.

'Like I can't touch anything? Yes, a bit.'

'Martha. This is your home.'

I nod because I know this is technically true, but the reality is I feel like I'm in a family photo and I'm out on the edges. I was a mistake for Dad and Zoe, I know that, and I was an afterthought, an add-on, to Dad and Sally and Oliver.

'I know you're not mine,' she says, 'not like Ollie is, but I do love you.'

'How can you?'

'Well, it's different,' Sally admits, 'but I do. If I didn't know it before, I knew it as soon as I walked in that bathroom and found you on the floor.'

'I don't know what love is.'

'I'm not sure either.' She laughs. 'Shall we look it up?' She picks up her phone and her fingers move over the screen. 'Here we are,' she says. 'Dictionary.com. Now then ...' she murmurs through a couple of definitions before saying, 'OK, here it is. "A feeling of warm personal attachment or deep affection, as for a parent, child, or friend." Based on that, I'd say I love you,' and with that she puts her arm around my shoulder.

It used to feel awkward when Sally hugged me, like we didn't really fit. But I put my head on her shoulder and it feels OK. She strokes my hair.

'I'm sorry,' I whisper and there is a whole heap of stuff in that sorry. I'm sorry she's had to find me and sort me out, that's the main thing, but I'm also sorry I've been a bit of a bitch to her. She seems to know. She nods.

'I understand,' she says. 'You thought I'd take him from you. Your dad.'

'Did you love him? Dad?'

'I still love him. I think I always will.'

'What's it like?'

'Love?'

'Yeah.'

'"A feeling of warm personal attachment or deep affection ..."'

'Ha, ha. You know what I mean.'

She thinks for a while. 'It's hard to explain. It's ... feeling like you want to be around that person all the time. It's caring what happens to them. Caring about them more than about yourself, I suppose.' She pauses. 'It's wanting them. *Needing* them.'

'No matter what?'

She nods. 'No matter what.'

I tell her about the box in the wardrobe. She asks me whether I want to show it to her; I shake my head no. I tell her how it makes me feel. Peaceful.

'Wow,' she says. 'In my day it was just eating disorders.'

I laugh in spite of myself.

'*Just* eating disorders?'

'Well, we didn't even call it that. Most girls just used to make themselves throw up, or only eat apples or something. You guys today are way more switched on. It's frightening.'

'Literally – we've got the Internet.'

'Hey, I'm not that old! And even when I was your age, we had … but look, it was nothing like it is now, anyway.'

'When you said most girls … about the throwing up and stuff. What about you?'

Sally is quiet for a long time.

'Well, I wasn't most girls. I did it properly. Unfortunately.'

I look at her and I can see how she would have looked when she was my age. And I notice for the first time how much weight she's lost since Oliver went.

'Do you want to talk about it?' I say.

She laughs, but it's a kind laugh.

'It's not about me, Mar,' she says, and I don't mind the 'Mar' this time. 'I just want you to know I understand. I mean, kind of. And you can talk to me.'

'I've messed everything up,' I say.

'What do you mean?'

'I think I've screwed up my exams,' I tell her, although that isn't what I mean. I mean, it's true, but it's the least of it. She tilts her head, nods. I can't tell her the rest. Can I?

'Well, if that's the case, we'll deal with it,' she says. 'You can re-sit them. We'll … I'll support you. And your dad will. You'll always have a home here. You know that, don't you? Whatever happens between me and your dad.'

'I guess.'

'There's something else, isn't there. Boys?'

'Kind of.'

'When you're young, you think that whatever's going on will last forever, but it won't. It doesn't. Everything passes.'

'Not this,' I say.

'Tell me.'

So I tell her everything.

'I'll go and see his parents,' is the first thing Sally says.

I laugh. 'They won't care. They're dealers too. He's always talking about how his mum is out of it half the time.' She has a look on her face I can't quite work out. I say, 'What?'

'What?' she echoes, shaking her head as though coming out of a trance. 'Oh, sorry. I was just thinking about all the ways we can fuck up our children.' She notices the way I react to her saying the word 'fuck', laughs, and pulls me to her for a full-on hug, which, I'm not gonna lie, is the best I've had in ages.

I'm still worrying about Dad. She didn't call him from the hospital, but now she has this new information, now she knows everything. Will that change things? I chew on the thumb at the end of my 'good' arm. I look at the other arm, wrapped in bandages, and I think about Ol and feel sad for him. I wonder for the first time how much his arm hurt, what kind of pain he felt in his little body.

'Don't tell Dad,' I mumble, thumb still in my mouth. Sally looks at me, frowning.

'Martha, I don't think—'

'Please.' I look up at the ceiling, trying to find the right words for what's in my head. 'I want him to … I don't want him to know all this about me. I want him only to think the best of me.'

Sally gives a big sigh. A look passes over her face, kind of like that weird look of recognition and confusion people get when they've just had a déjà vu.

'I'll have to talk to him,' she says finally, 'but I won't give him the details. OK?'

'OK.' I nod.

'But Martha, if anything like this happens again, I have to get him involved.' She pauses. 'Zoe, too. You understand, don't you?'

'OK,' I say again. 'Thank you.'

We sit up half the night trying to hatch a plan to sort out Brendan Lowe. It almost feels like fun, if I could just imagine for a bit that it isn't my actual life, just a puzzle we're trying to solve. My arm is stinging and I keep rubbing at it but that makes it worse. We say ridiculous, far-fetched stuff, like we'll hire a hit man to bump him off.

'I wish you'd come to us before,' says Sally. 'I'm really sorry you didn't feel you could.'

'You had enough going on. Right? And I so desperately wanted to be a grown-up,' I say. 'I thought I actually was a grown-up. Now, I just want to be a child again.'

'Well, technically you … wait a minute.' Sally sits up straight. We've been slumped under the blankets up to now; the fire has gone out and we're chilly but can't be bothered to relight it. 'That's it! That's exactly it.' She jumps up, tossing the cushion from her lap. When she looks at me her eyes are all shiny.

'You're a child,' she says, 'so that means that what this Brendan character has on his phone is basically child pornography.' I stare at her. 'Child pornography, Mar. Reckon the police will be quite interested in that, don't you?'

'The police?' I start. 'Shit, Sally, no—'

'We don't have to actually do it,' she says patiently. 'We just have to threaten it. Just like he did to you. About time we turned the tables on Mr Lowe, I reckon.'

Chapter Twenty-Seven

Richard

Mary calls. Then Sally calls. The phone calls I'd hardly dared to hope for, to say it's over, we are getting our boy back. I should be triumphant but I just feel sad.

'I can't welcome him home on my own,' Sally says quietly. 'Come. Please come.'

When I get there, she isn't on her own; Martha is there. The two of them answer the door together, shoulder to shoulder, practically arm in arm.

'Isn't it a school day?' I frown. 'Are you sick?' Martha looks a bit pale.

She opens her mouth to speak but Sally interjects.

'Study day,' she says. 'Well, you know, with a little break to welcome her brother home! Come on, I'll make tea while we wait.'

I stand in the living room, by the window, watching for Mary's blue Citroen. When I see it, I put down my mug and virtually leap out the front door. I hear Sally whisper to Martha, happily, 'He's excited.' She's misreading me: I'm angry.

'Richard,' Mary says, climbing out of the car and walking around to the rear passenger door. I can see Ol's chubby face behind the glass, 'good afternoon.'

I don't reply; words are burning to come out of me but they can wait. She lifts Ol out of the car seat and I take him in my arms, feeling the welcome weight and heat of him, then immediately turn to Sally, who has followed me down the path, her eyes full of tears. Martha hangs back in the doorway, watching, smiling.

'Here's Mummy,' I whisper to Ol, handing him to Sally. 'Here she is.' Sally envelops him in her arms, puts her face in his hair, breathing him in as though for the first time. Her eyes are closed and he's miraculously still, the two of them frozen for an instant, a perfect picture. She looks over the top of his head, at Mary, and mouths, 'Thank you.' Then she turns back towards the house, Oliver chuckling into her neck.

Mary moves to get back into the car, saying, 'We'll be in touch. To tie everything up.'

'Wait,' I say; I put a hand on her arm; she looks at it, then at me. 'So, this is it? You bring him back, it's all over? You can't take him again?'

She narrows her eyes.

'Not unless you give us any cause for concern again,' she says.

'And that's it? No apology?'

'Richard,' Mary says, 'I'm sure you know that we always regret any distress caused to parents, but for us, the welfare of the child is paramount.' I know instantly, from something in the way she says it, that it isn't that they don't think we did it; they are just too far off being able to prove it. Philip Lingwood has said we were lucky they didn't proceed anyway. In family courts, he said, '"Guilty beyond reasonable doubt" doesn't apply.'

'No offence,' I tell her, 'but I hope I never see you again.' She gives a half-smile, and says, 'Likewise.'

Back in the house, Ol flaps his arms and kicks his legs, his signal for 'put me down', and when Sally does he rockets up and down the long hall, his chubby limbs moving like pistons. He occasionally looks behind him, daring us to chase him, laughing in that gurgling, happy way that makes my heart leap.

'It's a wonder he doesn't wear holes in his knees,' I murmur, and we both stand rooted to the spot, just staring after him.

'He's home,' Sally whispers, and I put an arm around her shoulder, and she doesn't push me away.

It's simple, to Sally. At least, that's how she makes it sound.

'We're a family,' she says. 'Let's try again.'

Ol's napping. He didn't even make it up the stairs, just clambered onto the sofa and crashed out there. And there's an unspoken thought between us, that we don't want to put him in his cot. Don't want to let him out of our sight.

We're talking, in low voices, both of us all the while gazing at him, watching his little chest rise and fall with his deep, slow breaths. Martha has tactfully made herself scarce, though not before giving her little brother a gentle kiss and the warmest hug I've ever seen her give.

I want to believe that the things Sally is saying are possible. 'But how?' I say. 'How can we?'

'I'd rather be with you, knowing what you've done,' she says, 'than not be with you. I have to know it anyway. I might not be happy, but I'd be even less happy without you.'

This is what I've done to her, I realise. This is the choice I've left her with. You hear people say 'I hate myself', and now I know what that means. But that's the difference between Sally and me. Maybe it's the difference between women and men, I don't know. She would put up with anything, a bad marriage even, rather than be separated in any way from Oliver. Especially now. Now that she knows what that's like.

So we try again. I move back in. The first days and weeks are like having Ol as a new-born again. Both of us spend a lot of time just looking at him, and now that he's mobile, he spends a lot of time exploring. I suppose, although neither of us says it, he doesn't really remember being here before. We busy ourselves fitting safety catches to the cupboards, moving breakable items out of the reach of small hands, installing baby gates. I repaint his bedroom. It's not necessary, but feels good.

Meanwhile Sally veers between apparent ecstasy – in bed especially, where she performs like some X-rated actress, riding me enthusiastically, holding up her own hair, fondling her own breasts, gasping – and dark insecurity – the incessant texts and panicky voicemails whenever I'm out of the house. I tell her I accept that lack of trust will be part of our relationship for a while, but the truth is I'm afraid it will be forever, and I don't know what that will do, to either of us.

'You're playing away, eh? Never learn, do you?' Darren is brutally direct as always. I'm playing golf with him and Jerry, an ill-matched pair if ever there was one: the landscaper and the accountant, one scruffy, one smart, one outspoken, one quiet. Jerry just shifts about; he's not so good with the relationship chat.

'Yeah, all right,' I say, keen to change the subject. I look over the course, at the vast expanse of green, squinting in the late summer sun. It feels good to be out. 'We were having a shit time. I'm not proud of myself.'

'But it started before all the baby business, right?'

'What's your point? Just leave it, OK? Sally and me – we split for a bit and now we're back on. And everything's fine.'

But the truth is this thing I've done is hanging over me, an axe about to fall.

The golf course is partly out of mobile signal range, and a creeping anxiety comes over me between the twelfth and fifteenth holes, so much so that I start to sweat. I fluff my shots, can't get to the end of the game quick enough.

Because sure enough, when I'm back in range there they are, a succession of texts, first friendly then increasingly desperate:

Hi! Hope you're having fun xxx
When do you think you'll be home? X

Tried calling. Where are you?

Please ring me.

And then the pulsing, the vibrating of message alerts changes to a ring, the music muffled by my pocket. The guys look at me with a 'Can't it wait?' expression on their faces. I smile apologetically and pick up.

'Where are you?'

'Playing golf. I did tell you.'

'Still?'

'Yes, still.'

'What? I can't hear you very well.'

'It's a bit windy. Sorry,' as though I am to blame for the weather. 'There's a crap signal here,' I add, stopping myself from saying sorry again for my obvious culpability for the vagaries of O2 reception.

I promise her I'll be home soon, unsure whether she even hears me, then switch the phone off and drop it back into my pocket. I try to get out of having a pint at the end of the game, but it's expected, and the guys start to rib me so I give in. But I drain it quickly and jog from the clubhouse to the car.

Because this is how it is, now. How it has to be, until Sally trusts me again. I switch the phone back on and send a cheerful message: *On my way! See you soon sweetheart xxx*

But my stomach groans all the way back, and I notice as my hands slip on the steering wheel that I'm still sweating.

And then she asks me, one solemn, quiet night on the sofa, 'Why are you here? Why did you come back?'

I decide to be honest. I owe her that.

'Guilt,' I say. 'Guilt and fear. And the kids, obviously.' Then almost as an afterthought, I say, 'And love,' because I do love her, and need her to know that, but she cries and cries and I hold her, because we both know that love as an afterthought, love in fourth place, isn't good enough.

In the morning I get up and I move out again.

I think sometimes about how I'll be remembered. God, that makes me sound an insufferable wanker, like I think I'll have a place in the history books, like a prime minister or something. But bear with me. We all live on in our families and friends after we go. We all write our autobiographies, however small. Of course, as a rule history is written by the victors.

On the evidence so far, I admit it doesn't look good. It would be nice if, looking back, people could at least say I'd been a good dad. Yes. At least I can be a good dad. It can't be too late. And maybe that doesn't mean fighting Sally, but letting go. I've seen Martha grow up living out of carrier bags, trying to please everyone, from one home to another and back again, spreading herself between her parents. Can I really do that to another kid?

It's over, but it isn't over. When Mary calls, as promised, to 'tie things up', it comes out almost by accident that Ol is still on the child protection register. No one can tell us when, or even if, this will change. What this says to me, to everyone, is that although they've dropped the investigation, he is still considered to be at risk.

How can this be the case? Medical experts have testified, and social services have conceded, that there was no way it could be proven that Oliver was hurt deliberately. So they have to let it go, and yet they aren't letting it go.

They are leaving us with a label, the register hanging over us like a sign that reads: '(Probably) child beaters. (Probably) unfit parents.' Just because they can't prove it, doesn't mean they don't still think it. That's what the register says to me.

Sally feels it more than I do.

'It should be a comfort just to have Ollie home,' she says. 'That should be enough, but it's not. It's like waking from a nightmare but still seeing traces of it out of the corner of your eyes.'

I keep remembering what Lingwood said to me, early on. He said, 'In cases like this ... you might come off better if you admit blame.'

I need to make things right.

I call the social services office and ask to speak to Mary. An officious voice I recognise as Tim, the boy with a bumfluff beard who came to Ol's birthday party, says, 'Mr Townsend, I'm sure I can help. Mary's a bit tied up just now.'

'I'd really prefer to speak to her. Please ask her to call me when she's free.'

I'm about to hang up when I hear a muffled, rustling sort of sound, then Teenage Tim gives a sigh and says, 'Hold on.'

'Hello, Richard, it's Mary.'

'I want to tell you something. I mean, I want to make a statement.' My story is well-formed; I've rehearsed it. I tell her I'd gone out that evening, come back tipsy, got annoyed with Ol's crying and was 'a bit rough' with him.

'So you see,' I say, 'I'm ninety per cent certain it was me who hurt Oliver and I want you to do whatever needs to be done. And I want you to leave Sally alone.'

'I'm afraid it doesn't quite work like that.'

'What do you mean? How does it work, then?' I can hear her taking a deep breath.

'Well, if you're admitting harming your son, we'll have to re-open the case, obviously. There could be criminal proceedings.'

'Yes, I'm prepared for that.' I'm not; and I don't want them to re-open the case. 'Sally and I are separated now,' I add, 'I'm not living with them. So … even if you re-open it, you won't have to take him, right?' Mary pauses.

'Right.'

'OK. Then, do what you have to do.'

'Richard,' she says, 'I should make you aware, you were fortunate the police decided not to press charges last time. That was almost certainly because there were no additional injuries. But in the light of a confession, if that's what this is …'

'It's fine,' I say, 'I just want to make things right.'

'And why now, may I ask?' I can hear suspicion in her voice, and I try to keep the exasperation from mine. They've gone from suspecting me of hurting him to suspecting me of not hurting him. I can't win. I'm done with feeling powerless.

'Does it matter? I'm doing the right thing. I'll take the consequences.' *And you can't stop me*, I add silently.

I can give Ol a stable home life. And Martha too, for that matter. I can't give Sally the thing she wants most – a family – but I can give her the next best thing: a clean slate.

I put down the phone, hands shaking, but at the same time pleased that for once I've told a lie that will do some good.

Chapter Twenty-Eight

Sally

I know Richard is lying. And I know why he's lying. And I know I can't let on that I know. So I play my part, say to social services that what he said was 'credible' but that I strongly believe it was a one-off. I confirm that we've separated. I exercise damage limitation. Not saying too much, but just enough so that I will get what I want.

Oliver, mine for keeps. No black mark against us.

We had to give it one more shot, of course, but it was obvious to me he wouldn't stay. It was doomed. His guilt, and my jealousy, were corrosive poisons seeping into our relationship, edging inexorably towards its centre. We overdid it, in those few weeks he was back: frantic sex, excited future plans – Holidays! Another baby! An extension on the house! – but it was all hollow.

You imagine you can pick up where you left off, if you both want to, but you can't. Once it's broken, it's broken.

Before he left, Richard said, 'I've learned so much from being with you.'

'Oh, great,' I said. 'You've learned lots that your next girlfriend will benefit from. Well, that makes me feel brilliant. Good for you.'

'I'm sorry.'

'Just don't do that thing,' I said. 'You know, when you try to re-write history. Don't give me the whole "maybe I never really loved my wife" shit that you tried with Zoe.' He gave a hollow little laugh.

'Wow, how did you know?'

'Women know everything. Listen, it's wrong and it's an insult that you would even try. You did love me, you were in love with me. Either that or you've been a monumental liar and a psychopath all along. But I don't believe anyone can lie that well.'

'I did love you. I still love you.'

'I don't believe that either.'

'I do. It just breaks my heart that I can't make you happy.'

The thing neither of us wanted to admit, especially Richard, was that it was having Ollie that changed things between us. He didn't want to acknowledge it because it was like blaming Ollie for what had gone wrong. That was why I knew Richard would try to re-write the script: you couldn't *say* it was the baby's fault.

And it wasn't, of course – but it was the fault of the people we became after he was born. For all the books I read, and parenting classes we sat through, nothing prepared me for how changed we would both become.

In some ways, parenting on my own is easier. I didn't expect that. Life is quieter, Ollie and I have fallen into a routine that works for us, and I don't have to run things by anyone else, there is none of the asking for permission or seeking approval. The routine works for Martha, too, it seems: she rarely misses a meal, she sits at the table with us, helps feed Ollie. There are no arguments; Richard and I had seemed to disagree on everything, from feeding to sleep training to bloody haircuts. Suddenly I'm in charge. I've taken some leave from work but I know I will have to go back soon as I'm way over my twelve months maternity leave and running out of holiday. They've been patient but I don't know how long that will last. So I throw myself into looking for a nursery or childminder. I become in tune with my baby again, the irony not lost on me that soon I will have to leave him for ten hours a day, but at least I have a good sense of what he wants, what he likes and doesn't like. It's obvious, taking him to visit childminders, who he warms to and who he recoils from. He is turning into the strong-willed, spirited boy I saw in his eyes the day he was born.

It's the practical stuff that I wasn't ready for; once I get Ollie to bed at night, I can't just pop to the shops if I'm missing something. That kind of thing. But Martha helps. She even says that if I start dating again, she will babysit. She offers to help me set up an online profile. I laugh at this – dating is the absolute last thing I feel like doing. I am trying to be a better mother to Martha too. Between us three, Zoe, Richard and I have let her down.

I think about telling Richard, or even Zoe, what happened with Martha but she's begged me not to. She wants him to think the best of her, she says, despite everything. I see a girl, almost a young woman but still a girl, wanting her father's approval, and I feel a pang for my own teenage self. Nevertheless, I think he should know how far he's wandered from his responsibility. I call him one night when she's out with friends and euphemistically tell him she's had a few 'problems'.

'I can't tell you the details,' I say, 'I just want you to be aware.'

He sighs down the phone. 'She used to tell me everything.'

'Well, she's not a little girl any more. But she does still need you.'

He waits a while before saying, 'I let her down, didn't I?'

'We both did. I know I'm not her mum but I was here and I should have ... seen. Anyway, I'm here for her now. She can stay with me until you get settled. And afterwards, too, if she wants to. She's been passed from pillar to post so much. She needs to feel safe, now.'

When you break up with someone, you usually go your separate ways, but Richard and I obviously can't do that. We have to try and be friends – for Ollie. We do a weird verbal dance where we keep apologising to, and thanking, each other. We are polite to one another now, which is odd, we speak in the way acquaintances speak, and yet behind it, all those shared years and memories.

At least when someone dies you can go through grief in the proper way. There's a structure to it. There's a curve. Down and up.

This grief is different, with our false starts and attempts to re-model our relationship into something it was never meant to be. *Let's be friends.* Idiotic. Friends was never us. So there is an ending, but we are both still alive, of course, and what's more we are in touch, connected; there is no opting-out. So we re-appear to each other like persistent ghosts, and we re-grieve, again and again, on a merry-go-round of pain.

It seems odd that we will still know each other, see one another regularly, when we are old. 'Grow old with me,' he said during our wedding. Well, barring illness or accident that takes either of us early, it looks like I will, just not in the way we planned.

On the days he comes to see Ollie, I put make-up on. I spend ages pulling my hair into a carefully messy bun. I might wear jogging pants, to look casual, but I'll wear them with a vest top, show a bit of shoulder tinted with fake tan (I don't go to the effort of buffing, polishing and painting my skin for anyone else, so I guess it must be for him). I know that one day I'll care less what he thinks. One day I'll answer the door unshowered, wearing old pyjamas and streaky mascara. One day, probably. But not yet.

These days the measure of 'moving on' is how infrequently you feel compelled to check their Facebook page. Not that I can see much of Richard's as we're no longer 'friends' (how crazy is that, we've had a child together, we're bound by that, we've seen each other through the best and worst of times – but we're not 'friends' as defined by social media), but in the first days and weeks after we broke up I would pore over his profile pictures, old and new, looking for clues in that face I knew so well. I'm doing it a bit less, now.

But of course, I'm still waiting for a woman's face to appear next to his. The inevitable revelation that he's got someone else. Richard can't be on his own for long, and he can't keep it from me because we are tethered to one another.

When it comes, I know my heart will fall out of my body.

There's a singular sort of pain that comes with loving someone in such a way that you know they can never return it.

It's a bit like the love for your child. It's so complete. They will grow up and along the way, they'll be embarrassed by you, show you disapproval and reproach. Sometimes they'll even say 'I hate you'.

And you'll bear it because there is absolutely nothing else your heart can do.

It's a bit like that with Richard. Unconditional. Even when he was difficult and distant and critical, I loved him. Even when he cheated and lied and walked away, I loved him.

Does that make me weak, or strong?

I have decided I will carry the love like a boulder. In time you just get used to the weight.

So now it's just us. Me and my boy, and Martha. We're a unit. I don't know that I'll ever be able to trust or fall in love with anyone again but I'm not sure how much it matters.

Why couldn't Richard have become the man he is now while he was with me?

I like to tell myself that he'll never change; he'll cheat on the next one and the next one. But I don't think that's true; I think he *is* different. I just wish he'd got there with me.

Julia and I are becoming friends, proper friends, in a tentative sort of way. Ben is steadfast, of course, but he's in Portsmouth; he visits often, though, and he's getting really fond of Ollie. I suppose he's the closest thing I have to a boyfriend, although I have to stop myself from thinking of him that way. But Julia is local; it's good to have someone close by, someone who's a mum, someone who's a woman.

She says, 'You're not alone, you know,' but I am, deep down.

Then she says, 'You know, even if you had a man in your life, he might not be there for you in the ways you imagine.' I nod but I think that's easy for her to say, because she has one.

And then I think of her husband, who bought her that big house to live in but is never there. And then I realise maybe that's why she said it. And maybe we can help each other.

I know happiness is possible because I had it, for a time at least. When he was mine, and I was his. Why do we seek to possess each other, anyway? I don't know, all I know is that carrying his name, carrying his child, made me feel safe, protected. Owned.

Shortly after I had Oliver, Richard told me he was proud of me. I don't think he said that any other time, before or since. In fact quite the opposite (whether this was his fault or mine, I also don't know).

But in his arms, in his bed, under cover, I was happy. For all his imperfections, I loved him and don't suppose I will ever feel that way again. And by my side every day, the reminder, the mini-him, a gift so precious and yet so bound up in sadness. I will never get over that.

Once I hear the conclusion of the second social services investigation, once I know for certain what the future will be, only then do I ring Richard and say for the first time, 'I know you didn't do it.'

'Thank you,' he says.

Chapter Twenty-Nine

Martha

I finally tell Del everything. It's weird; it's like because I've now told one person, it's easier to talk to someone else. This thing I've been holding, that I thought had to stay inside me, is out and now that it's out, it feels smaller.

Del hugs me, then calls me a doofus for not telling her sooner. 'I *knew* something wasn't right,' she keeps saying, shaking her head, and 'I never liked that creep'. I tell her the bit I didn't tell Sally: that Brendan had hit me. Sally had noticed the bruise on my face but I told her I thought I'd hit it on the toilet when I fell in the bathroom.

'Right,' says Del, 'this ends. When are we kicking his ass?'

'Er, *we're* not,' I say. 'That is, you and me. I'm going to see him, though. With Sally.'

'Wow,' she says, 'you and the wicked stepmom really are getting on better, hey?'

'She's not so bad.' I smile, for once not flinching at the mention of Sally as an actual member of my family, but beneath that my insides are churning, because we are going to confront Brendan, and it's going to be tonight.

'I came to tell you I won't be doing any jobs for you any more.' He looks from me to Sally and back again. We're on his doorstep, and my heart is trying to hammer its way out of my chest.

'You've told *her*? Oh, Martha, I think that contravenes our little agreement.' He takes out his phone from where it is nestled, as usual, in his back pocket, and fondles it with his thumb.

'Oh, I'm not worried about that,' I say with forced cheerfulness. 'In fact, go ahead. Go on and post those silly pictures wherever you like.' He narrows his eyes at me, then laughs.

'Your wish is my—'

'Post them online –' Sally leans forward '– and I'll have the police round here so fast it'll make your fucking head spin.' The smile freezes on his face.

'What are you on about, you mad bitch?' His voice is still cocky but I see a flicker of doubt in his eyes, I think. The phone goes, slowly, back into his pocket.

'Child porn,' Sally says. She lets the words hang there for a minute, or maybe she's steadying herself. I could tell on the way here she was nervous but she's hiding it well now. 'Goes pretty nicely with drug offences, don't you think? Should add up to a decent stretch.' She steps towards him, so that her nose is almost touching his. I want to cheer. 'You do *want* to go to prison, right?'

'Oh, you forgot assault,' I say it brightly, as though I've just had an idea about where we might go for lunch. 'Or is it sexual activity with a child?'

'Actually, I think it's rape,' she says, swivelling her eyes towards him on the last word.

'You're both full of shit,' Brendan sneers, but he doesn't sound entirely convinced. Suddenly he looks like just what he is: a boy.

'OK.' I smile. 'Try it, and see. If I went to the police, with any charge against you, I'd have evidence because you'd have helpfully plastered pictures on the Internet.' I'm shaking, but I know I have to keep going. 'Fancy your chances in prison as a *child rapist*, do you?'

'You wouldn't,' he hisses, glancing over his shoulder and pulling the door almost closed behind him, 'I'll fucking kill you, you mad little slag. I know people ... I can get to you and you won't even know it. I can get to your family—'

'I'm her family,' Sally says, linking my arm, 'and I'm not scared of you, you jumped-up little shit.'

'Yeah, so go ahead,' I add. 'Just try it.'

'I still could,' he juts out his chin and I see his arm snake back around to the pocket with the phone on it. 'I don't have to put my name to the pictures. It's not like my *face* is in them.' He gives a horrible laugh, but his voice, a bit shaky, is giving him away. 'I can post them anonymously and still make your life hell. Everyone will see what you did.'

Slowly, as calmly as I can, I raise my right hand, in which I've been holding my own mobile. 'It's a good job we've been recording this conversation, then, isn't it?' He lurches forward, makes as if to grab the phone, but I step backwards and he stumbles. 'What was it you said – insurance policy?' I hiss.

Sally starts to pull me away, down the path. 'That'll do,' she whispers to me and then, loudly, to Brendan, she calls out in an overly cheerful voice, 'Bye for now then! Ciao!'

We walk calmly to the end of the street and as soon as we get there, round the corner and break into a frenetic run.

Del practically pisses her pants when I tell her what we did.

She's sitting on my bed, legs crossed, a can of Coke in her hand. She makes me tell the story again, from the start, and describe the expression on Brendan's face when Sally called him a 'jumped-up little shit'. 'Good for Sally,' she says with a hooting laugh, 'I love it.'

She says she's gonna quit the drugs. She often says that but she looks like she means it this time. I tell Del about the cutting. She looks at me, wide-eyed.

'I had a friend in Sweden who did that,' she says. 'Fuck, Martha.'

'I don't know how to stop. Sally says we should go running.'

Del starts to laugh, and I do too, but it doesn't exactly seem a crazy idea.

'She's funny, that stepmom of yours,' she says, and I nod agreement.

Sally has told me that running makes her hungry, so she used to run a lot when she was in recovery because she could control her weight but was forced, really, to eat, for energy and all that. It's more than that, though, she said; it's head space. That sounded nice.

'It'll be tough, mind you,' she mused, 'because we'll have to take Ollie, in the buggy.'

'That'll be a good work out, pushing him up the hills around here.' I grimaced. 'He got kinda fat at Grandma's.'

Turns out Sally was right. Nothing lasts, everything passes. In August two big things happened: I turned sixteen, and I got my exam results. The birthday was OK: Dad bought me a watch, which he let me choose myself, thank God, and Sally got me a really cool pair of Converse. Zoe got me paints, as usual, and a bracelet. Sally said I could have a party at the house, but I could tell she felt kind of anxious about it, so in the end I just invited Del round and a couple of the other girls and we had pizza and watched movies down in the den. It was low-key, although Del brought some cider, but that was OK. We all agreed that our eighteenths would be epic, though. I hope we're all still friends then. It was weird, leaving school; you realise you won't automatically see people every day any more. So we made a kind of pact, the four of us, me, Del, Lynsey and Pip. It was nice.

The exam thing was not so cool. I did OK, I got a handful of passes, but I messed up on a lot too. Dad was 'disappointed' (ugh) but he came round when I said I just wanted a year to re-sit the crap ones and decide what I want to do. I mean, I have the five A-C grades I need to get into the local college – just – but it doesn't feel the right thing for me. Or not yet, anyway. He said I could do a bit of work for him (again, ugh), and he would pay me, because if I wasn't going to go to school the deal was I should pay Sally rent. Everything felt very grown up all of a sudden, but I was OK with that. Dad said when he got a bigger place I could move in with him, but I quite like living with Sally in a 'girls' house'. Well, girls apart from Ol, of course!

Ol has grown up a bit and got less annoying. I joked that Grandma Bootcamp obviously did him good. Sally wasn't keen on that one. I guess at times I still wind her up.

I'd been scared I would see Brendan Lowe everywhere, but the whole summer it only happened twice.

The first time was in the pub. It was just me and Del; we were celebrating finishing our last exam. 'Beer only,' Del said, because like I say, she'd vowed no more pills or weed. She said 'beer' like it was something really healthy, like we were having a pint of aloe vera or something, which made me chuckle. Then I saw him, with his hangers-on, all talking too loudly and banging into things, already pissed at six o'clock in the evening. I started to shake a bit; I couldn't help it. Del noticed and followed my gaze. 'Do you want to leave?' she whispered, and I shook my head. She squeezed my hand.

The second time, he was in the Sainsbury's car park helping his mum to load bags into the back of her car. For some reason this really made me smile. He just looked like a boy. I watched him for long enough that it was like he felt my eyes on him; he looked up and immediately away, and

I got the weird feeling that maybe I hadn't seen him much because *he* was trying to avoid *me*.

We run, or I run, and Sally pushes the buggy and coaches me. 'Hips forward, shoulders relaxed,' she calls, puffing up the hill behind me, though not that far behind, because it turns out I'm pretty unfit. She's been teaching me to run on the balls of my feet when going uphill. She's taught me breathing exercises. It's getting easier, and I've mastered a pretty good technique, she says. She tells me running can be great therapy. One night, she said, 'Whenever you feel like … you know, you can go for a run instead.'

'And what if it's the middle of the night?' I said.

'Then just the breathing, OK?'

'Jeez, you sound like my mother,' I said, and laughed because she couldn't stop herself from pulling a face. 'I don't know, I could draw, or something. Get it out through *my art*.' I made fancy hand gestures and put on my most highbrow kind of face.

'Now *you* sound like your mother,' she giggled. 'Hey, whatever works.'

'I like the running.'

So here we are in the park, and it seems like autumn has crept up on us because from the top of the hill everything looks golden and there's an unfamiliar kind of mist starting to form. The sun is lower in the sky than it has been, although we run at the same time every day. I turn to Sally and I say, 'You know what? I don't want to run like this any more.'

'No?'

'Nope. I want to run like a kid.'

'Really?' She frowns as though she doesn't know what that's like, but she doesn't make fun of me. 'Go on then, show me.'

So I do: I run full pelt, fast as I can, arms windmilling, squealing 'Woooo!' all the way down the hill. My lungs burn and the wind whips my face, my feet struggle to keep up with the momentum in my body but I let the ground carry me, bouncing over every rock, taking long, striding jumps that are almost like skipping. It feels like flying.

I glance over my shoulder to see Sally and Ol, way in the distance, and Sally is clapping like a mad woman, and shouting something I can't hear properly over the wind, although I think I can just make out 'Be careful!', but she is smiling her head off and in that moment I feel properly happy, and cared for, and free.

Chapter Thirty

Richard

In the end we come to an agreement that seems to work for everyone. Sally, to my surprise, is keen to avoid police involvement and makes a statement to the effect that she's certain this was the only time I'd raised a hand to Oliver. I agree to go on a six-session anger management course and have counselling. I will have supervised access to Ol, once a week. Only once a week, but this will be reviewed periodically.

The important thing is that Sally is officially cleared, and can get on with being a mother. It will be just the two of them, now. Three of them in fact as Martha seems happy to stay there. This hurts, I won't lie, but then I see how settled she is, how well the three of them seem to fit together now, and I can't possibly argue.

My mother isn't pleased. She says, 'I have forgiven you many things, Richard, but I'm not sure I can forgive this.' I don't bother to ask which things she has so-called forgiven. We are sitting in her conservatory, the unusual autumn heat stifling the room, and we are drinking tea, of course. I've just told her the outcome of the social services decision regarding custody of Ol.

'It's still beyond me why you would admit to something you didn't do,' she says. 'David, speak to your son.'

My father looks up from his paper. I notice suddenly how, in his mid-sixties, he is looking much older.

'It sounds as though it's all been decided,' he says.

I nod.

'But why?' she cries. I don't often see my mother agitated; she is literally wringing her hands.

'I don't expect you to understand,' I say; she flinches at that, starts to say something, but I carry on. 'No. Listen. This was my chance – my only chance, now – to make Sally happy.' She scoffs. 'She's a good mum.'

'You do realise,' she seethes, 'that your precious Sally never even thanked me for looking after your son all that time?'

'Well, I imagine it was difficult for her to be grateful for a situation that she didn't choose, a situation she hated. If it makes you feel any better, *I'm* grateful. You did your best by Ol, I know. But things are different now.' I drain my tea. 'Things have moved on. Now, I have to go and spend some time with my kids.'

It is only when I pull up outside the house that I realise I've had a text from Sally. 'We're in the park,' it reads, no kisses, but a smiley face.

I find them by the swings. Ol has on a bright red coat and is clinging to the chains of the swing but laughing wildly. It's been a while since I last saw him; his hair has grown. It's curling over his ears. He sees me and makes an excited 'whee!' sound, arms outstretched, bouncing in the seat. I jog over and move to pick him up, glancing at Sally. She nods, a relaxed sort of smile spreading across her face. She looks different, too: every time I see her, these days, she looks a fraction healthier, happier. Her curves are coming back, and the colour in her cheeks. I'm glad.

'Hi, buddy,' I say as I lift him carefully out of the swing, one arm around his body, the other hand teasing his feet out one by one. 'Hi, pal. How's it going?'

He grabs my face – this is his latest habit – and gives me a toothy smile. I lower him onto the ground and say, 'Come on, then. Let's see those moves.' He's only been walking a few days. Sally sent me a video, and of course I've seen him on his feet before, navigating his two-legged way around the furniture. I've walked behind him holding his hands, staggering along with his toddler's pace as his little legs struggled to keep up with his body's forward momentum. But it's different seeing him in person, seeing him independently tottering, walking, running, every now and then looking over his shoulder as though to make sure I'm watching. I whoop and applaud and I feel like I could burst with pride.

'You're doing a great job,' I say to Sally, both of us watching him amble and tumble away down the hill.

'Thank you,' she says, turning to me, pushing the hair out of her eyes. 'You know, you could come over more regularly. If you wanted. When you're allowed. Spend a bit more time with him. I mean, that might be nice.'

'Yes. Yes, that would be nice.'

Epilogue

Sally

Dear Oliver,

Today you are two, and you are the greatest two-year-old boy in the whole world. Your dad and your big sister love you lots and your Uncle Ben visits when he can. As for me: you are my heart.

Here are some things you love, aged two: the water. You splash like mad in the bath and when the weather's nice I take you to Frensham Pond, to paddle.

You love Thomas the Tank Engine, you go crazy for the theme music, and line up all your trains with absolute precision. I worried for a while that you were a little obsessive but Julia tells me this is normal for little boys. I worry about you all the time.

I took you to the Watercress Line to see the 'real' Thomas and I'll never forget the look of joy on your face, although I don't suppose you'll remember. I hear we don't recall anything from before the age of three, and I'm partly grateful for that. Anyway, we had a wonderful day, although you cried when

Thomas let out his steam with a huge hiss. *You don't like loud noises. I never shout. Hardly ever.*

As I write this you are two, but you will be eighteen when I give you this letter and all the others I will write for you. Old enough, I hope, to understand. Maybe old enough to forgive.

It was only the third time I'd been out alone, without your dad, since you were born. I walked to the station that night, unsteady in my heels. I'd already had a drink, or two, hurried swigs of vodka at home. Dutch courage. I swung my empty arms, wondering what it would be like to never hold the weight of a child again. A phone call filled me with fear and I ended the conversation as quickly as I could. Images and sounds swam in my mind and I would spend the whole night drinking way too much, to drown them out.

I used to believe there was one true love for everyone. I believed your dad was mine. Now I know that the one true love exists between a mother and her child. I know this.

It seems a long time now, since that hole in my life when you were gone. I won't let anyone separate us again.

I wish I could know the future, so I could give you all the answers and protect you from the bad things.

I can't remember you, now, as a small baby. It seems you were always this age, always this big, this strong.

You don't seem like the same child who kept me awake, night after night.

And I'm not the same mother.

'Count to ten,' they say. Put the baby in a safe place, like in his cot, leave the room and count to ten.

It's bullshit. You can count to a hundred and still the wailing, the most excruciating sound you've ever heard, on and on and on and on. And tiredness doesn't cover what happens to you when you've not had an unbroken night's sleep for months. It's desperation. But also numbness, a sense of moving through the day in quicksand. Just trying to stay above the surface, keep breathing. I was alone. Resentment burned in me.

It happened quickly. An arm tangled up in a blanket, and what I couldn't see, was that it was stuck in the bars of the cot, and I yanked at you, too roughly, from the other side. I didn't hear anything break, but I knew something was different, something was wrong. I didn't soothe you; I regret that, now. I thought if I could close the door on it, on you, it would be like it hadn't happened. Richard would soon be back home, and as he got in, I was going out. If I could just go out, be somewhere else for a while, perhaps it would all be fixed when I got back.

Your cry, now you're older, is different. It's more of a whinge. It doesn't even come with tears.

I know sometimes I nearly lose it. It's tough on my own; there's no one to hand you over to, and I still find walking away from you hard. Sometimes I hear myself shouting, 'What? What is wrong with you?' Not often, though. Only sometimes. And afterwards I cuddle you extra tight and tell you Mummy is sorry for getting cross.

I wish I could know the future. All I know is, I love you. I love you in a way I never thought possible. I know no parent is perfect.

And I know this: I will never hurt you again.

Acknowledgements

Thank you

To my family, who, being Irish, are too many to mention, but special thanks are due to Mum, Stephen, and my late dad.

To all my friends, especially the three Annas and Jenny, who have all demonstrated extraordinary staying power. Old friends are gold.

To Kate Kelly, for helping me learn about pharmacy.

To the Hogs Back Writers, again, for listening and advising so brilliantly.

To the folks at the Bath Novel Award, without whom I wouldn't have got started on this crazy ride.

To all at Ebury, especially my editor Gillian Green, who showed great patience while helping me knock this book into shape.

To Juliet Mushens, almost certainly the greatest agent in the world, and a smart and warm human being.

Read on for an extract from
Joanna Barnard's award-winning

Precocious

also available from Ebury Press

One

We meet again in the supermarket. The drone of the tannoy announcements, the bustle of people, all seem to pause for a second while I register that it's really you.

'You look great,' I say. *You look old*, I think. You're holding a bag of frozen prawns, and a basket. Good. I stare at the basket. No trolley equals no family.

You're looking at me and for a horrible moment I think you don't remember me. Then you smile, and the smile is fifteen years older but the same cloudy, wry smile as then, as ever. Your wrinkles, your teeth.

'Fee, fi, fo, fum,' you say.

We embrace clumsily. You have no hands free and I have only one, so we sort of clang together and I end up patting you on the back as if in recognition of a job well done.

With my head buried momentarily in your shoulder I send a wish skywards that when we separate my hair will look neater, my face fresher, my waist thinner.

Pulling away from me, your polite questions begin.

'So, what are you doing now?'

'Shopping?'

I'm doing that thing where I say everything like a question – it comes out when I'm nervous.

You laugh in that way you used to when I could never tell if you were making fun of me.

'I don't mean right now, I mean, in life – for a career.'

'Oh. I work in publishing.'

I tell everyone this. I sell advertising space in the Yellow Pages.

'Publishing,' you consider this for a while, 'and the writing?'

But you say it with capital letters. The Writing, followed by a question mark, heavy with expectation.

'Oh, bits and pieces,' I mumble. The truth is I haven't written anything except emails for eight years.

The last thing I wrote was a letter I never sent. A letter to you, when I was twenty-two. Years had already passed and I was angry. I tried to disguise it as defiance. 'I would eat you for breakfast now!' I wrote, daring you to come back. I put it in an envelope and sealed it and it stayed on my bookshelf, so unlike the notes and poems I used to put in your pigeon hole or on your desk to wonder all day if you'd read them.

I'm brought back to the present by your question:

'What are you doing for dinner?' I look at my trolley full of food.

'No plans,' I say, 'nothing that can't wait.'

'Great. You can tell me your stories.'

And you're back.

*

A small part of me has wondered, from time to time, whether you might have died. But somehow I felt that I would have known – not found out, not seen it in the newspaper, not been told by someone – I would have just known. I would've felt it, in my gut. I would've felt a hot pain behind my eyes. I would have known.

I didn't think I'd been obsessed with you all these years, but now that you're back, the terrain between then and today takes on a different geography. I've thought about you, perhaps not every day, but most days, for however fleeting a time. I thought I saw you – lots of times – which was always disconcerting, even though a second glance would prove it to be only a piece of you, the flick of your hair, maybe, or the curve of your ear, on an impostor's face. I've heard your voice: unmistakeably you, the lazy sound of your vowels, your bored drawl. And each time when I realised it wasn't you, in the back of my mind was relief, and further back still a strange certainty that one day it would be.

So you didn't die – today you reappeared, very much alive, somehow smaller and with thinning hair, but still you, holding a basket. And now I'm following your car, steering with one hand and texting my husband with the other.

I will be late home.

The restaurant is made mostly of glass. Floor to ceiling windows look out onto a rain-soaked street. You slice through your steak, metal scraping china.

'Tell me about him,' you say.

'Who?' I push my food around my plate. I always did feel uncomfortable eating in front of you.

You say nothing but motion towards my left hand. I glance down at the perfect diamond and, without thinking, spin it inwards with a flick of the thumb so that I only have to look at two thin gold bands.

'Dave,' I say simply.

'Tell me about Dave.'

'Dave is ... a *grown-up*,' I want to say. I realise how ridiculous a statement this is to make to a man who is now in his forties, and laugh to myself. But that's how I think of Dave. Or at least, he makes *me* a grown-up.

Dave is one of those people who is meant to be married. He got close, with the girlfriend before me. She left him three weeks before the wedding. When we met, it seemed like he was looking for a sticking plaster. He wanted me, yes, but only a fraction of how much he wanted to be married. It was as though the quicker he fell in love and got someone to love him back – the quicker he got married – the easier it would be to convince himself that his heartbreak had never happened.

He even has a husband's name. Dave. A comforting name, something about the warm sound of the 'v'. A big man's name, but not threatening big, just warm. Comforting, comfortable big.

I had once thought I would end up with an Alec, or a Holden, or even a Heathcliff, but they are only characters in books, not real men you can marry. I thought I might marry one of the skinny, glassy-eyed, long-haired wraiths who kept me awake all night in my teens, smelling of patchouli oil and brown ale, running their hands along my back and quoting inaccurately from *The Prophet*.

But none of them asked. The one who asked was a Dave, the Dave who brings me flowers, who smells clean, soapy even, who quotes old Genesis love songs, singing shakily while I look down at him through my hair.

I tell you all of this and you listen.

'So that's why you got married? Because he asked?' I nod; I don't tell you that I also felt a bit sorry for him. The rings on my third finger feel tight.

'Maybe. Why not? Why does anyone do it?'

'I don't know.' You laugh that dry laugh, like a cough.

'*You* got married.' I sound like a sulky teenager. You say nothing but keep chewing. To fill the silence I say, 'It's just what you do, isn't it? It's what people do. *Normal* people.' I wave my fork at you and all around, as though to demonstrate the difference between these normal people and you. A flake of salmon lands on the tablecloth.

'Funny, I never had you down as a traditionalist, that's all.'

'Well, people can change in fifteen years.'

'Hmm. Not everyone is as stubborn and set in their ways as I am, I suppose.'

I feel exposed, accused of a crime I don't remember committing.

'Get married, have a baby,' you pause, 'that's next, I suppose?'

'No.' A little too quickly.

'Why not? Isn't that what they do, these normal people you're so fond of?'

'I just never wanted to have his baby,' I say, realising too late that I've emphasised the word *his*.

You give a slow, reptilian blink and then say, 'Whatever happened to vegetarianism?'

For a strange, surreal moment I think you mean generally; in society as a whole. I finger my brain. Have I missed something? Has there been a widespread decline in concern for animal welfare, recently documented in the cleverer late night TV discussion programmes, or worse, in the popular press, and I have not noticed? How could I have come to dinner so unprepared to discuss topical issues?

I look at you blankly and you nod at my plate.

'Oh,' I look down, 'I had to start eating fish. Vitamin deficiency.'

'Glad to hear it. Always thought it was nonsense, you giving up meat so young. You can't be a vegetarian until you've tasted a really excellent rare steak. Until that point you're simply not making an informed choice. Oh sure, it's easy to see the reasons for becoming vegetarian – but what about the reasons for eating meat? Until you've eaten veal – or foie gras – you simply don't know enough. Some cruelty is worth it.' You look at me, pop a forkful of steak into your mouth. 'The end justifies the means.'

I could swear I see blood oozing out at the sides.

'So if Dan doesn't mind ...'

'Dave,' I say; *you're not funny*, I think.

'If you don't think *Dave* will mind, can we go out again?'

'Are we becoming friends now?' I ask.

'Don't you mean again?'

'Are we becoming friends again?'

'Better late than never,' you grin.

'Fifteen years,' I say, 'that's late.'

I've had two glasses of wine. I don't drink and drive, as a rule; it isn't me. I like to feel in control. Something made me order the second glass and it's that glass, or that something, that I know is to blame when I reverse my car out of the pitch dark parking space and scrape the next car along.

Damn, damn, damn.

I get out, scribble my mobile number on the back of the supermarket receipt and leave it under the car's wind-screen wiper.

From across the street I hear the thud of a door, and footsteps, and now you are at my side, laughing.

'What did you do? Fee, Fee ...'

'It's just a bump,' I say irritably. I feel like a child. I feel shaky, inadequate, and can't look at you.

'I just wanted to say goodbye.'

'You already did. It was good to see you.'

You say something that I hear but immediately forget, because at once your hand is in my hair, and now on my throat, and there is kissing. I can't say you kiss me, or I kiss you, only that there is kissing, because I am watching it from far away.

And all I can think about is what I ate, and therefore what do I taste like, and does it feel nice to you, and I shouldn't be doing this, and I should be doing this, and...

At last.

Tonight I will do all of the same things I do every night.

Come through the door, stroke the dog, murmur 'hellos', exchange perfunctory kisses with my husband, wash the breakfast things that weren't done in the morning, have a cup of tea. I will say 'no, I've eaten, but I'll do something for you' and I will put some rice or spaghetti on to simmer while thawing out a sticky-labelled pot from the freezer. I do all the actual cooking at the weekends. I spend Sunday afternoons making chillies and stews and curries and broths and posting them, tightly lidded, colour coded, addressed to Monday, Tuesday and so on, into deep freeze.

Today is Wednesday.

Once I have thawed out, warmed up, talked about my day, I will put everything, including myself, away.

Tonight I will do all of the same things I do every night, but tonight is different. Tonight I feel like a ghost in my own life.

Dave often says: 'I can see right through you.'

It's one of his favourite phrases – he's said it for years. I used to take it literally, and I hated it; it made me look at the pale skin through which I can sometimes see my own veins. He would tell me, 'don't be silly', but all the while he would be absentmindedly stroking the fine purple lines on my inner wrist, my temple, my breast.

Then for a while I loved it: it made me feel completely *known*, and wanted. Safe.

Now it frightens me. What if he can? I feel high-pitched; a different, shiny version of myself. Does he notice?

I kick off my shoes and unpack the shopping, sliding melted ice cream and car-boot-warmed cheese straight into the dustbin with a smile. I prepare a bowl of spaghetti for Dave and a piece of chicken for the dog.

'I saw someone today,' I say casually. 'I mean, I bumped into someone.'

'Oh yes?' He lifts the fork to his mouth. The bowl is balanced on his lap, his eyes fixed on the TV. I watch the blood-coloured sauce tipping, from left to right, towards his trousers, towards the sofa cushions.

'Mm-hum. An old friend.'

'Right.'

'That's where I was. I mean, that's who I had dinner with. In case you were wondering.'

'I just assumed you were with Mari. So where do you know her from?'

'Who?'

'This friend. Who is she?'

'Oh. From school. It's a he.'

'Uh-oh, should I be jealous?' He puts the bowl down and nuzzles my neck, jabbing at the TV remote, eyes never leaving the screen.

'He was my teacher.'

'Ah, that's a no then. If he was your teacher, what is he, about ninety?'

'Cheek!' I pause, as if mentally calculating, as if I don't know your age in years, months, weeks and days off by heart. 'Forty-three.'

'Should I be jealous?' he says again.

'I don't think so,' I lie.

I lie awake: I, who have always been able to curl like a cat into any available space, any time, can't sleep.

You are replaying in my mind like a movie. How typical of you, to turn up like that, to put a spanner in the works, a cat among the pigeons, walking cliché that you are. I'm married. I'm happy. Finally I've put to rest the irritating feeling I've had for most of my life, the suspicion that I might be missing something, that around the corner, or tomorrow, I would find the thing that would satisfy me. I have done the done thing, and it is working. Has been working.

Then all of a sudden we were knocking each other over in the freezer aisle and I was hugging myself not from the cold, but for protection, and next I hugged you, and later there was the kiss.

Silence in the bedroom is an extra blanket: sometimes comforting, but not for long; usually too thick. Hot and scratchy. Through this deep cover my husband hears the sound of me rustling in his bedside drawer.

'Can't sleep?' he murmurs.

'Mmm.'

'Fee,' he lifts his head from the pillow, 'you had dinner with your forty-three-year-old ex-teacher?' Raises a quizzical, sleepy eyebrow.

'Like I said – he was kind of a friend. Aren't there any bloody pens in this house?'

Apparently satisfied with this response, he settles back into the pillow. 'Come back to bed.' Within seconds he is snoring softly.

I've always thought it is only when you spend the night with someone that you know whether you can love them. If you can bear their sour night-breath; if you can get used to their flickering eyelids and the knowledge that something is happening behind them that you can't know about; if you can lie and listen to their dream noises, you have a good chance.

I pad down to the kitchen like a thief, down to the bottom floor of our cavernous house. The dog barely stirs.

The kitchen takes up the whole of the basement. Copper-bottomed pans hang from the ceiling, so clean they look like they've never been used. In the windowless half-light they seem like weapons.

I pour a glass of filtered water (bottled is too expensive, tap too dirty, according to Dave) and attack the heavy oak drawers.

I need to find something to write with. The bill drawer – that's the one. On top of the neat pile of mail, a cheque book, a spiral bound note book and a rollerball pen. The itch in my head that I haven't felt for years is there, and I settle at the table to scratch it out onto the paper.

He was kind of a friend.

'If you trust me,' you used to say, 'I won't let you down.'

So I trusted you, and you did let me down, and later, you introduced me to your girlfriend.

It was the fifth year leavers' ball in 1994, that last summer before fifth year became known as year eleven at our school. There was a May smell of cut grass and keenly sucked ciggies behind the building. The fact that we were promised booze meant no one bothered to bring vodka in a Coke bottle. As it turned out, we only got one glass of watered-down wine each with dinner. I wore a pink and blue dotted puffball skirt and low cut white top. I was carrying a 'proper' handbag for the first time in my life and was rummaging in it as I tottered into school and straight into the two of you.

You coughed in my cloud of Lou Lou.

When I say 'girlfriend', she wasn't a girl, she was a woman, of course. She had ash blonde hair swept into a chignon and she wore her age like a badge pinned from a birthday card. It towered over me, gave her height.

'This is Fiona,' you said to her. 'The Genius.'

You both chuckled. She was not surprised – by my presence there, by your description. So you had talked about me.

I always thought teachers made fun of only the very dull (because they don't get it) or the precocious (who can give it back). Which was I supposed to be?

I left, and I left school, and until today I hadn't seen you since.